ETHEREAL AWAKENING

Jennifer Wells

This is a work of fiction.

Names, characters, places, and incidents either are products of the author's imagination or are used fictitiously.

Any similarity to actual events or locales or persons, living or dead, is entirely coincidental.

INDEX

PART 1

DISTRICT F199

CHAPTER 1

The Quail

As the sun neared the horizon, the sky suddenly erupted into thunderous rain.

The remains of the sun, half-submerged, lingered on the horizon.

Its intense heat flashing with lightning bolts that pierced the heavens and vanished within seconds.

Smoke-white rain veils descended, seizing the opportunity, and a dazzling torrential display of a "sun shower" unfolded.

This rain arrived unannounced but providentially, instantly dispelling the suffocating heat and stifling humidity that had lingered for days.

"Another instance of the Weather Mimic System... How many times this year?"

In the rain-shrouded city, elderly figures with graying hair gazed skyward, murmuring contemplatively.

New Pacific Alliance, an eastern island.

Among lush forests, a black umbrella moved swiftly through the rain.

The figure under the umbrella remained indistinct, a slender bundle protruding behind them, the black, anti-slip fabric dripping water relentlessly.

Despite the crude and rugged mountain path, their movements were as agile as a soaring falcon.

Halfway up the mountain, the umbrella shifted, revealing a fair and radiant face.

With lowered dark eyes, the young girl peered through the moist rain curtain, gazing down the mountain.

The presence of rain had prompted the local wildlife to seek solace in their nests, resulting in an unusual silence.

The only commotion emanated from the distant harbor.

This was a back mountain, seaside island, crisscrossed by an intricate web of transportation routes.

At regular intervals, massive cargo ships cruised the waters, while the Alliance's public air routes governed the skies.

State-of-the-art airships weaved through the skies, their iridescent neon signal lights creating a mesmerizing, dreamlike spectacle amidst the hazy rain.

But if one were to cast their gaze downward, clusters of cramped, affordable housing, the tang of salty sea air mingling with the polluted atmosphere, the weary and numb faces moving back and forth—like a sudden splash of cold water—all conspired to awaken a stark realization.

This was no utopia, hardly even a city.

The sky's grandeur sped up the decline on the ground.

The nascent bloom of a refined new civilization observed the struggles of its discarded predecessor with detached indifference.

District 199 perpetually earned a failing grade in the Alliance's comprehensive development assessment because of the gaping chasm between the two that birthed a dissonance.

F199 District, a forsaken realm undeserving even of its name.

District 199, which relied solely on seafood exports, gradually devolved into the Alliance's most desolate numeric enclave—a backward region that could be counted on one's fingers—because it missed out on the glory days of the "Radiant Thirty Years," a golden age of technological advancement in New Pacific Alliance's history, and lost out on the economic boom.

Paupers, alcoholics, chain smokers, gamblers...

Here, a sense of twilight gloom enveloped the indigenous, the dispossessed refugees driven out by the Alliance, and countless forgotten souls struggling to survive in the wasteland that was District 199.

They clung to a glimmer of hope, a faint dawn, by relying on the few transit lines bridging the old and new civilizations.

Once beyond the mountain's foothills, the rain suddenly ceased, as if crossing into a somber barrier.

The distinct briny aroma unique to District 199 washed over her.

The young girl folded her umbrella and meticulously shook off the rain before proceeding past a sentry checkpoint.

Near to there, a local, esteemed mariner furrowed his brows while smoking, his expression troubled.

Beside him, a young woman anxiously tugged at his sleeve. "Old Cheung, it's been nearly half a month since my son Ben set sail. You think he's alright?"

The mariner's brow furrowed as he exhaled a long plume of smoke.

"The Alliance specifically requested a local guide, and Ben's been sailing since he was eleven or twelve. He's the most experienced around here. Don't worry too much; he'll be fine."

The woman remained unconvinced.

"But my eyelids have been twitching for the past couple of days. I can't shake this unease."

She clung to his sleeve, her voice tinged with resentment.

"This job was your recommendation. You said that the Alliance's nonsense Ocean Current Research Team pays well and has minimal risk. It was your idea that convinced Ben. You can't just wash your hands of his fate!"

The mariner's face turned ashen from her grip, his response muffled. "Just give it a bit more time. The seas have been turbulent lately. If we don't hear in a few days, I'll send someone out to search."

The young girl's approach diverted his attention, and he wore a kindly smile on his weathered face. "Look who's back. Cora."

The girl respectfully called out.

"Cap... Captain Cheung."

Old Cheung grinned as he appraised her.

"Why are you all sweaty? Was it a tiring day?"

Cora shook her head meekly, her lips curving into a smile.

When she smiled, a faint dimple appeared on her cheek, making her look especially endearing.

Mrs. Travers, the woman next to them, turned her head and shot Cora a venomous glare, her eyes brimming with lingering anger.

Cora was sensitive to the emotions emanating from others. With a single glare, her smile vanished, and so did her dimple. She nodded to Old Cheung and remained silent.

Mrs. Travers was one refugee who had come to the District 199 years ago. She always looked down on the indigenous people, including Cora.

Cora felt that both Mrs. Travers and her chubby son were harsh, probably because she was reticent and spoke little. When they met, they would exchange snide remarks, and Mrs. Travers always had something negative to say.

Mrs. Travers' husband, Ben, was a local, kind-hearted and honest. He had worked for Old Cheung's transport team for a long time, and he had even given Cora candy when she was little.

Lately, many research teams had come to the District 199 — meteorology researchers, ocean current researchers, and even microbiology researchers.

Ben had the experience and would work hard, so he had taken on the role of a guide to earn some extra money for them. But who would have thought... that he would go missing?

Thinking about Ben's disappearance at sea, Cora walked forward in silence.

She passed by a fishing boat that had just returned, laden with a catch, and several strong young men in black shorts and rolled-up sleeves were busy unloading the cargo.

"Whoa! Ouch!" someone suddenly exclaimed, throwing a net overboard.

"What's going on, Sid? Quit overreacting," a concerned voice immediately asked.

"Bad luck, a fish just bit me."

"Are you kidding? You got bitten by a few perches? Trying to slack off, huh?"

"It's true! I swear it's a fish bite! Look, if you don't believe me!"

The person called "Sid" was met with laughter from his companions. His face flushed bright red as he ripped off his soaked glove and held out his hand to show them.

Cora had excellent eyesight. Following the sound, she looked into the distance and saw the fresh, bloodied wound on Sid's hand. In this line of work, injuries were commonplace, and the others didn't take it too seriously. They continued laughing and joking.

"Oh, it really is. This little guy packs a punch. Should fetch a good price."

"Sid, come over here and identify the culprit. I'll cook it up for you, give you some relief."

Not even the injured Sid seemed too concerned. After wiping away the bloodstains and re-donning his glove, he said, "This fish is quite a handful today, stronger than me. It's been tough pulling in the nets."

Cora shifted her gaze away, her steps leading her toward home. The vibrant surroundings behind her became less prominent, and her silhouette gradually vanished, leaving her with a sense of not fully fitting in.

After a few more steps, she belatedly cast her eyes toward the sky.

The fishing ban had just ended, and fall was on the horizon.

Yet, the blazing sun showed no mercy, dominating the horizon and emitting scorching heat as if desiring to reduce everything to ashes.

The scorching sun caused Cora to be drenched in sweat, with her head pounding.

She felt like a lump of cheap butter, on the verge of melting at any moment. Slowly, she propped open her umbrella again, this time to shield herself from the sun's relentless rays.

The searing sensation around her made her squint her eyes.

This summer was simply too hot.

Twenty minutes later, Cora, perspiring heavily, made her way through the cramped low-rent housing complex. She stopped in front of a run-down apartment building, her home.

She unlocked the door with her key, but before entering, she hesitated for a moment, dragging her feet.

Seeing no immediate movement, Cora stubbornly shuffled a few steps to the side and peeked her head toward her neighbor's apartment.

Why was Micheal so quiet today?

Micheal was a chatty quail who had become her close companion. Its beak was sharper than Cora's tongue, and it greeted her every morning and evening with spirited conversations.

It was like those birds guarding castles in old tales, always observing the princess's every move.

When Cora left home early in the morning, it would secretly chirp, "Go, Cora! Hang in there, Cora!" And when she returned exhausted at night, it would flap its wings excitedly, exclaiming, "Got into a fight again today! Another brawl!"

Given that Micheal was typically mischievous, what could be happening today?

Cora maneuvered to the base of the neighbor's wall, took a couple of steps back, crouched, and then, with a slight spring, effortlessly leaped onto the top of the wall.

From there, she deftly pushed aside the sparse fence and peered inside, whispering softly to her friend, "Micheal, Micheal!"

Micheal had its back turned to Cora, slumped in its bamboo cage, looking unusually lethargic. Upon hearing her voice, it took a while before it raised its head, struggling to flutter its wings and inch its way over. Its orange beak lightly pecked at Cora's palm, a greeting of sorts.

Cora cast a glance at the empty food tray. Although Micheal could mostly roam free, the neighbor's grandmother fed it every day, so it wouldn't go hungry. Was it in a bad mood because there was no food today?

Cora jumped down from the wall, picked a bunch of dark and lustrous grapes from the vines in her yard, and tossed them lightly over the fence, saying, "Micheal, have some delicious food."

After this back-and-forth exchange, Micheal seemed even more listless, curled up in the corner without moving, not even lifting its head.

Cora grew anxious, waiting, holding the grapes in her hands, hoping against hope.

Finally, she realized that Micheal genuinely didn't want to pay her any attention, and with a disappointed sigh, she reluctantly went back to her own apartment.

Once inside, Cora eagerly unwrapped the package on her back and laid it out on the table.

Slowly, the long object inside revealed itself—a fierce and menacing Tang sword, passed down from the era of the Old Civilization.

Cora's eyes widened, and she lovingly ran her fingers along the hilt, her expression one of pure longing.

After admiring it, she retrieved a thick sketchbook from under the table and meticulously drew.

She meticulously sketched every weapon she admired.

However, her interests were so varied that the sketchbook was growing thicker by the day.

In the new era, most traditional weapons had become impractical and people relegated them to relics and archaeological artifacts.

Cora was an exception.

While most people were fascinated by the innovative weaponry promoted by the Alliance in recent years, she had an insatiable fascination with the weapons of the Old Civilization.

The sword she was currently admiring was part of her master's collection, and she could borrow it after emerging victorious in a sparring match with her senior siblings.

However, she had to return it tomorrow.

Otherwise, she might have considered sleeping with it tonight, despite her master's strict prohibition before the journey.

As for her master, that was the reason Cora traveled the twenty kilometers back and forth every day.

Cora was exceptionally talented and had tremendous physical strength from a young age, so her grandfather had decided she should learn martial arts.

She had wandered with her grandfather for several years before finally settling in Yue Mountain (District E104).

There, she found a historic martial arts training center called Master Zhang's, her eventual master.

Supposedly, he came from a long-lost martial arts lineage, which gave him prestige and made him formidable.

Yue Mountain was an ecological landscape area and not suitable for residence.

So after some consideration, her grandfather had settled down with her in the nearby F199 District, known for its "dirty, chaotic, and poor" reputation.

They never moved again after that.

After thirty minutes of engrossed sketching, Cora stretched her arms and got up from the floor.

Her apartment was empty, save for a few oversized standardized pieces of furniture, making it feel somewhat barren.

She walked into the kitchen and prepared herself a large bowl of plain noodles, garnishing it with fresh green onions. She even indulged herself by making two sunny-side-up eggs.

After cooking, Cora carried her steaming bowl of noodles back to the living room.

With each bite of noodles, she would glance at the Tang sword on the table, then take another bite, and then reluctantly steal another glance at her sketchbook. It was an utterly satisfying meal.

Cora was an orphan, taken in by her grandfather. She had no parents or siblings, just herself.

A few years ago, her grandfather, her sole source of support, passed away.

She learned to live on her own, but because of her difficulty in social interactions. Over time, she had grown dependent on the quail companion she borrowed from the neighbor.

And she didn't really mind the lack of human conversation; after all, she wasn't much of a talker to begin with.

Because she stuttered, naturally.

After finishing her meal, washing the dishes, Cora sat back on the floor and retrieved an old holographic screen her grandfather had left behind. It was his last task for her before he passed away–she had to study for at least an hour every day.

Because of certain circumstances, she had dropped out of middle school a few years ago. But now, in this era of rapid advancement, she needed to keep up with the changing world. Her grandfather was worried she'd become illiterate, so he had set this strict rule for her– she had to study every day, at least to ensure her education wouldn't lag too far behind.

Cora scanned through the holographic screen, eventually plucking out a book titled "Particle Physics Advanced Microbiology," and read, feeling downhearted.

The sensory light above her head emitted a warm yellow glow, casting a drowsy atmosphere.

Cora barely got through a few pages before fatigue hit her. Today, in particular, Cora's eyelids felt as if they were coated in glue, battling to stay open. Perhaps it was due to overeating; she felt weak all over, and the drowsiness spread to her limbs.

"Clang!"

Suddenly, a loud crashing noise echoed in her ears.

The noise startled Cora, causing her to flip over and land on her back. It took her a good while to cover her head and slowly sit up, feeling rather groggy. But as she touched her head, she realized that something was amiss. Her head wasn't made of metal—why had she made such a loud noise?

Struggling to fully wake up, Cora propped her eyelids open and looked up in confusion.

To her shock, she found a large hole smashed through her window, shattered glass littering the floor. The damp and chilly night air wafted in, sending shivers down her spine, causing her hair to stand on end.

Was it hailing outside?

Carelessly tossing the dormant holographic screen aside, Cora quickly got up to investigate.

There was a blurry black shape rolling around on her windowsill, convulsing violently.

Cora approached cautiously, her guard up as she edged closer.

The black quail was trembling uncontrollably, its once sleek feathers now mostly gone, revealing mottled skin underneath.

Its black-bean-like pupils seemed covered by a hazy gray film, and it stared ominously ahead.

Opening its beak, it emitted a hoarse cry that seemed like a plea for help and a menacing growl all at once. But when its mouth opened, it revealed two rows of uneven, jagged teeth, stained with a sticky black substance.

It was Micheal!

Cora's hand gripping the windowsill tightened.

Before she could comprehend what was happening, the quail shuddered violently a few times, its head slumping forward, lifeless.

CHAPTER 2

Unusual Discovery

Cora had a dream.

In the dream, she lay beneath the shade of a grapevine. Michael, still his proud and arrogant self, pranced around her with lively jumps, occasionally pecking at her head with his sharp beak. It felt so real that when she opened her eyes, the sensation of his touch seemed to linger above her.

It had been an entire week since the night Michael underwent a transformation and died.

During these days, Cora had repeatedly attempted to knock on her neighbors' doors, but she received no response.

The tightly shut iron doors seemed to form a barrier of their own, shielding against any unwelcome scrutiny from the outside world.

Had they gone on a trip?

Perhaps that's why they hadn't been able to feed Michael. But if they were traveling, why wouldn't they take Michael with them? No, something didn't add up. Cora's knocking gradually ceased. Michael couldn't have starved, no way.

Dark memories surged like a nightmare–the grotesque, rigid body of the swan and its rows of protruding fangs. Whenever she recalled that image, her back shivered with a bone-chilling coldness.

Cora leaned her head against the closed door, her slender figure radiating an air of solitude. She had lost her only friend.

Behind her house, she laid Michael to rest on a slope, crafting a small mound of earth adorned with bamboo grasshoppers and grapes, his favorite treats. She had also written a note about Michael's passing and posted it on the neighbor's door.

Hoping the family would see it when they returned.

With a heavy heart, Cora stepped outside.

Regardless of the circumstances, she couldn't skip training at the martial arts academy.

If her master caught her skipping class, a sound thrashing was inevitable.

The sun had yet to fully rise, and a hazy mist enshrouded District 199. Occasionally, the sound of waves crashing against the rocks could be heard.

The neon lights above continued to shine without stopping, creating fragmented reflections on the indigo sea.

Passing by the harbor, Cora noticed an unusual scarcity of workers today.

Despite the laborious tasks, the work at the harbor was straightforward, didn't require identification, and the pay was decent.

It had always been a popular choice among the local youth. An almost-empty scene like today was quite rare.

She cast a puzzled glance and overheard a conversation in a corner. "... They're all on sick leave. The workforce has been dwindling lately."

"Did Sid not come today?"

"You haven't heard? Sid's dead!" "What? He was perfectly fine a few days ago. How did this happen so suddenly?"

"Someone poisoned Sid! His right hand rotted away completely! The police from District C were even called in. They came to deal with his body." Impossible... Why would people from District C bother cleaning up District F's mess?

"You don't know how horrifying his death was! I saw it with my own eyes! His eyeballs turned gray, his eye sockets protruded, and his whole body was as cold as ice."

The speaker lowered their voice, tinged with fear. "I heard they won't cremate him; they're sending the body to a forensic pathologist and an autopsy. Sid's parents fainted on the spot, and when they woke up, they were raving mad."

Cora's footsteps came to a sudden halt. Sid... Sid! The name sounded familiar, but it was only at this moment that she recognized it.

She remembered–the "Sid" they mentioned was the young man bitten by the fish that day. And the hand... the bloody hand... she recalled seeing it–the injured hand was his right hand!

In an instant, Cora's heart raced, and she couldn't stay in a place any longer.

She rushed towards the academy, driven by an intense feeling of urgency.

She had walked this path to Yue Mountain countless times, and she could navigate it even with her eyes closed.

However, today, whether or not it was her imagination, the surroundings were eerily quiet.

Even the familiar cacophony of insect chirping and bird calls was absent, replaced by a silence that sent shivers down her spine.

The scorching sun remained overhead. It is blazing heat causing sweat to trickle down her forehead, disappearing into the earth beneath her feet without a sound.

The cramped surroundings seemed to conceal boundless danger. Cora quickened her pace, reaching the mountaintop in a hurry.

Inside the academy, the atmosphere was as lively as ever, with occasional laughter from the trainees.

Cora leaned against the door frame, panting heavily.

Her tumultuous emotions gradually settled as she exhaled a deep breath, stepping over the threshold.

But after taking just a few steps, an intense feeling of impending danger swept over her–Danger!

A blinding red light suddenly burst from a corner, like a burning meteor, carrying a murderous intent as it shot toward her.

Cora's eyes narrowed, her upper body arching back significantly, her supple waist nearly folding in half.

In one fluid motion, she executed a graceful backflip, skillfully landing on her feet. The lethal red light narrowly grazed her forehead.

The assailant fired a missed shot and didn't linger, tauntingly muttering, "Junior stutterer, your reflexes are impressive."

Cora lifted her gaze to glance at him before averting her eyes again, remaining silent.

The stranger's tone was unfriendly.

"You can't even call for help properly? I remember you're a stutterer, not mute, right?" Cora pursed her lips and reluctantly spoke. "Ea... Eamon."

"Ea... Eammm... Eamon!" Eamon mimicked her speech, a malicious glint in his deep brown eyes. "So, it's true, a little trash from District F. Who gave you permission to address me by my name? Am I unworthy of being your senior brother?"

Cora didn't want to dignify his provocation. She turned a corner and headed for the backyard without a second thought.

Eamon followed, stepping forward and blocking her path with an annoyed expression. "I'm talking to you. Where do you think you're going?"

"I'm going to find... find Master."

For reasons unknown to Cora, Eamon's demeanor instantly turned cold.

"In a hurry to tattle, huh? Hah, just as expected of Felix's promised wife. He's not here, so you're trying to please his father, huh? Working hard, aren't you?"

The malevolence radiating from him was like the hiss of a snake lurking in the shadows.

Cora kept her head down, her fists clenched so tightly that her knuckles cracked.

If it weren't for the academy rules prohibiting fights between students, she would have kicked that smug face and turned annoying Eamon into a pig's head.

As the two locked in a standoff, a clear, feminine voice sounded from behind them.

"Eamon, why are you bullying our junior apprentice again?"

The newcomer was striking, her features beautiful, and she wore a sleek combat suit.

Her high ponytail exuded a sense of determination. It was their senior sister, Rita.

"Impressive, taking advantage of Junior Zhang's absence to break the rules, huh? Who told you to use a particle gun in the academy?"

Eamon's family was a powerful force in the Deep Forest (District C33), controlling several arms factories.

They possessed many illegal and restricted weapons.

He casually played with the gun's stock, a faint red glow flickering. "It's just defective merchandise that hasn't hit the market yet. I asked Junior Stutterer to test its power. Is that not allowed?"

As he spoke, he suddenly aimed the gun at Cora's head again. "Besides, she dodged it last time."

Dangerous particle energy coalesced before her, yet Cora stood her ground, unflinching. Rita, standing nearby, reached over and pushed the gun down. "Put that away. What if the Master sees you? Do you want to be kicked out?"

Eamon's gaze faltered briefly as he retrieved the particle gun with a bitter smile, muttering under his breath, "Junior Zhang's future wife is indeed precious."

Rita confronted him without fear.

"Just shut up already. You're always picking fights and causing trouble. Is it because you couldn't take part in The Azures' assessment this year? You voluntarily forfeited, so what does it have to do with Senior Brother Zhang and Junior Apprentice here? And now you're even attempting sneak attacks? You really have no shame!"

Azure Force, formally known as the New Pacific Alliance (NPA) Special Duties Force, was the most mysterious and talked-about a military unit in recent years.

It quickly gained popularity across all regions, sparking a wave of enthusiasm for military service.

Its selection criteria were incredibly simple: no restrictions based on origin, background, or gender. Citizens over the age of twenty could join.

However, the allure of these simple conditions was unparalleled.

Those selected through The Azures' assessment could directly gain citizenship in a B-level city.

This proposition drew countless individuals who saw The Azures as a ladder to change their destinies.

The higher the attraction, the fiercer the competition.

The assessment process for The Azures remained confidential, and the acceptance rate was extremely low, with most applicants being rejected without understanding the process.

As an elite military force, stringent physical requirements were a given.

The Alliance saw a rise in popularity of combat training after The Azures were founded.

Both Eamon and Rita hailed from District C, joining this training to qualify for The Azures.

The team from Yue Mountain Martial Academy that signed up for the assessment, led by Felix, had already set out.

"You!" Eamon was hit where it hurt, his face contorting. Yet, because of Rita's background, he refrained from acting recklessly.

Rita, utterly undeterred, raised her voice defiantly, "It's fortunate you gave up in advance. Otherwise, going and not being selected would be even more embarrassing."

With that, she grabbed Cora's arm and pulled her away.

Eamon watched the two retreating figures with a dark expression, sneering with disdain, "Idiots."

"People who haven't awakened their potential. What's the point of trying harder?"

The design of Yue Mountain Martial Academy was unique, featuring complex structures that required navigating long corridors from the front yard to the back hall.

On their journey, Rita paused before inquiring, "Junior Apprentice, aren't you... Junior Zhang's...?"

Cora turned to look at her, noticing a tinge of discomfort on her face, a faint blush rising to her ears. She wondered why Rita would blush. She and Felix were several years apart and not close. They interacted little, mostly because she struggled with communication.

Finally, she answered slowly, "No."

Rita's mood brightened as she affectionately put her arm around Cora's shoulder, clearly relieved by her response.

Passing by the cafeteria, they encountered a plump woman responsible for logistics. She carried a tray with several bowls of piping-hot ginger soup and greeted them warmly.

"Little Cora is here! Haven't had breakfast, have you? I prepared two eggs for you in the room. Help yourself."

Cora's eyes lit up, nodding enthusiastically.

Rita, pinching her nose in disdain, said, "Auntie, it smells terrible. Why are you cooking this?"

The plump woman sighed helplessly. "It's strange, right? On such hot days, so many trainees are falling sick with fever. I'm making some herbal medicine to help them recover."

"Could they be faking it, trying to get out of training?" Rita expressed her doubts.

It was indeed odd that so many powerful individuals suddenly fell ill for no apparent reason.

The plump woman clicked her tongue.

"Way. You know what Theon told me? He said he got pecked by a wild chicken yesterday, and now he's aching all over and can't even get out of bed. That rascal is just making excuses. I think he's just itching for attention."

"Hahaha, he's something else!" Rita had no sympathy, laughing uncontrollably, "And what about that chicken that pecks people?"

The plump woman joined in the laughter. "I slaughtered it. It wasn't laying eggs, anyway. It's a good way to nourish these sick kids."

"I'll help you take this over." Rita took the tray from the plump woman and then turned to Cora, instructing her, "Junior Apprentice, Master is in the meditation room. Why don't you go check on Theon while we talk?"

While they conversed, Cora had already taken the eggs the plump woman had prepared for her, stuffing them into her pockets—one in each.

CHAPTER 3

Strange Weather

Theon was the most trouble-prone among all the trainees. He was never one to shy away from scaling rooftops, catching turtles in the sea, or even daring to patch up holes in the sky.

Every time they compiled the list of wrongdoers, they would include his name.

The number of times he kneeled for punishment or received a beating grew, and Theon gradually realized a lesson: everyone else could be unreliable, but Cora always had his back.

Whenever he got into trouble, he would drag Cora along, ensuring that he wouldn't face punishment alone.

In the rest area, Theon was hooked up to an IV drip, lying weakly on his bed. Cora sat beside him, peeling eggs.

The background had the faint sound of morning news broadcasts, with the volume so low that the information came in bits and pieces.

"The Alliance Meteorological Bureau has issued a high-temperature red alert... cease outdoor activities... reduce travel."

"If any unusual situations arise... please report to the relevant authorities."

A plump woman at the door was giving a lecture to some misbehaving trainees, her booming voice drowning out the announcer's words.

"Arashi Research Institute... solar activity peak... starting... Weather Mimicry System."

The news briefly diverted Cora's attention, and when she looked down again, she found she had peeled the egg shells off the eggs in her hand. Theon on the bed was humming and mumbling, clutching his head weakly while chewing incessantly with his swollen mouth.

Given their history of facing difficulties together, she let his antics slide.

She reached into her pocket and took out another egg.

In the beds next to them, several trainees were engaged in a lively discussion about this year's assessment of The Azures.

The votes for Felix's successful passage had reached ninety percent.

Theon grumbled defiantly, "Next year, I'll show you all what I'm made of."

At only nineteen, he wasn't old enough to meet the registration age requirement yet, but he was already ambitiously planning his future.

He had wanted Cora to praise him a little, but when he turned to look, he found his junior apprentice absentmindedly holding a naked egg.

"What are you thinking about?"

"Se... Senior Brother, have you seen gray or... grayish-white eyes?"

"Of course I have," Theon answered absentmindedly, his gaze still fixed on the egg.

"Why do they turn gray?"

"Come closer, and I'll tell you."

Cora leaned soon.

Theon suddenly lunged forward and snatched the egg from her hand, exclaiming, "Why else? It's cataracts!"

Cora. "..."

He clearly hadn't given a serious answer.

She could tolerate his teasing and jokes, but not eating even a bite of the two eggs when she had prepared them was too much. Without a hint of emotion, Cora raised her fist, filling the room with a chorus of pained yells.

"Sister Apprentice! Spare us!"

"Sister Apprentice! Have you forgotten the bird nests we dug, the earthworms we collected, and the beatings we endured together over the years?"

"You forgot... cough, cough, cough!"

As the cries continued, Theon coughed violently. His cheeks turned bright red from the high fever, and tears streamed from his eyes. Cora looked at his pitiful state and found it hard to continue.

Theon seemed perfectly fine with the situation. After a few hearty coughs, he grinned and promised, "Tomorrow! Tomorrow, I'll give you four eggs to make up for it. Senior Brother always keeps his promises!"

Having finished with Theon, Cora finally caught sight of her master.

Master Zhang was the pride of Yue Mountain Martial Academy, a renowned combat master within the Alliance.

Despite his kind and approachable appearance, he had a fiery and uncompromising temperament, bursting forth like a firecracker.

As Cora slipped into the meditation room, she found Master Zhang amid seated meditation.

The atmosphere in the room was serene and solemn.

In the words of others, there was a certain aura around Master Zhang.

On the table sat a pair of gleaming, spherical objects.

Cora was reminded of the two unfortunate eggs she had peeled.

She reached out to touch them surreptitiously.

But with his eyes closed, Master Zhang's hand swiftly slapped hers away.

"You're drooling all over them! Have you not eaten breakfast?"

Cora covered her reddened hand, looking aggrieved. "I... I haven't eaten."

Master Zhang's left eye cracked open slightly, giving her a sidelong glance. "Are you so hungry that you're losing your mind? Thinking about touching my precious artifact!"

Seeing Cora's pitiful expression, he hesitated for a moment, then continued, "I haven't touched it yet. Go eat it."

Cora's eyes lit up, and she couldn't resist pushing her luck. She inched closer, saying, "Master, can... can I borrow that knife from last time, just to look?"

Master Zhang's expression instantly turned complicated. "No way. Why is it so sticky? Did it get covered in your saliva?"

Cora sheepishly lowered her head. Maybe, possibly, it really was her saliva. She had been scared that night and had slept with the knife.

Master Zhang let out a soft snort, seeing through her but not commenting. He stood up and took a couple of steps, retrieving two plastic bags from a low cabinet. "You're about to turn eighteen, right? Here, these are gifts from your master."

"Why are there two... two of them?"

"One is for you, and the other is for... Senior... Brother Zhang."

Cora's birthday was the day her grandfather found her.

Coincidentally, it was also Felix's birthday.

And since she had learned martial arts on the mountain, they had celebrated their birthdays together.

This was also why everyone jokingly referred to her as "future wife."

Master Zhang maintained his composure, although his tone was stiff.

"When he returns, find a moment to give it to him."

"Why don't you give it to him yourself?" Cora couldn't understand why she had to be the intermediary. She and Felix weren't really close.

Master Zhang's eyes widened, and he barked sternly, "If I tell you to do it, you do it! Stop with the pointless questions!"

Cora shrank back, intimidated by his reaction. Her master was quite fierce.

After a long day of intense training at the martial academy, with her palms sore from two rounds of punishment, Cora trudged back home.

Just as she passed the outpost, she noticed a crowd gathered at the pier. Standing on the outer periphery, she overheard discussions about the return of Old Cheung's team, who had been sent to search for Ben.

The murmuring crowd grew larger and larger, and before she knew it, Cora was pushed into the inner circle.

The sight of so many people gathered and talking made Cora feel uncomfortable. She was about to slip away when a heartbreaking scream cut through the air.

"Where's Ben? Why is it just you who came back? Where's Ben?"

Mrs. Travers's voice was hoarse as she clung to the surviving member of the team, who was now disheveled and ragged. No one else could pry her off. The survivor, his clothes torn and shoulders covered in layers of black bruises, had a vacant expression.

He alternated between crying and laughing, repeating over and over again, "They're dead, they're all dead, hahaha!"

His collar had been torn off halfway, revealing layers of black bruises on his shoulder. His pupils were dilated, and when the harsh sunlight hit his eyes, it reflected an eerie grayish-white hue.

"We've arrived."

Right at that moment, the District 199 security officer hurriedly arrived with three people in tow.

The first two were dressed in police uniforms, looking arrogant and proud.

However, when they spoke to the middle-aged man who followed behind, their demeanor shifted to one of utmost deference.

The middle-aged man wore a plain work jacket, his face unfamiliar, not a native of District 199.

He frowned as he observed the deranged researcher, and his expression quickly changed.

He raised his voice sharply, commanding, "Back away! Everyone disperses!" The crowd was still bewildered, but in the next second, the frenzied researcher suddenly went berserk.

Previously, he had been pushed around by Mrs. Travers, lying prostrate on the ground. But now, like a fish on a chopping board, he flipped over and leaped to his feet, launching an indiscriminate attack on everyone around him.

Mrs. Travers, being the closest, was the first to suffer. She lost a sizeable chunk of flesh from her arm as the researcher bit into her.

In the blink of an eye, his teeth gleamed, and within a few breaths, uneven and jagged fangs had sprouted between them.

The lower half of his face was punctured, a gruesome mess of blood and tissue.

"Mon... monster!" The scene was horrifying, and the witnessing crowd turned pale with fear.

People scattered in all directions, stumbling over each other and falling.

The monster took advantage of the chaos, pouncing and tearing, turning the scene into a chaotic frenzy.

Cora remained frozen in place as the fleeing crowd collided with her shoulders and back. While chaos ensued, she felt as though her feet were glued to the ground.

The man's eyes... had turned grayish-white.

In the critical moment, the middle-aged man brought by the police sprang into action. A sudden gust of wind swept through the area.

Before Cora could fully comprehend it, the man's coat fluttered, and he almost instantly appeared before the rampaging monster.

Cora rubbed her eyes in disbelief and took a few steps back, seeking refuge on a nearby fishing boat. He was so fast! She hadn't been able to catch the full trajectory of his movements!

Caught in the fierce wind, the frenzied monster was lifted high into the sky, ensnared within a whirlwind that trapped it like a vortex. It was utterly powerless to retaliate. Its already tattered clothes were torn to shreds, and its expression grew increasingly violent.

In contrast, the middle-aged man remained unscathed in the center of the storm.

He pressed his hands, manipulating the airflow to create a wind barrier that suppressed the monster's movements.

However, as time passed, the strain on the man's face became more clear. Beads of sweat formed on his forehead, and about ten minutes later, the struggling in the vortex gradually subsided. The monster's eyes slowly closed, and it appeared lifeless.

The middle-aged man let out a sigh of relief. He withdrew his outstretched palms, causing the gusts of wind that had mysteriously emerged to dissipate instantly. The monster plummeted from midair with a loud thud, kicking up a cloud of choking dust.

Turning around, he nodded slightly to the people behind him who were maintaining a state of alertness. "It's alright now. Take it away."

Unexpectedly, one of the policemen suddenly paled, panicking as he yelled, "Watch out!"

The middle-aged man whipped around! The barely conscious monster had roared back to life behind him, its sharp claws swinging toward him.

The man couldn't dodge in time. In his haste, his coat pocket was slashed open, drawing a few strands of bright red blood.

A sharp gust of wind sliced through the monster's neck, severing most of its head.

The remaining portion dangled precariously, threatening to detach from its neck.

This time, the monster was truly motionless.

The middle-aged man's expression soured as he stared at his wound for a couple of seconds. Then he turned and strode away.

"Get out of here!" His composure had dissipated, replaced by a trace of indescribable fear in his eyes.

The police officers dragged the monster's body away, and Cora slowly straightened up.

The ground was now littered with debris–clothing fragments, viscous brown fluid, and streaks of blood intermingled, emitting a nauseating odor.

The crowd that had gathered just minutes ago had scattered in all directions, leaving no trace.

The researcher... had turned into a monster? Who was the middle-aged man? How could he control the wind? Cora's understanding was in complete disarray. What on earth was happening?

Exhausted, Cora made her way back home.

As she passed by Michael's grave, the once plump and juicy grapes had withered and rotted, but the straw cricket still looked vibrant. She squatted down and adjusted the cricket, murmuring softly, "Michael, did you as well... turn into that kind of... monster?" Dead people wouldn't answer her questions, nor would dead birds. Cora would remain without answers.

The neighbor's door was shut tight, and a paper note stuck to it flapped in the wind. Were they still not back yet?

She pounded on the door, but there was an only silence that stretched on for a long time. No one answered. She looked around–the desolate surroundings were devoid of people.

Cora glanced at the low wall, took a deep breath, and prepared to jump. But just as she was about to leap, the smooth wall surface flickered, and an onslaught of bright light overwhelmed her vision.

Cora looked up in astonishment.

At sunset, the sun, unwilling to sink into oblivion, erupted with blinding radiance as if it would never rise again.

The scorching light intensified, accompanied by an all-encompassing searing sensation that pushed the limits of human senses.

Cora felt the same dizziness and disorientation she had experienced a few days ago under the scorching sun.

This time, it was even more unbearable.

She felt like she was suffocating, the air around her growing thin. Even the flow of blood through her veins felt like it was incinerating, consuming her inch by inch.

She couldn't even vault over the neighbor's wall. Gritting her teeth, she retreated, but the intense white light overwhelmed her vision.

Brief blindness left her unable to see anything.

A distant sound, a faint shattering of streetlights, reached her ears. Then the world fell into complete silence.

She couldn't hear anything at all.

Cora collapsed onto the ground.

Her body was burning hot, her skin flushed red. Her head grew increasingly heavy, and she struggled to remember her surroundings. Finally, she found her way to her own front door, pushing it open with every ounce of strength left. Cora crawled inside, shivering, as she closed the door behind her.

The unbearable heat caused her to lose consciousness and give in.

CHAPTER 4

The Awakening of Power

Cora endured three consecutive days of unbearable burning torment.

For most of that time, she lay on the ground, nearly breathless, trapped in a state of deep unconsciousness. Occasionally, in fleeting moments of wakefulness, she could sense the lingering pain coursing through her body.

It felt as if someone were wielding an iron saw, slicing through her tendons and veins, and then haphazardly piecing them back together between her bones, the process repeating endlessly.

Her lips cracked from dehydration, and her clothes were soaked through with cold sweat, clinging damply to her back.

The blood in her limbs alternated between scorching heat and a freezing chill, causing sensations of both burning annihilation and numbing frostiness.

The agony reached such heights that Cora would futilely close her eyes and tilt her head back, releasing soundless screams as her feeble body writhed and convulsed on the floor.

In fragmented consciousness, Cora's fleeting thoughts hinted at her impending demise.

Like Micheal, she'd perish in a remote and shadowy corner, vanishing from this world without a sound, her existence forgotten by all.

No one would remember her, and no one would commemorate her as she did for Micheal—burying him, erecting a monument.

She would live her life in solitude, only to die in obscurity.

Three days later, in the quiet room, Cora's curled fingers twitched, and she slowly opened her eyes. She hadn't died. She was still alive.

The prolonged agony had finally come to an end, but her spirit remained somewhat fatigued.

Grasping onto the table, Cora unsteadily rose to her feet.

Her thoughts and awareness felt as if they had been thoroughly cleansed, becoming exceptionally sharp.

There seemed to be a subtle change within her body, though she struggled to put it into words.

Outside, the window revealed an impenetrable fog that obscured the sky.

The boundary between heaven and earth grew increasingly chaotic.

In this environment, one could easily be plagued by illusions.

Could the bizarre experiences of the past few days have all been products of her imagination?

However, the constant ache in her joints reminded Cora that it wasn't an illusion.

Three days ago... the brutal and bloodthirsty creatures, the intense solar storm, and the sudden onset of high fever and unconsciousness were undoubtedly actual experiences.

It wasn't her imagination.

"I need to go outside," Cora thought. "At the very least, I need to find out what's happened." The misty surroundings seemed to be haunted by countless hungry souls, like specters roaming in search of something elusive.

The outside might not be safe, but Cora knew she needed a self-defense—a knife, preferably. Her thoughts were scattered, ideas racing through her mind. Unbeknownst to her, the wooden table she was holding onto was quietly undergoing a transformation. With her palm at the center, the entire table emitted a soft blue light.

In the next moment, the wooden table vanished, and in its place— Cora held a kitchen knife. A broad spine, a straight edge, razor-sharp cuts...

It was a bone cleaver!

Perfect for heavy chopping.

Cora tightened her grip on the handle, her gaze dazed. "Where did this come from?" she wondered. She had just imagined the structure of a kitchen knife in her mind so vividly... Why had a physical replica appeared?

With a puzzled expression, Cora swung the knife forward. As she did, a surge of energy coursed through her body like ocean waves, followed by a resounding "boom." The ancient wall across from her crumbled in response.

"Wow, impressive!"

The ethereal knife flickered for a few moments before gradually dissipating from her palm.

Cora, sensing a fleeting resonance, marveled at the strange sensation she'd just experienced.

She felt power-energetic, radiant, and indescribably new.

It cascaded from her like a gushing fountain, an unstoppable torrent from deep inside.

It was strong, yet elusive, to control. It would take more practice.

Looking around, Cora confidently reached toward her single bed.

With a thought, the ethereal light emerged again, transforming the iron bedstead into a brilliant blue staff.

Its tip emanated a frigid chill, radiating an icy brilliance and harboring an immense, thunderous potential.

Cora's eyes lit up as she dashed around the room, turning everything within reach into various weapons.

Knives, guns, swords, spears, axes... everything she'd seen before or could conceive of manifested before her eyes.

Only when the last piece of furniture had transformed did Cora pause, her energy depleted.

A wave of overpowering tiredness engulfed her all of a sudden.

Awake for barely half an hour, she collapsed once again.

Upon her next awakening, Cora refrained from using that newfound power.

Although her actions had been reckless, leading to mental exhaustion and fainting, she'd pieced together her current situation in a twist of fate.

Cora understood that her ability to conjure weapons at will stemmed from a mysterious energy within her body.

This uncanny power could be summarized as the deconstruction and reformation of matter.

By channeling her mental strength and comprehending various weapon structures, she could disassemble a specific medium or attribute, then reconstruct it based on her intentions.

She referred to these manifestations, under her control and command, as "Ethereal Artifacts."

Bathed in a luminous blue light, these artifacts possessed astonishing killing power.

The collapsed wall in her house provided undeniable verification.

However, her ability to deconstruct and reconstruct was limited by the intrinsic nature of the object.

No matter how audacious her imagination, a small teacup wouldn't transform into a massive, several-hundred-kilogram axe.

At most, it would manifest as a slim, leaf-bladed sword.

Sustaining the Ethereal Artifacts relied on her own mental energy.

If she lost consciousness and fell into a coma, all artifacts would vanish. As for how long she could maintain them, she had yet to test.

Cora's understanding hit a ceiling.

The deeper principles and specific origins of this power remained elusive beyond her current knowledge.

After organizing her thoughts, Cora quickly freshened up and decided it was time to step outside and assess the situation.

No matter what had transpired in the world beyond her home, she couldn't remain hidden indoors forever. She was deeply concerned about her master of Mount Yue and her senior martial siblings. She wondered if they had been affected by the solar eruption.

With a deep breath, Cora cautiously pushed open the door. Because of the pervasive mist, the surroundings were eerily silent, and visibility was limited. She turned her head, gaze landing on the neighbor's house on the opposite slope. This time, she refrained from knocking on their door, a sense of foreboding telling her that no matter how long she knocked, no one would answer.

Leaping gracefully, Cora scaled the wall and entered the

backyard.

Once she crossed the fence, she quickly took a few steps and then doubled over, dry heaving onto the ground.

It was foul!

A putrid stench hung heavy in the courtyard's air, flies swarmed, and the scent of decaying fish and shrimp, left out in the open for a long time, mingled with a pungent aroma.

Cora covered her nose and cautiously moved further inside.

The deeper she ventured, the stronger the nauseating smell became.

Half-eaten leftovers and bowls littered the pergola in the courtyard. The milky fish's head tofu soup had long since spilled and dried into clumps, leaving only the jagged fish bones.

Cora stared at the discarded food for a while, her thoughts racing. The lack of tidying up, the remnants of food—it wasn't at all indicative of someone going on a journey. Something had happened.

The main door of her neighbor's house wasn't properly closed, a thin gap allowing Cora to peer inside.

Darkness shrouded the interior, obscuring everything.

Cora's ears perked, and she faintly heard heavy, labored breathing from deep within the house.

Something large was dragging its weight across the floor.

The sinister atmosphere, the heavy breathing, and the slow crawl of something inside immediately set off alarm bells in Cora's mind.

She halted her steps, her heart racing. After scanning her surroundings, she reached out and touched the sturdy pergola.

With a shimmer of blue light, the pergola vanished, leaving in its place a sturdy two-meter-long sword. Holding the weighty weapon in her hand, Cora finally felt a semblance of safety.

Using the sword's tip, she pried open the gap of the door. The rusty bolt emitted an unpleasant creaking sound. The creature hidden in the shadows within heard the noise and turned toward her in unison. They were crouched on the ground, their bare skin mingling with dark metallic fur. Their cloudy gray-white eyes betrayed no consciousness, emitting rapid, anxious breaths.

Cora stared at the clothing on the creatures.

Her neighbors were an elderly couple with a young grandson.

They interacted little, but in daily trivial matters, they would help each other out.

Micheal, the quail they raised, had been her only friend.

The monsters before her were mangled beyond recognition, some parts of their bodies oozing pus turning a sickly bluish-black.

Despite the decay and stench, their tattered clothes were eerily familiar — the same clothes her neighbors often wore.

Chills ran down Cora's spine as a horrifying realization dawned on her.

Perhaps they had turned like this, just like Sid and the deranged researcher from the pier. Sid was bitten by a bird, and the researcher encountered a shipwreck. What about them? Were they attacked by something else, or was it... Micheal?

In her distracted moment, the creatures caught a whiff of the scent of a living human and crawled out from the shadows toward the entrance.

The two twisted and bizarre forms drew nearer, and the leading creature emerged, exposing its entire visage to the chaotic sunlight.

Cora's instincts screamed that something was amiss. Two... wait! She jerked her head up, her teeth chattering. Their house... what happened to their young grandson?

The creature in front of her, its pale eyes fixed on Cora, its silver hair tangled and matted, fingers a bloody mess, its abdomen distended like a pregnant woman at full term, oozing a suffocating bloodiness.

Cora's grip on the sword tightened, the blue light flickering, emitting a soundless lament.

The monsters were agitated by the sudden illumination, lunging forward.

Cora parried with her sword, the claws clashing against the blade, producing intense friction.

The monsters stumbled back to the ground, and Cora retreated two steps.

Such incredible strength!

The attack only further enraged the creatures. They split in two directions and closed in on her.

Cora rolled sideways, evading the assault, then swung the

gigantic sword in retaliation.

The sharp blade stalled as it struck one creature's heart before veering a few inches down, slicing a deep gash across the monster's abdomen.

Should she kill them? Could she bring herself to slay her former kin without hesitation? Dark liquid oozed from the wound, yet the creatures seemed impervious to pain, relentless in their assault.

They were no longer... human.

Cora clenched the sword with both hands, leveraging its weight to spin her entire body like a rapidly spinning top. The creatures were thrown off balance, toppling backward. Seizing the opportunity, Cora rolled away and shut the door behind her. She jammed a steel pipe from the corner into the bolt, then added another one, trussing it.

For a moment, silence enveloped the room before the sound of pounding on the door and the enraged roars of the monsters pierced the air.

CHAPTER 5

An One-Way Ticket

Cora lurked in a corner of the junkyard, remaining still and holding her breath as she observed. After leaving her neighbor's house, the thick fog had disoriented her, and she had unwittingly ended up in this area.

Her destination was the villa district halfway up the mountain, but in order to reach it, she had to traverse the junkyard before her.

Faintly, from within the mist, she heard the gnashing of teeth and the creaking of bones being chewed.

About five or six meters away, a few figures ambled past, uncoordinated and awkward, one after another, mindlessly stumbling into piles of discarded tin cans.

Through the vague mist, Cora made out their faces and her heart sank. They were the "monsters."

She couldn't stay here any longer!

Seizing the opportunity when the monsters crossed paths, Cora dashed forward, keeping low and moving swiftly.

The wind kicked up a few pages of paper as the lingering creatures simultaneously turned their heads, but within the expanse of white, they didn't catch sight of anything and continued aimlessly wandering.

Cora used her sword to clear a path, sprinting several hundred meters and breaking into a sweat.

Her damp hair clung to her neck, and even her eyelashes were damp with mist. She had run too fast, and unable to slow down, she collided head-on with someone. The impact sent a buzzing sensation to her forehead. Reacting instinctively, Cora bowed apologetically. "So-sorry!"

The person stiffly turned around, their pallid pupils slowly fixing on her, drool dripping from their gaping mouth...

Cora. "!!!"

Her heart raced, and with both hands gripping her sword, she swung it forward with a forceful swipe. "Bang!" She sent the creature flying, then turned and ran. She scrambled up a nearby column and leaped onto a rooftop.

The slower monsters couldn't catch up and only scratched angrily at the walls. Cora's legs wrapped around the column as she ascended, not making a sound, her heart pounding.

After a while, the agitated monsters, lost in the thick fog without a target, spun around in place for a few fruitless rotations before wandering away in confusion.

Cora let out a relieved breath and swiftly vaulted onto the roof. This area was on the outskirts of District 199, quiet, with scattered standalone villas. It barely qualified as the local "rich district." Cora was here to inquire about the situation from Old Cheung, but the problem was, she had last been here two years ago and couldn't remember the exact location of Old Cheung's house.

Cora crouched on the roof, squinting her eyes as she tried to make out the house numbers. "27... 28... 29, 29!" With the direction confirmed, Cora jumped down and made her way to Old Cheung's house. When she reached the doorstep, she took a few steps up and paused. She glanced down at the giant sword in her arms and felt that it might not be polite to show up like this. With a thought, she made the sword disappear.

"Knock, knock, knock..." She knocked on the door for several minutes before the iron door creaked open slightly, revealing the gleaming latch in the center and half of Old Cheung's wary face.

Cora urgently spoke, "Cap-Captain Cheung! Neighbor, bit-bit someone... Just encountered a monster, chased after me..."

Her words became more hurried, her stutter worsening as she struggled to explain.

She couldn't seem to make herself understood.

Old Cheung looked surprised, "But why, young one..."

The latch was removed, and Old Cheung examined the surroundings before motioning for her to come inside. "You better come in first. Come in and explain."

Cora bent down and squeezed through the door, accidentally bumping into something hard on the floor, nearly stumbling face-first.

The living room was quite disheveled, with several large suitcases scattered on the ground, partially filled with various men's and women's clothing and daily necessities.

Old Cheung locked the door again, checking multiple times, then turned back to Cora. "With everything being so dangerous outside, monsters everywhere, how did you make it here?"

Cora was still trying to figure out how to explain herself when she heard something she didn't expect.

What did he mean by "monsters everywhere"? Did that mean it wasn't just her neighbor's house and the junkyard? Was the situation worse than she thought?

Old Cheung noticed her confused expression and analyzed, "Take your time to explain. What happened earlier? And where have you been these past few days?"

"I-I've been at home the whole time, s-sick. That day..." Cora organized her thoughts and recounted her unexplained high fever and the strange changes she observed in her neighbor's couple.

Just as she hesitated whether to mention her awakening ability, Old Cheung waved his hand, interrupting her with a serious tone, "I understand, young one. You've been holed up at home, so you know nothing. Two days ago, the Alliance issued an urgent announcement. Because of a once-in-a-century solar storm, the Earth's magnetic field has been disrupted by an unknown energy, leading to mutations in some organisms."

He paused here, his tone growing heavy and mournful, "As for those monsters that eat people... although the announcement didn't explicitly state it, everyone is saying that 'doomsday has come.' Nowhere is safe outside, District 199 has already fallen, and those who have the ability have long fled."

Cora's gaze swept over the suitcases on the ground. Old Cheung was in District 199, so he could certainly be considered as someone with the ability.

Unaware of her thoughts, Old Cheung's face displayed concern as he continued, "We're preparing to evacuate on a starship shortly. Since things are so perilous now and there's news that monsters are everywhere, we should leave quickly. 199 is no longer safe, and I'm guessing the situation in District D is similar. The number of trips to District C is limited, and if we don't catch this afternoon's ship, it might become impossible to leave in the future."

Cora listened quietly as he rambled on, blinking as she realized what he meant.

Old Cheung also seemed to notice his own implication and abruptly stopped speaking, looking a bit embarrassed. "Young one, uh... over the past few days, we couldn't get in touch with you either. Since you've come looking for us, maybe you should consider... coming with us."

"Hey, Dad!" Old Cheung's daughter-in-law emerged from the inner room with a baby in her arms, interrupting him brusquely, "You come with me." The two of them walked into the study, and Cora could clearly hear them slam the door shut, their argument carrying through the door panels.

"What are you thinking, trying to be a good Samaritan at a time like this? Where are we supposed to find extra starship tickets to bring her to District C?"

"No need to buy a ticket for District C... get one for District D..."

"District D? You make it sound so easy. Going to District D won't cost any money? Besides, at a time like this, where can you even find tickets?" "We'll figure something out..."

"Dad! Are you completely out of your mind?" The sharp female voice gradually turned into a plaintive sob. "If you take her with you, who are you going to leave behind? Your feverish son? Your grandson who's not even a year old? Or me, your non-blood-related daughter-in-law?!"

"It's not like that..." Old Cheung's rebuttal grew weaker and weaker, eventually fading into an awkward silence.

Cora studied the patterns on the floor with lowered eyelashes, silently repeating the word she had heard.

"Starship."

The starship, the most advanced flying terminal of the Alliance, is one of the remarkable creations born from the "Glorious Thirty Years," and the most prominent and eye-catching feature in the sky above the isolated island, adorned with neon lights.

It was the sole passenger route connecting to the outside world.

In a place like F199 district, it was easy to get in, and ticket prices were practically negligible. However, leaving was as difficult as ascending to the heavens.

Even for a trip to the relatively affordable District D, the cost was quite substantial.

Cora's wallet was cleaner than her face, ringing with poverty.

With her financial situation, she couldn't afford a starship ticket out of District 199 in this lifetime, or even the next.

After coming out of the study, Old Cheung didn't dare to meet her eyes. Their argument had been so loud that Cora must have heard it all.

He awkwardly explained, "Young one, at present, these tickets have become priceless commodities. I've put in everything I have, exhausted every avenue I could, and secured only four starship tickets."

"I... I understand," Cora reassured him, her tone more gentle, "Thank you, Cap-Captain Cheung. My grandfather used to say that you're a good person."

Upon hearing these words, Old Cheung's expression changed drastically.

Cora's mention of "my grandfather" felt like a sharp knife, accurately piercing his heart.

Six years ago, Old Thornton, his face ravaged by illness, stood before him and entrusted him with a smile. "Cheung, you keep this money. Cora doesn't understand the ways of the world, and we don't have any other relatives. When I'm gone, take care of her. When she grows up, if she wants to stay in District 199, this money will be enough for her lifetime."

"What if she wants to leave?"

"She can go out and explore, visit District C or D, wherever she wants. Since she doesn't have any identification, you'll have to help her buy starship tickets. As for District B... it's not suitable for her. Tell her not to go there, and say it's my request."

Old Cheung accepted the money, and at first, he followed Old Thornton's instructions to take care of Cora. He looked after her well-being, her education, and martial arts training on Yue Mountain. He even sent her to school in District D. However, Cora returned halfway through her high school years, refusing to go back. Old Cheung had asked her many times, but she stubbornly shook her head, insisting she didn't want to leave again.

And so, that money became a thorn in Old Cheung's heart. He could see and touch it, but he couldn't have it. One night, Old Cheung woke up from his sleep, determined to decide. At first, he thought about using just a small portion of the money to purchase new ships, expand his transportation fleet, but then... his son got married, they bought a house, his grandson was born...

In the end, it all came down to money. Who didn't spend money on their family? His business grew bigger, his family became happier, and he gradually had less time for Cora.

Returning to the present, Old Cheung's heart pounded. Cora was just a child back then, and she wouldn't have known about the money Old Thornton left him.

Observing Cora's expression, he tentatively began, "Young one, before your grandfather left..."

Surprised by Cora's limpid gaze, Old Cheung felt his heart skip a beat. Gritting his teeth, he admitted, "He left some money before he passed away, entrusting me to take care of you. Over the years, your living expenses, education, and training expenses, every expenditure, your grandfather kept meticulous records of them."

"That money... wasn't much to begin with, and now, if you go out and ask around, you won't even be able to buy a starship ticket. I truly saw you as my granddaughter, and I really have no way... no way to help you..."

Old Cheung's daughter-in-law stood at the doorway of the study, her cold eyes watching, a wailing baby in her arms making sharp, piercing cries.

Cora remained stunned for a moment before nodding slowly.

She did not know that her grandfather had left her money. She had always been grateful and close to Old Cheung, who had taken care of her all these years. Now that the truth was revealed, she felt a sense of understanding. The Old Cheung family had left District 199, and from the start, their plan hadn't included her. It was her rash decision to visit them that had made the situation awkward.

In terms of closeness and priority, every person's motivations were ranked.

Cora had already grown accustomed to being at the bottom. She was the "distant" one, the "estranged" one, the one easiest to discard.

If it weren't for the impending doomsday, Cora would never have considered leaving District 199 or thought about starship ticket prices. Old Cheung could have taken this secret to the grave, and in her heart, he would have remained the kind and caring old ship captain from the past.

Cora smiled and looked up, "I can't... I can't leave. I have to go... to Yue Mountain, to find... my master."

Old Cheung seemed to release a burden, immediately echoing her words enthusiastically, "Yes! That's right! You can still go find your master. Or you can ask him if there's any other way. He's definitely more capable than I am!"

The electronic clock on the wall pointed to 1:00 in the afternoon. Old Cheung discreetly glanced at it a few times.

Cora comprehended his suggestion and politely stood up.

"Then, Cap-Captain Cheung, I'll be going."

Old Cheung replied somewhat hesitantly, "Oh? Leaving already? Alright...alright."

As she was about to leave, his expression became complex, revealing his inner struggle.

This fragile girl, left alone on an island infested with monsters, had only one certain fate—death.

Perhaps out of guilt or unease, memories of Old Thornton's pale face resurfaced in Old Cheung's mind. He hastily whispered in a lowered voice, "Listen, tonight at 8:00, there will be a military evacuation team at Fool's Wharf. If you can find them, go with them. It's your only chance to leave this place!"

Cora's limpid gaze met his, and she repeated calmly, "Thank you, Captain."

The iron door slowly closed behind her, and Cora stood on the steps, exhaling deeply. Turning around, she walked back home, packed her belongings, and when everything was ready, she stepped once more into the boundless mist.

The incessant wailing of air raid sirens echoed throughout District 199, yet the streets and squares remained eerily silent.

Buildings along the road were tightly shut, and ships in the harbor jostled against each other chaotically.

A pungent, salty stench filled the air, accompanied by sporadic bursts of short and abrupt screams.

Cora dared not stop and hurried toward Yue Mountain. As she neared the entrance, a feeling of unease washed over her. Suddenly, she halted her steps. Inside, it was deathly quiet, without a rustle of wind or a chirp of birds, not even the usual shouts of training from the disciples.

Complete silence.

Cora's heart raced, and she took cautious steps forward, her breath held. However, every room she entered—courtyard, corridor, training hall, resting room—was empty. Finally, she arrived at the innermost part of the martial arts school, outside Master Zhang's chamber. A disgusting smell made its way to her nose.

CHAPTER 6

The Fallen Academy

The entire martial arts academy lay eerily silent, a palpable sense of oppression hanging in the air.

Cora pushed open one room after another, checking for any signs of life.

There was no one in the kitchen, but it was in disarray, with broken dishes strewn about. In the student dormitories, the doors and windows were wide open, with streaks of dried black blood in the corners, but there was nobody around.

The training grounds were deserted, equipment strewn about, traces of combat everywhere. No one.

With each room she searched, her expression grew more solemn.

Her heart sank like a stone in icy water, sinking deeper into the abyss.

Finally, she reached the deepest part of the backyard and heard faint noises coming from the meditation chamber. Could they be in there? The door was unlocked, and Cora cautiously pushed it open.

Upon first glance, the room seemed ransacked: furniture overturned, cabinets toppled, low table shattered, even the incense holder's ashes scattered across the floor.

But her gaze shifted further inside, and in the next moment, her pupils contracted!

Master Zhang was kneeling deep within the chamber, a bowl-sized hole in his chest.

The blood, bright red and congealed, had formed a dark pool around him. Propping himself up with a sword, his head hung low, body motionless. He bore no resemblance to the lively figure who would often reprimand her with raised eyebrows. He stood like a statue, robbed of life.

Cora stumbled forward, desperately covering the hole in his chest, her voice trembling.

"Master, Master Zhang..."

In the entire Yue Mountain and the entire NPA, who could kill her master? How could Master Zhang possibly be dead?

His body had already grown rigid, tilting slightly when touched, his grip on the sword loosening, the blade clattering to the ground.

Cora reached out to steady it. But her discovery of another door blocked by him immediately diverted her attention. It led to the storage room behind the meditation chamber.

The storage room had long been abandoned because it was far from the training grounds, and it now only held miscellaneous equipment or items.

Cora gazed at it with a dawning realization, and after a moment, she understood that Master Zhang's posture in death was a sentinel's vigilance.

Perhaps prodded by the noise behind it, the door rattled even more violently, the successive blows soon interrupting her train of thought.

"Bang—"

"Bang, bang—"

The bamboo door quaked and creaked under the strain, threatening to give way at any moment, and a low, frenzied roar echoed from beyond. Something was trying to break free.

Cora held her breath, bracing herself.

"Clang—!!"

A deafening crash rent the air, the bamboo door collapsing in a cloud of dust as a horde of fetid-smelling creatures surged out. Cora quickly counted, and there were dozens of them, packing the room to capacity.

As the foremost creatures charged at her, Cora leaped up the wall, kicking them back with a powerful aerial strike that sent a cascade of them sprawling.

Upon landing with grace, she intended to follow up with another attack, then make her escape. But her movement suddenly ceased.

The creatures lay sprawled before her, their grotesque features and vacant expressions fully exposed.

"Lynn, Senior Lynn!"

Cora cried out in astonishment.

In that moment, the creatures had a respite, scrambling to their feet and those in the rear catching up. The room was dimly lit, but it was enough for her to see their faces clearly, even amidst their pallor.

"Ono, Senior Ono..."

"Auntie..."

Despite their haggard and horrifying appearances, Cora recognized every one of them-the senior students she'd sparred with, the gentle senior who cared about her well-being...

These creatures, now mere shadows of their former selves, had once been her friends.

As Cora faced this nightmare, the creatures advanced relentlessly. With her retreat thwarted, she could only backpedal, each step taking her further into a corner.

The light of recognition flickered in her tear-filled eyes as she shouted their names, hoping to reclaim their lost consciousness.

In District 199, she had been an isolated figure, with Old Cheung as her sole companion; no one else will engage with her. But it was okay, because she had the Yue Shan Martial Arts Academy, where most of the people didn't mock her. And they would sing her "Happy Birthday" every year.

Yet now, the senior brothers and sisters who had once sung birthday songs for her couldn't recognize her anymore.

The swarm of creatures closed in, and Cora retreated further, only to find herself trapped against the wall. Should she escape? Yes, she could escape, but then what? All these... "creatures" couldn't be left unchecked. The door to the meditation chamber couldn't contain them. Was she supposed to let them all loose? If Master Zhang was still alive, he'd surely berate her with a fiery rage.

In that momentary lapse of attention, a swift figure stepped on the head of one creature behind her, launching toward her. This one differed vastly from the others, both in size and aggression. Its spikes glistened with menace, its maw dripping foul-smelling saliva. Its clawed hand gripped Cora's shoulder, and its mouth lunged for her neck.

The stench of decay was overwhelming, and death's scythe was about to fall.

Cora pressed her palm against its ashen face, locking eyes with its cloudy, gray ones. Tears streamed down her face as she cried out its name.

"Theo... Theon..."

The person who had laughed carefree, even when sick, to make her smile. The one who had promised to compensate her with four eggs, who had been playful. Now, all it wanted was to bite into her veins with savage intent.

"Theon" emitted a guttural "gnawing" from deep within its throat, its sadistic bloodlust undeterred, its claws sinking into her collarbone. Blood spurted out, and Cora winced in pain.

She broke its arm with a swift twist, and its attack faltered momentarily.

Cora seized the opportunity to escape its grasp, rolling away in the opposite direction.

But the arm-broken "Theon" hesitated for just a moment before launching another ferocious attack.

Unfeeling and relentless, it couldn't feel pain or reason.

Cora was locked in an endless battle, wounds covering her body like a tapestry of pain. Limbs, torso, heart-shards and debris filled the air, tainted by spatters of foul blood. No matter where she struck, no matter how she fought back, the relentless onslaught of the creatures' biting didn't cease.

Tears went from scalding to icy, then eventually dried up as Cora sadly realized that the situation was dire.

It wasn't a matter of her being devoured alive by these creatures or dying here. It was her killing all the monsters and surviving or succumbing to this endless struggle.

Exhaustion took its toll, and a failed dodge resulted in another wound on her lower back, crimson liquid seeping into the floor.

Cora lashed out, countering, and the nearest creature was sent flying several meters, causing her to crash to the ground beside Master Zhang.

Cora's widened eyes subconsciously turned toward her master, whose own unblinking gaze met hers-calm, devoid of sorrow or joy. It was as if he waited for her to decide.

"I'm sorry..."

Cora turned her head away from his gaze, whispering weakly.

She didn't know if she was apologizing to the deceased Master Zhang or the unrecognizable senior brothers and sisters.

I'm sorry.

But she wanted to live.

A gust of wind brushed past her ear, and in the nick of time, Cora yanked the long sword from the ground—its hilt flaring with an otherworldly blue light that transformed it into a sharp Tang sword.

This broad-bladed sword was perfect for close-range combat, and in this tight encounter, Cora used her core strength, lifting it high above her head, and with a decisive swipe.

The creature's movement froze, and it was nearly bisected from top to bottom. Its shattered trachea spewed thick, dark blood, and it twitched for a few moments before collapsing.

Cora's heart skipped a beat as realization dawned-no wonder she couldn't kill them.

Trying to attack in another place was useless.

However, the deaths of their kin didn't deter the remaining creatures, who continued to charge relentlessly.

Armed with the knowledge of their fatal weakness, Cora acted decisively and slashed with precision.

She struck at their vital points.

Her expression was unwavering and her actions bear a striking resemblance to a wrathful demon coming out of hell.

Half an hour later, dozens of creatures lay motionless, their lives extinguished.

All but "Theon."

Unquestionably the fiercest, it still exuded a potent aura even with a severed arm and leg.

The stump of its arm revealed decaying tissue, oozing a dark, viscous fluid.

It locked eyes with Cora, and despite its injuries, it crawled toward her with a twisted and malevolent determination.

Cora's eyes were dry, having shed all tears long ago. Her hand holding the sword trembled at her side.

Fourteen years of martial training, and for the first time, her hand shook uncontrollably.

It should all... end now.

Cora raised the sword slowly, its faint blue glow casting an ethereal light on her stony face.

She closed her eyes, the blue light flashing brightly from the tip of the blade as she swung forward

Chop! Slash! A few drops of the creatures' foul liquid splashed onto her eyelids, tracing paths through her tear-streaked cheeks.

In the dim meditation chamber, Cora meticulously arranged the bodies of the creatures, placing their severed heads back in their rightful positions, preserving the dignity of their former selves.

She sat amidst the bloodstains, gazing silently at their faces, which were no longer contorted in rage.

Her gaze suddenly froze, a glint catching her eye within one creature's head. It was a fleeting reflection of light. Cora's powerful strike had obliterated its head, leaving it as shattered as a melon.

She leaned down, retrieving a crystal from within.

It was small, about the size of a lychee, with a hexagonal shape that seemed both opaque and translucent, an intriguing enigma.

Cora eagerly searched through the other shattered skulls, but none held anything similar.

Wasn't every creature supposed to have one?

She scrutinized the ruined heads one by one, finding three in total. While two were similar, the third was slightly larger, its internal structure a more transparent white. This one came from Theon's head.

What were these things? Gemstones? Cora stared at the crystal in her palm, befuddled by this unfamiliar realm beyond her understanding.

As she pondered, a faint noise outside the window startled her. It was as if someone were watching her. Again? Cora's spine tensed as she gripped her sword, brandishing it outward.

Thud—!

An icy surge of intent burst forth, shattering the window into pieces. In the ensuing haze, a half-human-sized avian creature stood on the windowsill, its gaze fixed intently upon her. It had a chicken-like form, yet two enormous wings sprouted from its back. A tuft of white feathers crowned its head, and its mismatched claws glistened with a metallic glint, while whip-like tail feathers rested quietly.

The giant bird lingered in place, its silent vigil seemingly unending.

Its chilling vertical pupils bore into her, as if observing Cora's despair, her exhaustion, and then her resolute surge of aggression.

Cora's scalp tingled, her heart racing as she sprang to her feet, gripping the sword horizontally before her—a taut standoff between girl and beast.

Strangely, the creature seemed uninterested in attacking.

Its tiger-like claws shifted slightly, and after regarding Cora for a few seconds. It disdainfully turned its head, fluttered its wings, and vanished into the sky.

Cora clutched the ashen-white crystal in her hand, staring at the distance where the giant bird had vanished. A single thought kept looping in her mind.

This world truly has gone mad.

CHAPTER 7

Aberrants and Anopower

Behind the hill, Cora buried the inhabitants of Mount Yue Martial Arts Academy.

Clumsy and determined, she only knew to bury her head in the task. Sweat and blood mixed as they splattered onto the yellow earth with each rise and fall of the iron shovel.

She tightly pressed her lips and performed repetitive and mechanical movements, as if she were an inexhaustible humanoid machine.

After finishing digging the holes, she began carving tombstones, her fingers blistered and aching by the time she etched each person's name.

There were twenty-three small mounds of earth.

They held her fellow senior disciples, Master Zhang, and all the connections she had in this place.

While counting the numbers, Cora unexpectedly made a discovery: not all the Martial Arts Academy's people had died there.

Mount Yue was in District E104, not easily accessible in terms of transportation.

The Academy provided accommodations for the students.

So, many people like Theon, who were devoted solely to training, lived their lives entirely on the mountain.

There were also people like Eamon and Rita, who held themselves in high regard, only coming up the mountain for scheduled training sessions and rarely lingering at the Academy.

Cora had found no trace of these two among the monster corpses. She guessed they had narrowly avoided it.

In addition, there was Felix, a senior disciple, along with his group, who were taking part in The Azures assessment. He had taken with him the elite members of the Academy.

Cora wondered where they were now.

With the chaos outside, would they even return?

Cora grabbed a water hose and cleaned the bloodstains on the walls and floor carefully.

After finishing cleaning, she checked the entire Academy, finding that the TV had no signal.

Though the water and electricity were functioning properly.

She found a screen in one of the student dorms. She wasn't sure whose it was. It didn't have a password, and there were many open tabs. Cora scrolled through and discovered that online discussions were already in turmoil.

Everyone was posting anxious comments about "doomsday" and "zombies." Some criticized the Alliance for its lack of action, others urged people to stockpile for self-preservation, and there were desperate pleas for help.

Not being adept with electronic devices, Cora grasped only the basics. She came to know that the outside world was experiencing the same terrifying monsters, although the situation was comparatively less dire than in District 199.

At least most cities hadn't lost control.

Cora considered and attempted to search for the Alliance's official news account.

The latest pinned message had been posted two days ago, announcing that the Alliance had opened hundreds of emergency shelters.

Residents could locate and navigate to them for refuge. She scrolled to the bottom and clicked on the details link, but the screen suddenly displayed.

"No access permission."

Power and status not only determined the distribution of wealth, but also controlled access to information.

Just like her, the owner of this screen was also denied the small privilege of seeing the emergency shelters.

Cora set down the screen and then realized she was covered in dirt. Blood had splattered during the fight, and she had become quite messy. After digging in the dirt for a while, she had an unpleasant odor clinging to her. She took a cold shower in the bathroom, scrubbing herself clean. Afterward, she bit into a bandage and dressed her wounds.

Cleaning, stopping the bleeding, applying ointment, and bandaging.

The blood of those monsters, or whatever it was, appeared black and flowed slower than normal human blood.

Remembering the panicked expression of the middle-aged man who had been injured at the pier, Cora looked down at her wound, uncertain of the consequences.

Night fell, and the sky gradually darkened without her noticing.

Cora packed an 80-liter backpack with warm and moisture-resistant clothing, a small amount of non-perishable food, a wide-mouth water bottle and purification tablets, a fire starter, a flashlight, a portable first aid kit, a sleeping bag, and a tent.

She thought for a moment, then added a compass. As for weapons, her extraordinary ability was her most potent arsenal, so she brought nothing physical.

Before departing, Cora hesitated for a long time while holding a pen. She had wanted to write something, but what could she write? Who would read it? Write about witnessing Master Zhang's tragic death? Write about how circumstances had forced her to take lives, killing all twenty-two members of Martial Arts Academy? Once today was over, Mount Yue Martial Arts Academy would no longer exist. Who could she seek forgiveness from? No one would forgive her. They had all turned into monsters.

In the end, she left the pen untouched. Cora locked the gates of the Academy and gave it a deep last glance before turning and walking away.

At eight o'clock in the evening, Fool's Dock was brightly lit, and the departure channel was congested. There were no walls that couldn't be breached, and the news of the military passing through the port had leaked out tonight.

Several green military trucks parked at the end of the road, serving as makeshift barriers.

Standing beside the trucks were a few tall figures in conspicuous military uniforms.

They wore camouflage pants tucked into combat boots, exuding a resolute aura and a fierce presence.

The Alliance had not proclaimed a rescue mission in District 199.

Technically, this group was just passing through and not obligated to organize an evacuation.

However, they had still chosen to take as many residents as possible. This "taking" was, of course, conditional. Each resident had to pass through a careful inspection by them before being allowed onto the starship behind.

Cora was all alone, trailing behind the group with her bags and belongings, craning her neck to look around.

There were two lines moving faster than she had expected.

In silence and obedience, everyone advanced while carrying bags and luggage.

Along the way, someone checked the color of their pupils and examined their bodies for wounds and sores.

At the forefront of the line was a folding table with a small black box on it, about the size of a radio. Every person who had passed the preliminary check had to step up to the table. They spread their arms like getting a chest CT scan, and the black box scanned them. The side of the black box was connected to a display screen. From Cora's position, all she could see was a jumble of red and green lines intertwining.

During the short time she observed, three more people passed the front of the line, but the lines on the display screen remained unchanged. One man, stern-faced and in his thirties, who seemed to be the leader, adjusted his lips. These three people were all assigned to the back half of the starship.

Cora fixed her gaze on the ordinary black box, lost in thought. Just as she was contemplating, she was suddenly shoved forcefully from behind. "Move! Don't block the way!"

The person behind her was not holding back, applying full strength. However, despite the forceful shove, Cora, who appeared fragile, stood her ground and remained unmoved.

Instead, the person who pushed her stumbled forward a few steps because of his excessive force, froze momentarily, and then recovered, glaring menacingly at Cora.

Cora, in an attempt to go unnoticed, cast her eyes downward and retreated, wordlessly clearing a path for the other person.

She recognized the man, Victor Blackwood. Behind him was a fair-skinned young boy, his son Damian.

Victor had made a fortune in his early years through illicit smuggling operations.

Supposedly, he had connections even in B-level cities and was the richest man in District 199.

He always wore a peculiar-shaped gold watch on his wrist and a flashy gold belt that supported his round belly. He would walk with his nose in the air, looking down on everyone. Although he was petty and vengeful, he had a reputation for holding grudges. Cora had heard Old Cheung talk about his domineering deeds and didn't want to get into trouble at this critical juncture. She moved aside without a word to make way for him.

"Consider yourself lucky!" Victor was accustomed to his arrogance.

Seeing Cora's timid appearance, he mumbled a few words without saying much. He pushed and jostled his way through the queue, brazenly cursing and cutting in line. He led his son toward the front.

The crowd dared not speak up, reluctantly giving way to him. His son blushed and lowered his head in shame, allowing Victor to pull him forward.

The two of them quickly passed the checks along the way and stood in front of the black box.

First was Victor. Just like the residents who were checked earlier, the black box didn't react.

However, when Damian stepped up afterward, the long-dormant

black box suddenly flickered to life.

The tangled red and green lines on the display screen still meandered at the bottom, but several green curves undulated like rolling hills, oscillating with renewed vitality, as if an electrocardiogram of a lifeless heart had come back to life.

The man standing beside the box, arms folded, slightly straightened his posture and cast a glance at Damian.

"You go to the rear section."

The starship that had been commandeered was a regular civilian model.

Its interior was clearly divided into two sections: standard and deluxe.

The standard section was larger, but the seats were cramped. The deluxe section had smaller seats, each enclosed within a small compartment.

Brown-tinted glass with privacy film covered the compartments, emphasizing passenger privacy.

The two sections were not interconnected, and even the entrances were separate.

Upon hearing the result, Victor's face lit up with joy before anyone could react. He was about to move forward, leading his son. However, the man reached out and stopped him.

His stern face was filled with seriousness. "You go to the back."

Victor's eyes widened, his tone growing frantic. "This is my son! We're together!!"

The man in front of him remained expressionless, repeating, "You, to the back cabin."

Victor's frustration twisted his mouth, but he surreptitiously glanced at the muscular arms of the man before attempting to assert himself.

"Sir... Captain, could we work something out? Can we discuss this...?"

He reached into his briefcase, pulling out a thick stack of money wrapped in newspapers, discreetly trying to slip it into the man's hand. The man pushed it back, his tone icy. "To prevent conflict, Aberrants and regular people need to retreat separately. It's protocol."

"Aberrants."

Cora, who had moved midway through the line, perked up at the unfamiliar term.

Unable to bribe his way through, Victor's face elongated, his tone growing more forceful, "Whose orders are you following? Get your superior here to talk with me! Do you... do you even know who I am? I have connections in Zone B! I must get into this luxury cabin today!"

He shielded the slight figure of Damian behind him, mirroring Victor by refusing to let him board. Seeing this, a young soldier nearby swiftly drew his weapon, a line of guns now pointing at Victor, "Captain, please advise..."

Victor trembled, but the memory of tickets being canceled despite being bought in advance and the collapse of transportation in District 199 caused a flash of determination to cross his eyes.

He clenched his teeth, refusing to yield.

The stern captain glanced at Damian, who had lowered his head, signaling the soldiers to lower their weapons, yet he refrained from giving the order to let Victor pass, effectively leaving him hanging.

As Victor's standoff caused others to shift lines, the remaining people maintained a relatively steady pace.

The line was shortening, and just a few more people before it was Cora's turn.

But a new disruption arose unexpectedly.

"Ma'am, please remove your hat for inspection!"

A tightly wrapped woman forced her way through from behind, charging forward heedlessly.

She cradled a young boy wearing a duck-billed cap, face buried into her neck, unmoving.

The woman's surprising strength cleared a path through the crowd, overturning a folding table along the way. The black box placed on it wobbled and set off a piercing alarm. Then it toppled to the ground, its connection to the display screen abruptly severed.

In the blink of an eye, Cora's widened as she saw it all unfold. In that fleeting moment, the red lines on the black box rebounded as if hitting rock bottom, suddenly soaring to the peak.

"Please undergo inspection!" The soldiers with loaded guns responded swiftly, immediately surrounding the woman.

Blocked and trembling, she dropped to her knees and kowtowed repeatedly, her voice pleading, "I beg you, please save my baby! Please... take him away."

Despite her desperate pleas, her actions were uncontrollable, and half of her body twitched eerily.

Someone stepped forward, wary, and unraveled the scarf that had concealed her head.

A surprised gasp followed.

"Captain, she's undergone aberration!"

As the woman's face came into view, Cora was taken aback; it was Mrs. Travers.

However, Mrs. Travers, at this moment, bore no resemblance to her former self.

Her face had turned ashen. Her veins seemed to bulge with an unnatural ferocity, and drool incessantly dripped from her mouth. Her violent convulsions shook the ground, and even though her child clung to her shoulder.

She remained eerily still.

Another soldier approached and lifted the baseball cap covering the boy's eyes, then turned to the Captain and slowly shook his head, "The child, too."

Mrs. Travers raised her head abruptly, her eyeballs bulging in their sockets.

Her once clear irises had grown murky and her facial muscles strained and contorted as if unable to contain her emotional turmoil.

"Lock it down!" the Captain shouted sternly.

As one, the soldiers hoisted their guns into the air.

Amidst the disorder, individuals scattered in fear like startled animals, and within this turmoil, Mrs. Travers accidentally collided with Victor and his son.

Damian, who had been looking down, unexpectedly lifted his head at that moment. Seeing Mrs. Travers' transformed visage, his face drained of color.

His pupils trembled violently, and in response to the overwhelming stimulus, he let out a scream that pierced everyone's eardrums, "Ah—!!"

An invisible surge of energy surged through the air, emanating from Damian as its epicenter.

The temperature plummeted, and over a dozen sharp ice spears shot up from the ground, hurtling towards Mrs. Travers and the young boy. Because of his lack of control, some veered off course, shooting in all directions.

"Not good! The kid's Anopower is out of control!"

"Itch, damn, it's an ice-type. This just got complicated."

Amidst the icy landscape, the Captain remained composed, issuing a series of gestures.

Trained individuals heeled him closely, the very ones who had stood by the trucks earlier, the very ones who had stood by the trucks earlier.

A lean man stepped forward, moving against Damian's surge.

Ice spears, stopped by an invisible barrier, shattered upon contact.

"Everyone, get inside!"

The simple-looking soldier slammed his fists into the ground, creating hollow earthen rings reminiscent of old-fashioned tents that materialized out of thin air.

Frightened residents rushed into the makeshift shelters. Victor, overcome by fear, was dragged in like a lifeless fish. Cora jogged behind the crowd, her gaze fixed on Damian.

These soldiers in military garb were all "Aberrants," each possessing extraordinary skills!

Suddenly, her peripheral vision glimpsed a figure.

With lightning speed, the stern man skillfully navigated through the ice spears, concealing himself behind his team.

He advanced relentlessly towards Damian.

His ghostly speed and movements far surpassed those of an ordinary person, rendering him almost invisible.

Amidst the ice, gusts of wind, and flashing lightning, his presence bore down on everyone present with an overwhelming pressure.

Damian found himself engulfed in unease, his pupils occasionally catching the agile figure of the man.

However, his eyes couldn't track the movements of the man, forcing Damian to shake his head frantically, inadvertently causing the ice spears at him to tremble and waver, launching wild attacks in all directions.

In the next second, the man materialized behind Damian, his hand striking down.

Damian's terrified scream caught in his throat, and his vision blackened as he lost consciousness.

The ice spears vanished, and the team members rushed forward, using special ropes to secure Damian, ready to transfer him onto the starship.

The earthen mound crumbled with a resounding crash, returning to dust.

The soldiers comforted the remaining civilians, rapidly conducting checks and evacuations.

Victor had long been reduced to a puddle of fear, his earlier arrogance evaporated.

Trembling, he was herded into the standard cabin, unable to even meet his son's gaze.

Cora's heart raced.

Amidst the hail of ice shards, an invisible barrier had flung Mrs. Travers out. Her child slipped from her shoulder, landing beside her. As sharp shards of ice descended, her child was at imminent risk of being impaled.

In the blink of an eye, Cora seized a broken piece of wood from the ground, her palm emitting an azure glow.

It materialized into a shield, intercepting the impending attack.

With a swift thought, the shield dissipated into nothingness.

Cora wasn't sure what "aberration" meant, but Mrs.

Travers was markedly different from the monsters she had encountered earlier.

Unless Cora remembered incorrectly, Mrs. Travers had been bitten at the harbor.

Despite days having passed, she remained conscious and capable of coherent speech.

Could that be normal?

Cora's thoughts were muddled, a sense of oddity gnawing at her. Yet, amidst the urgency, there was no time to dissect the situation. Her instincts took over, and she saved young Travers on reflex.

As the ice shards were halted, Mrs. Travers dashed forward, scooping up her child. She didn't utter a word, and her ashen eyes briefly met Cora's before she turned and fled.

With everyone's attention riveted on the icy battlefield, no one noticed the slight commotion here.

Mrs. Travers likely realized the futility of boarding and was making a desperate escape, leaving without a backward glance.

Cora stared at her fading figure until the distant urging voice reached her, "Miss, come over for inspection!"

She acknowledged and was about to move forward when her foot accidentally kicked something, causing it to roll away some distance. It was the black box, slightly battered from the melee, one edge slightly crumpled. However, the indicator light stubbornly remained lit.

Was it still functional?

Cora picked it up, studying it with curiosity.

Suddenly, the black box reacted to some stimulus. The red and green lines on the screen danced wildly, resembling a disco dance, up and down in chaotic succession. Before long, the lines froze into rigid straight lines, like a system crash, then-Bang! A puff of smoke erupted, and the box had simply malfunctioned!

Cora had no word.

"..."

Cora thought, this is trouble! Can she discard it now?

CHAPTER 8

The Abandoned

Cora faced the tall figure in military attire, standing by the folding table.

Resting on the table was the charred and short-circuited black box, which she nervously nudged forward to suggest her innocence.

The tall man cast a brief glance at the scorched mess of wires and then back at Cora, a surprisingly bright smile spreading across his face as he suddenly exclaimed, "Oh."

Cora's whole body trembled as she whiffed her head and gestured, "N-no, it wasn't me!"

"Mmm, not you," the tall man chimed in, his smile remaining, as he turned to report, "Captain! The detector's malfunctioned!"

The stern captain walked over, crouching down to inspect the smoking ventilation slots of the black box. He pressed the switch, and the indicator light flickered twice before sputtering out, giving a sense of hopelessness to the situation. As he looked at Cora, his attention was drawn to her hands, resulting in a furrowed brow.

"Really, it w-wasn't me, it just, it broke on its o-own!" Cora stammered, her heart racing. She really had done nothing, but what if they accused her of damaging it and demanded compensation?

"Give me your hand," the captain commanded in an icy tone.

Cora obediently extended her palm, her hands wrapped in white bandages from her knuckles up to her T-shirt sleeves. Apart from her fingertips, not an inch of exposed skin was visible.

"Undo the bandages," the man instructed in a matter-of-fact manner.

Cora hesitated for a moment before slowly unwrapping the layers of bandages.

Her slender palms displayed a few deflated blisters, and there were a few minor scratches on her arms, appearing longer than they were deep and already scabbed over.

"How did you get these injuries?" he inquired.

"Accidentally s-scratched myself," Cora replied.

The man didn't respond, maintaining a stoic expression as he observed Cora intently.

She met his gaze, her eyes bright and pupils dilated, and her attention occasionally drifting toward the black box in worry.

Despite the ordinary scrapes and scratches, they appeared quite normal, and there were no obvious signs of mutation. The captain seemed lost in thought, remaining silent for a while, his gaze as though trying to burn a hole through Cora.

The tall man couldn't bear the tense atmosphere any longer. "Captain, don't be so hard on the girl. Look at how frightened she is; she's stuttering and all. Hahaha!"

Cora thought, I already stammer even without the added pressure.

"Did you awaken your Anopower?" The captain unexpectedly broke the silence, his voice cold and his tone conveying a sensation of grinding stone.

Cora's heart skipped a beat, and she quickly thought. Did he see it? How much did he see?

She had covertly created the shield with the wooden plank, and the entire process took less than two seconds. How did he notice?

Unsettled, Cora didn't want to reveal her secret of having Anopower, at least not now. After the incident with Old Cheung, she had grown even more cautious and couldn't trust these people, who were not only strangers but also fellow Aberrants. She wasn't sure of their strengths, and if they took action, it could get complicated. She had other hidden secrets...

The tall man, overhearing the conversation, observed Cora's anxious demeanor, examined her, and muttered skeptically, "I'm not so sure. Look at her slim arms and legs; she doesn't really seem like..."

Several burly men carrying the bundled-up Damian walked by, swiftly boarding the luxury cabin of the starship, leaving the tall man to trail off awkwardly, poking his nose, clearly reminded of the torment that Damian, with his similarly "slim arms and legs," had subjected them to.

The captain ignored the tall man's muttered words and cut straight to the point, stating, "You saved that mutant."

A chill ran down Cora's spine, her mind racing as she pondered. Did he see? How much did he see? She subtly transformed the wooden plank into a shield, a motion that lasted less than two seconds. Yet, he mentioned it as if he had witnessed it all.

"The mutants all eventually turn into zombies, without exception. Saving them serves no purpose," he continued.

Aha, maybe he didn't see my shield transformation?

Cora relaxed slightly, but her sense of relief was short-lived, as the captain's chilly demeanor delivered a quick blow to her confidence.

She insisted stubbornly, "Th-they aren't, aren't zombies."

Cora couldn't offer an eloquent argument, but she had a hunch that Mrs.

Travers and the young boy differed from the typical zombies.

They didn't seem like monsters destined for extermination.

The captain remained noncommittal. "It's only a matter of time."

Not again! Cora thought. It seemed like he hadn't seen the shield's transformation. She sighed with relief before his icy attitude brought her right back down. She continued to explain, her tone sincere and determined, "T-they're not, not like that, really."

While she couldn't put her thoughts into eloquent words, she had a deep feeling that the fate of Mrs. Travers and the young boy differed from that of ordinary zombies. She couldn't explain it, but they were distinct, and she couldn't just stand by and watch them be treated like monsters.

Vincent, unsure why the captain was being unusually harsh with the girl, tried to ease the tension. "Don't be so tense, young lady. We mean no harm. See, we're from Azure Force, the 11th Division of Azures. I'm Vincent Anderson, and this is our captain, Jeremy Wolfgang. You can call him Captain Wolf."

With his right palm turned upward, the man generated a faint sphere of lightning, saying, "If you've awakened Anopower too, you're welcome to join us. We can take you to the next shelter. The seats in the front cabin are available."

Cora stared at the lightning ball in his hand, pursing her lips. "I-I don't have Anopower."

"If you don't, then you'll have to stay at the back," Jeremy said, turning away and walking off.

Vincent followed suit, casting a glance back at Cora as she prepared to board the regular cabin.

"Captain, do you really suspect she has Anopower? I mean, I mentioned Azures; if she has Anopower, it would be safer for her to join us. There's no need for secrecy, right? She seems like an ordinary person," Vincent reasoned.

Jeremy's response was chilling. "I only suspect. It's best if she doesn't."

With his Anopower, Jeremy's already keen senses became even more perceptive. On a recent occasion when he teleported, he felt a strong, unfamiliar energy surge in a particular direction.

It had been fleeting, and only Cora and two other mutants were in that vicinity. By the time he looked, nothing was there, and they had already been rolled several meters away with the mutated boy.

Although the detection device had malfunctioned, Jeremy could still detain Cora and conduct further testing later.

However, their team had an urgent mission, and they couldn't afford to waste time here. In the end, Cora was just a suspected Aberrant and wasn't worth making a fuss over.

Jeremy had personal reasons for not trusting her.

She had disobeyed orders to save a mutant, which contradicted Azures' principles.

Starship's Ordinary Cabin.

The passengers here were numb or vigilant. When Cora stepped in, she attracted little attention. She glanced around, saw several rows of seats vacant at the back, and then lowered her head, heading to the very last row. She settled into a corner seat.

It didn't take long before the engines roared to life, propelling the Starship forward into the endless night.

This was a low-orbit starship, equipped with operable windows. Some passengers in the front seats had cracked their windows open, allowing the warm breeze of late summer to waft in. The cabin was filled with a heavy, damp air, an atmosphere of melancholy and gloom settling over each person's head. Cora caught the sound of a few muted sobs.

A pervasive shadow had cast itself over everyone's heart.

Distant from home, facing an uncertain future, no one knew whether they would survive, or for how long.

Cora looked out the window.

The mist had cleared, and tonight, the moon was absent. The sea stretched out in an abyss of blackness. The faint lights of a distant island gradually sank, merging into the night until they blended seamlessly.

This also meant that District F199 was growing further away from her.

Goodbye, my homeland.

Cora whispered her farewell silently in her heart.

About an hour after the Starship embarked, Victor seemed to regain his composure, reawakening.

He fumbled his way up from his seat, determination guiding him towards the frontline where the dutiful soldier stood. It seemed as if he knew that his cash power had ceased its influence by now. He produced a pack of premium cigarettes, and with a certain purpose in mind, he approached the soldier.

"Hey there, buddy. Mind if I ask you a question? Where's this starship headed?"

The soldier took the cigarette, running it between his fingers, catching a whiff before pushing it back.

"A nearby D-grade city."

Victor's hand shook as he held the cigarette box.

His voice dropped to a whisper, laden with disbelief. "D-grade?! Why D-grade? Aren't we supposed to be heading north... to the base?"

The last few words were almost inaudible, revealing Victor's obvious intention to keep the conversation private.

The soldier turned his head, a half-smile playing on his lips.

He didn't provide a direct answer. "Yep, it's D-grade. We're being settled in a nearby D-grade city for now. The next batch of rescue teams won't be here for another two days, after which we'll take you to the nearest emergency shelter."

Victor's expression grew darker. He leaned in and exchanged words with the soldier, his emotions showing a hint of excitement.

However, the soldier's attitude remained cold, his demeanor impassive. He shook his head, repeating the same phrase. "I'm not sure, just following orders from above."

Most of the passengers in the carriage had no inclination to sleep, so when Victor returned to his seat, his face darkened with concern, those seeking information immediately surrounded him.

"Mr. Blackwood, you're resourceful. Can you tell us where we're headed?"

"Where else could we be going? We're just swapping one place to die for another!"

"Weren't the military personnel supposed to lead us in retreat? Transfer us to a safe place?"

"Do you seriously believe that? Do you think safe places are just easy to come by? For people like us, it's all up to fate!"

While he said "up to fate," his expression was one of frustration and mockery.

"Mr. Blackwood, what do you mean by that? Do you have some kind of insider information?" An eager middle-aged man inquired.

Victor fixed a penetrating gaze on the questioner.

"Do you think the apocalypse arrived out of the blue?"

"Wasn't it said to be caused by solar activity...?"

"Nonsense!" Victor's voice trembled, anger lacing every word.

"So many emergency shelters, so many military Aberrants. Do you think all of that could be organized in just two or three days? Let me tell you, they've known for a long time! Those people knew all along! And now, the apocalypse is finally here. Aberrants have become the elites, while us ordinary folks are just disposable lives, mere playthings for them. In the end, we all turn into mindless zombies!"

In a corner, a faint blue light flickered in Cora's palm. A narrow, sleek dart danced skillfully between her fingers, its sharp edge grazing her fair skin.

It moved with a dexterity akin to a child's toy.

Upon hearing Victor's remark about "Aberrants being the elites and ordinary people's lives being expendable," the dart executed a graceful spin, emanating a chilling aura.

Victor's sharp words rebuked the middle-aged man, who had been the first to inquire, leaving his face soured.

"Mr. Blackwood! It's true that our lives are expendable, as long as we survive. It doesn't matter where we end up," he remarked, a hint of disdain in his eyes. "But isn't your son an Aberrant? Why don't you have a way out?"

Victor's eyes lit up, as if he had found a lifeline. He seemed deaf to any further conversation, muttering to himself. "Yes! I still have a son. My son is an Aberrant!"

The atmosphere in the carriage grew heavy once again as Victor's revelation settled in.

Some stared off into the sealed-off luxury cabin, others whispered in hushed tones about the origins of Anopower and why they hadn't been so fortunate.

However, no one had any concrete answers, and nobody dared to inquire of the armed soldiers at the front.

Around four in the morning, the Starship came to a silent halt.

Most of the passengers in the ordinary cabin had fallen asleep by this time. A few still awake had their eyes closed, weariness clear on their faces.

The slight mechanical sounds of movement were easy to overlook, yet Cora suddenly opened her eyes, as if alerted by some intuition, rousing from her half-slumber.

She opened the window, stepping onto the ledge with both feet, moving like a nimble gecko. Clinging to the window's edge, she leaned out and climbed onto the top of the Starship with a few agile movements.

Through the dim morning light, she saw something astonishing: the Starship was automatically separating!

Darkness shrouded the luxury cabin carrying the Aberrants, with its red lights flashing.

In a matter of seconds, it reconfigured itself into a compact and independent craft.

It then switched trajectories,

veering in another direction and distancing itself from them.

Cora refrained from shouting and alerting everyone to the abrupt situation.

She remained on the top of the Starship, watching as the other craft vanished from view, gradually fading into the distance.

She turned her attention to her surroundings, and a realization hit her—she recognized the landmark building at the city center.

A nearby D-grade city? It was actually here.

As the first rays of dawn broke through, a civilian starship slipped into a food factory warehouse on the outskirts of Flower City (District D56).

The warehouse, spanning about 500 square meters, had been transformed into a makeshift refuge.

Three of its walls were enclosed, leaving only an entrance on the south side.

A group of armed Alliance soldiers patrolled the entrance, with their vigilance extending two kilometers outward.

On the surface, the security measures seemed nearly impregnable.

All the passengers disembarked from the Starship, passing through the inspection queue, and entered the warehouse like docile lambs. Cora lingered at the end of the line, her steps slowing down, creating some distance from the others.

The place seemed secure, but entering might mean there would be no turning back. Their movements would be restricted, and...

Cora touched her collarbone, feeling a slight ache. It was a constant reminder of her encounter at the martial arts studio yesterday. Although the journey had been uneventful until now, it was still preferable not to be surrounded by so many individuals. She just wanted to survive dragging no one else down.

By capitalizing on soldiers' shifting positions to maintain order, Cora discreetly pulled back.

Then, with a swift motion, she slipped into a dark alley.

PART 2

FLOWER CITY

CHAPTER 9

Fight for Survival

Convenient transportation and abundant natural resources blessed the Flower City (D56 District), in the southeastern part of the NPA, making it a rare habitable city within the D-tier.

When mentioning the most celebrated characteristic of Flower City, one must acknowledge its exceedingly intricate radial road network that directs towards the core of the city.

Cora was no stranger to Flower City. She had attended school here, walked its bustling streets and quiet alleys, and experienced the city's summer rains and winter snow.

If it weren't for the events that transpired later... she might have become even more intimately familiar with the city.

However, the Flower City of today bore no resemblance to its former vibrancy.

As Cora journeyed from the outskirts towards the center, the density of zombies grew ever thicker.

The once lively central business district now stood devoid of life, its stores either ransacked or barricaded behind closed doors, many secured with thick chains. The city, once teeming with activity, had transformed into a desolate wasteland almost overnight.

Walking along the main road, Cora kept a safe distance from the zombie horde. She sought alternate routes, leaping nimbly across rooftops within the residential areas, navigating her way through the urban landscape. Unexpectedly, she came face-to-face with a young boy in an adjacent building.

Their eyes locked momentarily through a protective window grille. The boy's pupils widened in shock, and just as he was about to scream, an adult behind him quickly covered his mouth, ushering him away from the window. To them, any lurking creature outside was as threatening as zombies.

Cora paid little heed to their reaction. Instead, her attention was drawn to an abandoned supermarket. A leap from the third floor brought her closer to her aim. The glass doors parted slowly in response to her infrared signal, dimming the already faint interior lighting. To her surprise, she found people inside!

Three or four men were sifting through the shelves, dressed in attire that showed they were residents. Judging by their appearance, they seemed to be survivors scavenging for supplies.

At the sound of the door opening, they all turned their attention towards Cora, hastily brandishing makeshift weapons — knives, rolling pins, and similar implements.

Cora swiftly assessed the situation and discovered that the supermarket had already been picked clean of supplies. She had no desire to engage in conflict recklessly.

Raising her hands in a non-threatening gesture, she maintained her gaze on the men while slowly retreating from the store.

Though provisions were scarce, Cora was grateful to secure a source of clean drinking water. Exiting the supermarket, she surveyed her surroundings and remembered that there was a delivery station for an online shopping platform nearby. She had seen advertisements for it when the platform first launched.

The location was discreet; she recalled... at the end of a particular alleyway.

Following the rough direction from her memory, Cora navigated a series of turns until she stumbled upon the delivery station.

Astonishingly, the station remained undiscovered by others.

Cora picked the lock and stepped inside. The air was thick with the sour stench of decaying fruits and vegetables. She refilled her water supply and selected items with longer shelf lives, such as cakes, dried fruits, ham, and biscuits, stuffing them into her bag. As she reorganized the contents of her backpack, a faint noise caught her attention from outside. Cora zipped her bag closed and crept to the window, parting the blinds to peer outside.

At the entrance of the alley, two blurry figures wrestled. A burly, bald man dragged a frail woman along, hurling insults and attempting to seize a bag from her grasp.

"Let go!" he bellowed, his anger clear.

He beat the woman until she clung desperately to her bag. Eventually, he wrested it from her grip, turning to flee. The woman, her hair disheveled and body hunched, continued clutching the man's pant leg.

Her voice trembled as she begged, "Give it back! I worked so hard to find these... please, I beg you!"

The bag's contents spilled onto the ground, revealing loose cans of powdered milk, followed by baby bottles and diapers, and finally, a few stray packets of instant noodles.

With the bag in hand, the bald man sneered at its contents. He unleashed a brutal kick, smashing the woman's head against the ground. Blood flowed from her forehead, and as he turned to leave, the woman clung desperately to his pant leg.

Her voice grew shrill as she cried, "You monster! You won't get away with this! Even in death, I won't forgive you!"

Yet, within seconds, a piercing scream reverberated through the air.

Cora's heart sank. "This isn't good!"

Almost on cue, a dozen zombies, drawn by the commotion, surged into the alley. They descended upon the struggling figures, tearing into them with frenzied hunger.

The gruesome tableau unfolded before Cora, accompanied by the woman's anguished cries, making it a sight that was nearly impossible to bear witness to.

Both figures met their demise at the hands of the zombies, yet the zombies persisted, lured by the overpowering scent of fresh blood.

They congregated, pressing into the alley until there was scarcely room to move. The nearest zombie had already reached the door of the delivery station, passing Cora by mere inches.

"No, there are too many. Waiting any longer won't do."

With her bag secured, ensuring nothing would spill out, Cora pushed open the door to the delivery station.

The faint creaking sound immediately attracted the zombies' attention. Dozens of pallid faces turned towards her as one.

Cora met the oncoming zombies head-on, standing her ground.

"Swoosh, swoosh!" A couple of throwing knives darted from her hand, piercing the eye sockets and necks of the nearest zombies. Their movements faltered momentarily.

She seized a kettle within her reach, which instantly transformed into a nearly three-foot-long staff as she swung it downward with force!

The tallest zombie's head went flying, its neck severed from its body. Cora tossed the head into the pile of zombies and, using the staff like a makeshift weapon, cleared away the others surrounding her. By the time she reached the alley's entrance, she held the staff's end with both hands, sweeping it in a 180-degree arc to knock back the zombies who hadn't yet joined the fray. In a matter of moments, a significant portion of the zombie horde lay incapacitated.

In just a few minutes, Cora had devised an escape route.

Leaping over the nearest rooftop, she quickly distanced herself from the grisly scene.

That night, Cora found herself atop an abandoned water tower in the industrial district, taking refuge.

Far removed from the city and its inhabitants, the zombies couldn't reach her here. As she lay on the cold concrete ground, staring up at the chaotic night sky, Cora's mind felt adrift.

Ever since that fateful day when she learned of the impending apocalypse, Cora had been lost. Her grandfather's last words had been to "survive at all costs." But after awakening from a three-day slumber, everything had fallen apart.

She hadn't comprehended what was happening before zombies started chasing her, before the Cheungs abandoned her, before her master died, and before the martial arts school was lost. After that? What should she do to survive in this apocalypse?

It had been almost two days and nights without closing her eyes. Cora was feeling overwhelmed, her sleepiness gradually taking over.

Just before drifting off, she shifted her position and kept repeating in her mind, "It's been this long already, and I'm still doing fine. I shouldn't turn into a zombie, right?"

Regardless of the situation, she stayed put for another couple of days. She would hold on until that rescue team arrived, whatever it was. At the very least, she was familiar with Flower City and believed she could tough it out for a while. She needed to uncover the mystery behind her Anopower...

On the second day, Cora continued her exploration to the west.

As the first light of dawn broke, she arrived at Academy Street in Flower City. Once bustling with many shops, the area had surprisingly left behind very few supplies, likely having been scavenged already.

As Cora approached a certain intersection, she could hear faint rustling noises ahead. Her right hand discreetly brushed against her pocket, where a few shurikens remained.

She turned the corner, and there on the ground was a huddled figure. When footsteps were heard, the figure stopped moving immediately.

After an eerie silence, the figure slowly lifted its head, turning it in Cora's direction. With pale gray eyes and a disfigured face covered in smears of unidentifiable flesh, its jagged teeth still held fragments of something.

Sensing fresh prey, its dilated pupils widened, and it leaned in towards Cora with a guttural growl.

An unpleasant stench wafted through the air, causing Cora to wrinkle her nose. Just as she was about to take action, cries erupted from behind her.

"Over here! There's a zombie here!"

Several teenagers dressed in Flower High School uniforms suddenly appeared, wielding baseball bats.

Two nimble boys dashed past Cora and swiftly dealt with the zombie, all the while nervously yelping and stomping their feet. They soon noticed Cora and cautiously circled around her.

"Who's she? No, wait, is she human or a zombie?"

"She should be, she should be human..."

"But she was just standing with the zombie! What normal person would be face-to-face with a zombie like that, playing kissy-kissy?"

"Who's going to ask her? I'm not going to...!"

"No, why are you all looking at me? I said I'm not going to!"

Finally, the guy who had repeated "I'm not going to" several times was pushed forward. Summoning his courage, he nervously stammered, "Hey, l-l-little miss, are you, uh, a person?"

Cora withdrew her hand from her pocket, about to respond, when the guy suddenly panicked.

"Oh no! She's not talking! She's really scary! I said I'm not going to, waaah!"

"?" Cora took a deep breath and explained, one word at a time, "I... am... human."

Tears welled up in the guy's eyes as he continued, "Then h-h-h-h-how come you were alone outside?"

"What are you all doing, stopping here?" Several more people arrived at the intersection, joining the group of students.

Among them was a strikingly beautiful girl who, upon glimpsing Cora, exclaimed in surprise, "You're... Cora?"

Cora slowly looked up upon hearing that voice.

"Irene, do you know her?" a round-faced girl asked in confusion.

With an embarrassed tone, Irene called out, but then quickly averted her gaze from Cora's icy, dark eyes, turning her attention to a certain boy's back.

The boy was facing Cora and seemed visibly tense.

Biting her lip, Irene clenched her clothes' corner and approached Cora, extending her hand and offering a deliberately warm smile. "Cora, you disappeared without a word back then. We were all surprised. Later, we heard you went back to your hometown to work. How come you're back now?"

Cora stared at their interlocking hands expressionlessly until Irene awkwardly released her grip. Cora then turned her gaze toward the guy, continuing her monotone response.

"I got separated... from the r-retreat team and ended up... alone."

"Oh, I see," the guy replied in relief, not expecting Cora to engage with him.

"Ha!" Someone laughed, and the glances toward Cora turned subtly strange. "What is it, a st-st-st-st-stutterer?"

"I heard survivors from a different district came over these past few days, talking about central management."

"Didn't they say central management? Then why is she wandering around alone?"

"Who knows, but she seems pretty fearless. The girls in our class would scream their heads off if they saw a zombie..."

Cora stood among their laughter, her expression unchanged.

"JP, did you see?" a young man with neatly curled hair, looking more mature, asked quietly. He was Ray Jean-Pierre, referred to by his followers as "JP."

Ray's gaze was complex as he silently stared at Cora, his old scar on his brow more pronounced in the sunlight.

He clenched and relaxed his hand, unexpectedly inviting, "Cora, our school has a safe zone with around a hundred people. Do you want to come with us?" He added, "We have Aberrants."

"Ray! Why are you telling her all this? She's not from our school!" another boy grumbled discontentedly.

Ray touched the ring on his finger, sending a stony gaze that immediately silenced the complainer.

The unexpected encounter with Ray and Irene had drained Cora's mood to the bottom of the valley. She felt annoyed, utterly annoyed, and had no desire to interact with them.

Her feet were already taking her away, but upon hearing that last sentence, she hesitated.

Aberrants? She had wandered around Flower City for two days, unable to find anyone to gather information from. They had Aberrants; maybe they knew something.

Cora nodded. "Sure."

CHAPTER 10

The Alpha of the Scout

Each member of a strange group of students walked down the deserted streets of Flower City holding baseball bats.

At the forefront was Ray, the leader of this high school band, his companions obediently following his lead—except for Cora.

Cora, being audacious and untamed by the twists and turns of social intricacies, walked beside Ray without hesitation.

She paid no mind to the individuals trailing behind or the array of expressions adorning their faces.

As they strolled along, an eerie silence hung in the air. Only after a considerable distance did Cora and Ray exchange a few words. Cora chose to be reserved, always keeping her words close, while Ray surprisingly remained subdued.

In the past, he'd been boisterous and defiant, impossible to ignore. But now, after nearly three years, he'd mellowed considerably. His very essence seemed to have transformed, as if reborn, a fresh outlook allowing him to face Cora anew. It seemed like someone had wiped away the slate of past grievances, and he even explained their current situation.

"The day the sun erupted coincided with the start of the school year. Many people suddenly collapsed. We had no inkling of the gravity of the situation. We dismissed it as ordinary heatstroke, tending to the afflicted in the infirmary. That same night, the first zombie appeared, followed by others. Within a mere two days, the school fell into complete chaos."

"You mentioned... Aberrants."

"Yes, there are three Aberrants among us."

"And how many regular folks?"

"One hundred and twenty-three," Ray's gaze darkened, "Just a couple of days ago, there were almost two hundred. Some were reluctant to remain in the school and tried fleeing—either to their homes or to nearby shelters. But once they left, all communication ceased... So fewer people have ventured out these past few days."

Cora, understanding the serious repercussions of students losing contact at this crucial point, prudently decided not to delve deeper.

"Cora, are you... holding up?" Ray abruptly turned to her with the question.

Cora gave him a bemused look. The question seemed out of place, leaving her at a loss for words. If she claimed things were going well, she'd be spinning a yarn. Her life had crumbled, leaving her adrift, homeless. But to admit things were going poorly? Well, she would have been zombie food long ago if that were the case. How could she be standing here, chatting with Ray, if she'd been bitten and turned into one of those creatures?

Ray, seemingly aware of the inopportune nature of his query, fell silent for a moment, then swiftly changed the topic.

A quarter of an hour later, they stumbled upon a western-style restaurant. They pried open the lock of the outer shutter, preparing to divide into two groups for a thorough search. "We haven't checked out this joint yet. I'll take a few folks to the main hall and the second floor. Holden, you guys scour the kitchen."

"Keep it quiet. Don't alert any zombies."

Ray quickly organized the teams. Twelve people in all. He led seven, while the remaining five trailed behind Holden. Irene was assigned to Ray's group but wisely kept her distance from Cora, opting for silence as she pondered her own thoughts.

When it was Cora's turn, Ray hesitated briefly. "Cora, why don't you go with Holden to the kitchen?"

Holden, the one with the scorched tin foil, didn't voice any objections. His gaze lingered on Cora for a couple of seconds. The main hall faced the street, and the second floor boasted many outdoor balconies. Compared to the kitchen, it was undoubtedly riskier. Ray assigned Cora to Holden's team, a tacit understanding among the group that they were watching over her.

Cora was unfazed, content with wherever they placed her. With the teams now organized, she nodded in agreement and positioned herself behind Holden.

The kitchen lay deep within the restaurant. They traversed the main hall and walked along the corridor for a while until an excited voice cried out, "Hey, there's a walk-in freezer here!"

Holden swiftly decided. "Let's go check it out."

As Cora moved to follow, Holden extended his arm to halt her. "Stay put, okay? Don't wander."

This was Holden's third time coming out of the freezer. He was more cautious than the others, his thoughts racing further ahead.

Having a delicate girl among them, especially one connected to Ray, left him feeling uneasy. He hoped Cora would remain still, like a fragile doll, avoiding any potential complications.

Cora sensed his hesitation and retreated with measured steps.

"Sure."

One by one, Holden and another boy emerged from the freezer, carrying beef, lamb, fruits, and vegetables. They handed their findings to a round-faced girl, who sat on the floor sorting and packing the supplies into backpacks. Cora sat to the side, watching them work.

Inside the cramped kitchen, two boys entered succession, scanning their surroundings for supplies.

"Wow, this restaurant's kitchen is tiny. Probably doesn't have much left."

"Should we head outside, then?"

"What's the rush? If we head out now, we'll have to help with the moving." the basket of potatoes had sprouted in several places. The tall boy picked up a small one and mimicked a basketball shot, tossing it into the hood of the stuttering guy's hoodie. "Three points! Nice shot!"

The stuttering guy's face twisted in distress. "Jacky, knock it off!"

Jacky paid him no mind and continued, "It's alright, we've got JP and the others outside. Hey, Little Fire, no need to hide!"

"Little Fire" referred to Flame Tillman. He had an aversion to pain and was twisting and dodging to avoid the flying potatoes. One of the small spuds veered off course and bounced a few times on the counter, making a dull thudding sound as it struck something. Both boys looked in surprise at the point of impact. Several zombies swayed to their feet, one of them wearing a white chef's hat and round as a small mountain.

Jacky's jaw dropped, leaving him stunned for several seconds. These zombies wielded frying pans and knives!

"Oh! Little Fire, run!" He dashed for the door, shouting as he clung to the door frame. "Hurry over here, Little Fire!"

Flame stood close to the door, facing off with the chef zombie. In his state of panic, he stumbled and the chef zombie seized his leg.

Flame kicked and struggled, trying to kick the zombie's face, screaming in terror, "Help! Help!"

The commotion quickly reached the outside. Holden and his group rushed out of the cold storage, and even Ray's team hurried over.

Jacky's voice trembled with urgency. "JP, help Little Fire!"

The kitchen door was narrow, allowing only one person to pass at a time. Inside, the space was tight. Ray rubbed the ring on his right hand, hesitating. He wasn't particularly adept at close combat. But when he looked up, met the expectant gazes of everyone, his breath caught.

He finally issued a hoarse command, "After I go in, retreat immediately."

But someone was quicker than him.

Cora had been idle, swinging her slender legs as she watched the girls packing. Suddenly, a scream echoed from the kitchen. Without thinking, she propped herself up on the table and jumped out. She burst into the kitchen, delivering a series of swift kicks to the rotund belly of the chef zombie, sending it stumbling back. She swiftly snatched up a bucket from the sink and slammed it down onto the zombie's head with a resounding thunk.

As it flailed around, disoriented, Cora grabbed Flame by the back of his collar and pulled him along. "Let's go."

Flame, weighing over 160 pounds, was flung out of the kitchen like a ball. Zombies followed closely behind, and Cora attacked their weak joints. Snap, crackle, crunch, the sound of bones breaking echoed as she incapacitated the zombies. She snatched up Flame's dropped baseball bat, swung it heavily at the chef zombie's head just as it freed itself from the bucket. It toppled backward like a bowling pin, knocking over a group of zombies nearby. Cora used the opportunity to close the door, lock it, and barricade it with tables. She turned around to face a group of bewildered teenagers, their eyes wide with shock and fear. Cora offered a helpful reminder, "It's dealt with. Let's go, move!"

An unsettling stillness enveloped them.

After a while, someone couldn't contain their amazement.

"It's like," Jacky stammered as he supported Flame, swallowing hard, "scarier than the zombies."

Ray stood at the forefront of the group, gazing at Cora's slender figure. The old scar on his brow seemed to ache faintly. He couldn't help but smile wryly. He had been mistaken. Cora, capable of single-handedly taking down a whole class back in the day, hardly needed his protection.

"Pack up, let's get out of here, quickly."

The journey back to the school went surprisingly smoothly, perhaps because Ray and his group had familiarized themselves with the route and encountered no more zombies along the way.

The high school students behind them were whispering, and no one dared to mock Cora to her face anymore. Lin Xia, the round-faced girl who had been in Cora's group before, tugged on Irene's sleeve and exclaimed in amazement, "Irene, who is this classmate of yours? She's really impressive."

Irene lowered her eyelashes, her voice soft and indistinct. "Is that so? She's always liked to fight."

As they neared Flower High School, Cora finally voiced the question she had been pondering for a while. "I have a question."

"What's your question?"

"You said that the school is filled with zombies, so why is there still a safe zone?"

"Well... you'll see in a moment."

They didn't approach the school through the main entrance, but took a detour along the side slope. Looking down from the slope, Cora was momentarily speechless at the sight before her.

Hundreds, even thousands, of zombies in school uniforms had taken over the playground, dormitories, and classrooms.

The density was hair-raising, and they roamed like ghosts, nervously turning their heads, sniffing the air for the scent of living humans.

This was the largest group of zombies Cora had seen since the apocalypse began, and it was the most chilling sight she had witnessed. After all, they had once been vibrant teenagers with promising futures, the hopes of the Alliance. Now they were lifeless, soulless corpses.

A weight settled upon everyone's faces.

Flame's sorrow was almost overflowing from his face. "In our class, except for me and Jacky, everyone... even the teachers who tried to protect us, zombies bit them."

Even Jacky, who had been laughing and joking all along, had red-rimmed eyes as he turned away.

Ray pointed in a certain direction. "The safe zone is over there."

He showed a sports hall near the edge of the school. They built the sports hall near the edge of the school, fully enclosed and using the latest earthquake-resistant and fire-resistant materials from the Alliance. A high-voltage electric fence surrounded it.

Cora gazed at the sea of zombies outside the Flower High School, her heart sinking. "How do we get in?"

"Come this way," Ray led the group, and the others followed him. They circled around the slope, and as they got closer, Cora noticed a hole in the high-voltage electric fence. It looked like intense flames had burned it through. The hole was large enough for an adult to pass through, but a couple of zombies wandered nearby.

"Step back," the group halted in the forest, close to the zombies. Ray's voice was stern.

The others took two steps back, brushing away, but Cora remained isolated in her spot. She surveyed her surroundings, moving slowly until she was in line with the rest of the group.

Ray took off his ring and walked towards the zombies. Cora

keenly noticed a faint reddish mark at the base of his middle finger. Just then, Ray raised his hand, and a two-meter-long snake of fire burst forth from his palm, instantly forming into a fiery whip that lashed out at several zombies. The smell of burning flesh filled the air as their skin sizzled, and the zombies wailed before collapsing to the ground.

It was at that moment Cora realized–Ray was an Aberrant!

After Ray dispatched the zombies, he turned and looked at Cora. He seemed to want to say something, but the others were already cheering.

"JP is so cool!"

"That AOE skill, taking out zombies is so satisfying!"

With the minor obstacle cleared from their path, the group passed through the gap in the electric fence and quickly reached the back wall of the playground. Ray took out his phone and typed a message.

Two minutes later, the unimaginable happened: the wall in front of them rapidly dissolved, revealing the shape of a door that had appeared out of nowhere!

A portal, perhaps?

"Cora, welcome to the safe zone," Ray said, then pushed the door open without hesitation. One by one, they entered the portal. The door closed behind them, existing for about ten seconds before vanishing as suddenly as it appeared.

Cora glanced at the wall and found it to be as smooth and undisturbed as it was before.

CHAPTER 11

Different Anopowers

In the gymnasium, around a hundred people sat or stood, all looking over. "JP is back!"

After the door had completely disappeared, Cora noticed a boy standing beside her. He had a somewhat pale complexion, but his eyes were bright. The boy wore a deep blue sports headband and had just pulled his hands back from the wall.

For a few moments, Cora locked eyes with him.

Ray noticed her gaze and leaned closer, whispering into her ear to explain, "His name is Simon Liu. His Anopower is 'Portal,' which allows him to create a door on any flat surface for twenty seconds. That's how we enter and exit the Safe Zone."

Cora wasn't used to someone being so close to her, so she just made a sound of acknowledgment and took two steps in the opposite direction.

Creating a portal with Anopower? No wonder this place could be a Safe Zone. Smart-controlled doors barricaded with heavy objects secured the east and west entrances of the gymnasium, enclosing it on all sides.

Along with Simon's Anopower, they could control the flow of entry and exit, minimizing direct confrontations with the zombies.

The group of thirteen made their way toward the center of the gym, where a young man was waiting for them.

"Mr. Sheridan, we're back!" The members of the scout surrounded him as they saw him.

"We hit the jackpot on this trip. We found steaks! Lamb legs! Finally, we can have some meat!"

"Mr. Sheridan, there are more and more zombies outside. When is the Alliance's rescue team coming?"

The mood shifted from high spirits to despondency upon hearing the last question.

Staying here for another day increased the danger, and their hope hinged on the belief that the Alliance wouldn't abandon Flower City easily.

Ryan Sheridan, a thirty-year-old teacher from their school, stood with an average build and wore rimless glasses that gave him a cultured appearance. He was patiently listening to the students, slightly tilting his head to take in their words.

Once they were finished, Ray recounted the events of the day and gestured toward Cora.

She became the center of attention. Initially, the remaining people in the gym hadn't noticed her presence.

With Ray's gesture, however, many curious eyes turned her way.

Mr. Sheridan finished hearing Ray's account, and then leaned toward her, gently beckoning, "Cora, come over here."

The members of the scout subtly moved aside as Cora stepped forward. She moved a bit slower and found herself exposed. Walking a couple of steps ahead, she turned into the center of everyone's focus.

Mr. Sheridan had been her homeroom teacher and knew about her stutter. He didn't mind her reticence, and just gazed at her through his glasses, lost in thought.

"Mr. Sheridan, Cora saved me today!" Flame, eager for Cora to stay, spoke up.

"Yeah, we encountered zombies, and she took down several by herself. She's really amazing." Jacky chimed in.

While the others didn't voice their support, their hopeful expressions were clear. Cora's swift combat skills had left a lasting impression on them. Having someone capable of such feats join them boosted their sense of security.

"Mr. Sheridan, let Cora stay," Ray proposed.

"Let's not rush things," Mr. Sheridan smiled, soothing the group. He turned his caring gaze toward Cora and asked gently, "From what Ray told me, you got separated from the evacuation team, right? Flower City is dangerous now. We try our best to ensure the safety of every student. If you're willing, would you consider staying here temporarily?"

Mr. Sheridan spoke eloquently, making everyone feel at ease. His eyes behind the glasses held a persuasive power that made it hard to resist.

Cora immediately looked in another direction, prepared to give her assent.

"No! I disagree!" A pretty and spirited girl descended from the stands. Irene tried to grasp her sleeve, but the girl brushed her hand away and continued, "Mr. Sheridan, it's already dangerous enough here. Why should we let in someone unknown? What if she seeks revenge or causes trouble?"

Ray wrinkled his brow at the sight of her, patiently explaining, "Angela, Cora isn't an unknown person. She's our classmate." "Classmate? Does she even consider us classmates? Don't forget why she dropped out in the first place!"

"That's enough!" Ray cut her off sharply.

Angela, scolded by Ray, was taken aback for a moment, as though slapped in the face. Her father was a member of the school board, and the haughty little princess was used to being treated with respect. When was the last time someone confronted her like this, especially Ray?

Mr. Sheridan dismissed the others to handle supplies and turned to Angela, speaking in his usual composed manner, "Miss Chou."

Angela looked up, her anger clear in her expression. She met his calm gaze and shivered, her overwhelming arrogance dissipating instantly. Her snappy retort and foul language vanished.

Mr. Sheridan spoke slowly, aiming to persuade her, "At a time like this, all of us should unite and put aside personal differences. Think about it. Cora joining us could be a good thing."

Angela, not knowing how, nodded along.

Mr. Sheridan offered a satisfied smile and turned to Cora, "You've had a long day. Go rest for now. The rows over there comprise your former classmates. You can join them."

Cora fixed her gaze on Angela, sensing something peculiar about her.

How could Angela change her personality so drastically after three years? She was seething with anger a moment ago, almost wanting to pounce and bite, but now she suddenly became so obedient?

Interrupted by Mr. Sheridan, Cora also turned her gaze toward the stands. She noticed her "old classmates" looking both fearful and embarrassed, none daring to meet her eyes.

"No need," Cora thought with a cold smirk, finding a corner with no one around and leaning against the wall to rest.

On the west side of the stands, someone curiously approached the group from Class Three, asking about the latest gossip.

"Who's that? So arrogant. JP's new girlfriend?"

"F**k," another person trembled, "Don't mess with her. She's a jinx... She's the one who gave JP that scar on his head!"

When Irene brought supplies to Angela, she saw her sitting at the edge of the stands with vacant eyes. Irene adjusted her facial expression to appear concerned and whispered softly,

"Angie, are you still upset about Cora?"

Angela looked confused for a moment before gradually snapping out of it. "Who? Oh, her. What a jinx. Mr. Sheridan agreed to let her stay. Why did you guys have to encounter this disaster?"

Sitting down beside her, Irene spoke, "Actually, it's not a big deal to come across her. Ray insisted on bringing her back, and he took care of her all the way. We were gathering supplies, and she just needed to watch."

Hearing this, Angela's anger surged back, and she stood up to confront Ray. Irene grabbed her arm, saying, "Angie, don't act impulsively. If you go find Ray now, he'll only dislike you more. Ray is an Aberrant now, and you can't provoke him like before..."

Angela pouted, "I just don't get it. How can she have the nerve to let Ray bring her back?"

"Because she can fight! But Angie, things are different now. Even though she can fight, she's not an Aberrant anymore. Some situations are beyond even an Aberrant's abilities. Without Ray protecting her, who knows what might happen..."

Irene paused, unable to finish her sentence.

"What might happen? Hey, wait a minute, can you just say it all at once?" Angela scowled at her.

Irene clicked her tongue inwardly, mentally cursing, "Idiot. I hinted so clearly, and she still doesn't understand?"

Then, she smiled gently, "Angie, do you know Siegfried likes you?"

Leaning against the wall, Cora activated her Anopower, gently manipulating each subtle change within her body.

She sensed an energy cluster approaching with her outwardly projected psychic sense.

Opening her eyes, she caught Little Fire placing a jerky bun in front of her.

Upon being discovered, Little Fire scratched the back of his head, blushing as he said, "Thank you for saving me today."

Cora retracted her Anopower and succinctly replied, "No need."

"It's necessary. Thanks to you today, I was terrified."

Flame gestured his gratitude repeatedly, carefully observing her expression.

Initially, he had been a little scared of Cora, but after the life-and-death situation, a newfound closeness developed.

Cora couldn't help but think of Michael for a fleeting moment, his incessant chatter going on uninterrupted just like this.

However, Flame's nonstop talking went on, and Cora couldn't take it anymore.

Finally exclaiming, "Hey, can you just... shut up?"

Flame looked like a parrot with its neck pinched, abruptly silenced and appearing pitiful.

Cora sighed inwardly, "I really, really want to talk. Can you, uh, fill me in on the... situation here?"

"Sure thing." Flame brightened up again. "I entered the Safe Zone on the first day. What do you want to know?"

"Aberrants."

"We currently have three Aberrants. JP, you already know about him. JP is a fire-type Aberrant; he can manipulate flames into long whips. Fire-types are effective against zombies, so I declare JP as the strongest fighter among us."

Cora raised an eyebrow, noncommittal.

"Then there's Simon. His power is to create portals. The door we used to enter just now was his doing. But he needs a twelve-hour interval between each use, and he used to pass out at the beginning. So, we only go out every other day."

Cora recalled depleting her Anopower initially and realized that Simon's unique ability required a lot of energy. It made sense that he could only use it twice a day.

"And the other one is Siegfried." Flame pointed in another direction, where a burly male student was helping a female classmate set up mats for sit-ups. His biceps bulged like two small hills.

"His Anopower is super strength, I think? Siegfried Zahn was used to playing American football. Now, he can lift the entire podium with one hand! See over there."

On the west side of the smart-controlled entrance, the entire podium had been uprooted and piled behind the door. It likely weighed several hundred kilograms. Cora had initially found this strange, but it turned out to be the work of Aberrants.

"However, luckily for you, you encountered JP today," Flame couldn't help but mutter.

"What... what do you mean?"

"Do you not know? JP isn't just strong with Anopower, he's also trustworthy. He takes us out responsibly every time, so everyone will follow him. But Siegfried had a terrible reputation before. He's impulsive and gets angry easily. Last time he led a team out, some people didn't come back..." Flame continued explaining.

Cora directed her gaze towards Siegfried, who had completed the task of moving the mats and was now engaged in conversation with a few guys near the stands.

She wasn't sure what they were saying, but they were laughing uproariously.

Angela shot him a scornful look nearby, and then Irene approached and began conversing with him.

Cora shifted her gaze back to Flame and continued asking, "What about Sh... Mr. Sheridan? It seems like you all... listen to him."

"Yeah, when the zombies first appeared, we were all terrified. Fortunately, Mr. Sheridan was there. He organized our retreat and came up with the idea of the Safe Zone. We take turns going out to find supplies, and he's the one who assigns people to different tasks."

"So, do you know how Anopower... awakens?"

"We don't know. The Alliance hasn't officially explained it. It's all hearsay, some true, some not. If it weren't for JP and them being real Aberrants, I probably wouldn't have believed it, either."

"But I noticed they have one thing in common!"

Flame suddenly lowered his voice, leaning in with a mysterious air as he revealed to her, "I don't know about other Aberrants, but the night JP and the others awakened their Anopower, they all had a fever. Siegfried woke up first, around 11 p.m., then Simon, around 3 a.m., and JP woke up latest. It was almost noon the next day."

CHAPTER 12

A Trap

Fever as a precursor to Anopower awakening?

Lost in thought, Cora pondered this question, tuning out the rapid stream of information Flame was sharing.

He rambled on about the rules of the safe zone, the scheduling of outings, gossip among classmates—all of it barely registering in her mind.

Having finished sharing his intel, Flame quenched his thirst and headed back to Jacky's side for water.

Cora lowered her gaze, lost in contemplation.

If fever truly heralded the awakening of Anopower, then her three days of high fever, during which she almost succumbed.

Could it impact her Anopower? What exactly was the Anopower she had awakened?

As she solved one puzzle, new questions popped up like weeds. Cora's head was spinning.

Ray eventually approached her again, braving the scrutiny of many eyes, to deliver food and a mattress.

Cora used to think of him as a mobile nuisance, but three years had passed, and he still had that same irritating demeanor. She couldn't be bothered to acknowledge him.

Perhaps sensing her impatience, Ray left after placing down the items. Cora showed no gratitude and simply ate the bread from her own bag.

As night fell, the wind and rain subsided over the sports field. Everyone lay on their mats, lost in their thoughts, drifting into slumber one by one. Cora picked up her backpack, her surroundings shrouded in darkness, and slipped into the equipment room.

The stifling heat within the equipment room made her tug at her shirt hem as she unwound the bandages from her body.

As the gauze separated from her skin, there was a faint tugging sensation. After all the bandages were removed, Cora was momentarily stunned. The deep wounds on her body, once exposing bone, had remarkably healed in just a few days. Fresh, tender flesh had grown, and poking at it was hardly painful at all.

Could this result from her Anopower awakening?

Her body's recovery rate seemed to have sped up.

Cora had been reluctant to travel with the military personnel mainly because of her injuries, especially the gruesome ones on her back and abdomen.

At first glance, they looked like mangled flesh, so she deliberately wrapped long bandages around her arms to divert attention there and downplay the other wounds.

After all, being injured by zombies, and with her uncertainty about potential mutations, she didn't want to draw any attention, especially from the formidable and vigilant Aberrants.

The consequences of such attention could be dire.

After reapplying the ointment and treating her wounds, Cora covered the door and nestled back into her original corner.

Later in the night, she fell into a fitful sleep with her backpack as a pillow, until the tranquility of the safe zone was shattered by a loud exclamation.

"There's news! The Alliance has issued a statement!"

Intermittent flashes of phone lights illuminated the area as people, awoken by the commotion, hurriedly checked the official announcement.

"It's true! A rescue team is less than 80 kilometers away from Flower City!"

"They're saying they'll first clear out the peripheral zombies and then dispatch Starships for urban rescue. Survivors can upload their locations." "This is fantastic! We can finally get out of here!" The girls embraced each other, jumping and crying tears of joy.

The entire safe zone was filled with hope of survival.

Sleep was forgotten as everyone gathered to agitate. Mr. Sheridan summoned a group of students for an emergency meeting, apparently discussing plans to establish contact with the rescue team.

Cora had little interest in their meeting. She rolled over and faced the wall, continuing her slumber. She knew that rescue teams were coming these days, having learned of the possibility when she escaped from Zone F199.

The news becoming reality was just another reminder of the impending transition to another place of wander.

What she didn't expect, however, was that shortly thereafter, the same group that had just finished their meeting started walking towards her.

"Cora, wake up! We need to talk to you about something, Cora?"

Charlotte Lincoln, acting as their spokesperson, called out softly, but Cora, nestled with her bag, continued to slumber deeply, showing no response.

She had actually been awake since they drew near, but the collective hum of their voices irritated her, triggering her morning grumpiness. She wasn't too keen on dealing with this group of people.

Mr. Sheridan squatted down in front of her, seemingly aware that she was awake. His tone remained calm as he spoke. "Cora, are you willing to wake up for a moment? We have something important to discuss."

Although he seemed to seek her opinion, a sea of faces behind him stared at her expectantly.

Everyone was waiting for her response, and Cora, unable to pretend to be asleep any longer, slowly opened her eyes and yawned —a deep yawn.

She was tired, her eyes welling up with tears because of the exhaustion.

By the time the group of people approached, she had already woken up.

But with so many voices buzzing around her, her irritation got the better of her. She didn't feel like acknowledging them.

Mr. Sheridan paid no mind to her rudeness. He continued to cajole in his warm tone, "Cora, each person has a role and contribution within our team. You've just joined us, and as a teacher, I believe in fairness. I know you're capable, and we've discussed this with Siegfried; he agrees to your involvement."

From the corner of her eye, Cora noticed Flame frantically shaking his head at her. Ray stepped forward, his lips tightly pressed together, "Mr. Sheridan, let me lead the team today."

Siegfried, who had already been in a sour mood, sneered at Ray's proposal, "Come on, Ray, you think you're better than me? You're the hero, and I'm the scumbag?"

Mr. Sheridan intervened just in time, extinguishing the brewing argument.

"While searching outside is crucial, safeguarding the safe zone is equally important. Ray, I trust you, and I hope you have faith in your classmates' abilities."

Ray seemed like he wanted to argue further, but Holden quickly pulled him back, murmuring something to him. Both Aberrants glared at each other, a tense standoff.

Despite the imminent argument, Mr. Sheridan remained composed and lowered his voice soothing, "Cora, let me speak my mind. Ray is dependable and responsible; I have confidence in his leadership. As for Siegfried, he has a stronger personality. While you're outside, monitor him. I know you're quite skilled."

When he mentioned "you're quite skilled," there was a hint of deeper meaning in his tone.

Cora's heart skipped a beat, unsure of what Mr. Sheridan's last words conveyed.

Mr. Sheridan turned away and declared in a louder voice, "Siegfried, you'll lead the team today. But remember, we cannot afford to lose anyone else." He seemed to smile, but his eyes held a bottomless depth, carrying a sense of warning.

In the dimly lit sports field, a few pendant lights illuminated the area, casting shadows over everyone's faces, making it hard to discern their expressions.

Cora's gaze swept across Angela and Irene in the distance, passing Flame and Charlotte closer by the tense standoff between Ray and Siegfried, and then finally landed on Mr. Sheridan.

Each face concealed its own thoughts.

What plans were they devising? What were they worried about? What were they afraid of?

Grandpa was right. Dealing with people was truly the most exhausting thing in this world. Cora heaved her bag with one hand and pushed herself up from the ground. "Got it, I'll go out," she said.

By touching the wall, Simon triggered a surge of intense energy that transformed into a solid door.

He patted Siegfried's shoulder. "Send me a message when you're back." Siegfried gave a thumbs-up in response.

Right before opening the door, Siegfried suddenly pulled his hand back and grinned playfully at Cora. "Hey there, I heard you're quite skilled. How about you go first?" Going out was undoubtedly riskier than coming in; who knew what horrors might await beyond that door?

"Sure," Cora replied lazily, not bothering to expose his ulterior motives.

She nodded, and without giving him a second glance, pushed the door open and stepped outside.

Audacious, far too audacious.

Anger contorted Siegfried's face almost beyond recognition.

This time, the team comprised eight people, including Cora. All of them were boys, and she didn't recognize any of them except for one—Holden, who somehow tagged along. While others weren't paying attention, he came over and whispered a warning to her, "Siegfried might cause you trouble. Be careful."

From Flame's gossip, Cora knew Holden was a repeat student, older than the rest of them, and seemed to have a weighty demeanor. He was on good terms with Ray, and Cora felt neither fondness nor dislike towards him. She simply nodded in acknowledgment.

"Sieg, should we head to the Starship port first?" One of the team members asked shortly after leaving the school.

"No rush," Siegfried replied, casting a sidelong glance at Cora.

She trailed behind them, eyelids drooping, projecting an air of detachment that kept people at arm's length.

"Thornton," Siegfried drawled slowly, looking at Cora. "We still have time. I thought we'd scavenge for supplies first. What do you think?"

Cora lifted her gaze. Her eyes were similar to pieces of turquoise as she stared at Siegfried, causing him to feel unsettled in an inexplicable way. Slowly, she nodded. "Sounds good."

Given their upcoming visit to the Starship port, their scavenging progressed more efficiently.

The team made their way along College Street, and not long after, they stumbled upon a commercial street.

The shops in this area may have been small, but they were tightly packed.

A few of them stopped in front of a row of shops. Siegfried surveyed the area, suggesting with a sly smile, "Thornton, how about we split up and each take a shop? You go first."

He didn't move, and the group behind him dared not budge, clearly intending to pressure Cora into agreeing.

Cora casually chose a gift shop and grabbed the door handle. She twisted back and asked, "One person per shop, but who gets to claim the supplies?" It was best to clarify such matters in advance. She wasn't one of them and wouldn't accept their system of collective distribution.

Siegfried's smile wavered between amusement and something else. "Whoever finds them gets to claim them."

Cora was satisfied.

"Fine."

As she entered the shop, Siegfried whispered a few instructions to his entourage, and the remaining members dispersed, entering neighboring stores.

Holden was searching for supplies when he faintly heard some commotion outside. A sense of unease crept over him, causing him to drop what he was doing and rush out. Sure enough, Siegfried's men had found some thick iron chains from somewhere and had wrapped them around Cora's door, creating multiple layers of locks.

"Siegfried, what are you doing?!" Holden realized their intent and moved to dismantle the chains.

Siegfried's robust arm swung over, punching him against the wall. He squatted down, his eyes dark and menacing as he glared at him.

"I'll warn you, mind your own business."

Holden shouted in anger, "Have you lost your mind? Aren't you afraid of causing a fatality?"

"What I want is to teach her a lesson. Why are you so concerned?"

"If anything happens to her, not just Ray, even Mr. Sheridan won't let you off the hook."

Mr. Sheridan's attitude towards Cora had been noticeably courteous, and Siegfried paused, momentarily recalling the boasting he had indulged in the previous night. This only fueled his anger further.

"You think I'm a fool, just letting one and all walk over me? Lock it up!"

Chains as thick as a bowl's rim wound around the door handle, forming an impenetrable web. Despite passing a significant amount of time, there was no sound from inside. A sense of unease crept over the group. "Sieg, what if there are zombies inside...?"

"If there were zombies, wouldn't she have screamed? Wait until she begs me, properly kneels down, admits defeat, and then I'll let her out. Let's see how arrogant she remains."

Before anyone could respond, urgent pounding erupted from inside. Heartbeats quickened as everyone's gaze remained fixated on the door.

One of the team members muttered in disbelief, "Why isn't she shouting?"

For several intense seconds, the pounding continued. Then the door shook violently, causing the chains to clank together in a symphony of metallic collisions.

Gradually, the sounds subsided, and there was silence from within.

The profound stillness felt like a heavy stone hanging over their heads.

The burden became too much for someone to handle.

"Sieg, do you think... something might have happened?"

Siegfried hadn't expected Cora's resolve to be so unyielding, refusing even to beg for mercy. He wasn't as foolish as he appeared on the surface, and he truly didn't want to take things to the point of no return. But in this situation, he found himself trapped.

He clenched his teeth and endured for another five minutes, sweat trickling down his face. Finally, unable to withstand the psychological pressure any longer, he relented.

"...Go open the door."

Out of nowhere, a thunderous crash echoed from within, freezing everyone in place.

"Bang—"

"Bang—"

"Bang—"

One crash, two crashes, and then three consecutive crashes, causing the entire door to splinter down the middle, debris flying in all directions.

Amidst the dust, Cora emerged like a Valkyrie descended to Earth, carrying a massive azure war hammer three times her size on her shoulder. She stood before them.

She fixed her gaze on Siegfried and his group, a faint tug at the corners of her lips.

"War... booty."

Cora swiftly kicked and sent a few decapitated zombies flying at Siegfried.

CHAPTER 13

The Meteor Shower of Shattered Beliefs

As the zombies lunged forward, Siegfried's muscles bulged, and with a powerful thrust of his arms, he sent several of them flying. However, his companions behind him weren't as fortunate.

Cora's throws were cunningly precise, and they ended up being surprised by the headless zombies.

Blood-soaked necks met their faces, and their screams echoed with heart-wrenching agony. They hadn't realized that those zombies were already long dead.

"You're an Esper," Siegfried declared with intensity, kicking aside the obstructing zombies, his gaze locked on Cora, each word dripping with emphasis.

Cora remained silent. Her lean frame flowed into her forearm, and with the ease of handling a toy, she swung the massive hammer into the ground. A powerful surge of residual energy swept over them. Siegfried's shoulders felt as though they were carrying a thousand pounds, and his feet involuntarily sunk into the earth. Clenching his teeth, he exerted all his might to resist the overwhelming force.

She was intimidating him, daring to do so! How dare she!

Siegfried, being an Esper himself, understood all too well the terror that Cora's imposing presence brought. He couldn't even move his fingers now, and her Esper level far surpassed his.

Not only was Cora an Esper, but she had also awakened the same power as him—a power-based Esper. This was why she could exert such a comprehensive suppression over him. He realized how laughable it was that he had even considered confronting her earlier.

The consecutive events visibly shook the members of the group, despite their daring. The relentless onslaught had drained the color from their faces.

Cora slowly emerged, dragging the enormous hammer behind her and helping Holden up from where he had fallen against the wall. Siegfried had held back when dealing with Holden, but Holden's back had been scraped raw, and his limbs bore some minor injuries. While these were not serious, his complexion was far from pleasant.

He spoke urgently before he even regained his footing, "This commotion is drawing too much attention; we need to leave immediately."

Siegfried, reckless as he might be, wasn't entirely foolish. When reminded of their perilous situation, he realized that now wasn't the time to quarrel with Cora. Besides... he wouldn't have the upper hand, anyway.

So, with a stern expression, he ordered, "Let's retreat."

The group quickly planned and hurriedly traversed the commercial street. Their pace quickened as they moved along, but it became apparent that Holden was struggling as they went. Beads of sweat formed on his forehead, and Cora glanced at his ankle before offering him a hand. Holden instinctively declined.

"It's fine, just twisted it."

"Oh." Since he didn't need the help, Cora simply retracted her hand.

Holden. "..."

He was just being polite; why did this person take everything so seriously?

Left with little to say, he continued, "Ray was originally supposed to come, but I volunteered to go in his place. I never expected you to be an Esper..."

Holden's emotions were a jumble. He had initially volunteered because he had witnessed Cora's strength and figured that nothing major would happen. He thought he could just stand by and get some credit from Ray, making it a good deal all around. However, he hadn't expected Siegfried's reckless behavior and the fact that Cora herself was an Esper. He ended up injured and caught in the middle of their scuffle, much to his chagrin. "Why did you have to come out? I could've managed on my own."

As expected, Cora didn't show an ounce of gratitude. Instead, her face was filled with disbelief and a healthy dose of disdain. Holden's ankle throbbed even more.

Cora had revealed her Esper identity for a reason. First, she believed that Mr. Sheridan had already seen through her secret, and she didn't want to be manipulated. Second, she wanted to avoid unnecessary trouble. People like Siegfried, when they reveal their hostility, were looking for attention and were quick to bully those who seemed weak. She had noticed the change in Siegfried's behavior since he no longer dared to taunt her along the way.

The group continued on in silence, walking intermittently and searching for supplies along the way. By the afternoon, they had reached the vicinity of Starship Port.

A bespectacled boy couldn't help but ask, trembling, "Have any of you felt that something's off?"

Everyone paused, carefully considering their experiences thus far.

While they couldn't pinpoint exactly what they felt wrong, there was an undeniable unease in the air.

Holden mused, "Could it be too quiet?"

Indeed, it was eerily quiet. During their previous outings, most of Flower City's infrastructure had been functioning normally.

They had encountered unmanned buses, traffic navigation robots, and colorful nighttime scenes.

Even during the night Cora spent in the water tower, she had witnessed the fountain show at Flower City Theater from above.

Yet today, as they walked, the broadcasts in the malls, the music in the amusement parks, and the large-scale projections on advertisement screens—all had vanished without a trace.

The bespectacled boy's face turned pale, and he fumbled to retrieve his phone. "I've lost a signal on my phone. How about you guys?"

"I don't have any signal either."

"Neither do I."

They finally realized what was amiss.

Water, electricity, and the network—everything that signified modernization—had all ceased to function.

The city's systems became completely paralyzed on September 9th, Year 46 of the New Era, on the seventh day after the solar eruption.

From this point onward, Flower City transformed into a dead city.

The true apocalypse had arrived.

Amid the deathly silence, Siegfried spat out in frustration, "Let's go check Starship Port."

"Yes! And there's the rescue team. Didn't they say it's within 80 kilometers? The NPA won't abandon us!"

As if clutching at the last straw of salvation, Siegfried and his group hurriedly made their way towards Starship Port.

A lotus flower inspired the design of Flower City's Starship Port. The entire structure gleamed in a soft silver-white, with the blooming flower buds at the top serving as control centers and boarding platforms.

The scattered flowers in the middle formed the takeoff lanes. However, at this moment, the petals held only a few isolated starships, and an almost eerie silence enveloped the entire port.

Siegfried's group didn't enter the port; instead, they found an observation platform on the outside, where they could have a clear view without the threat of zombies.

"There are people," Cora crouched atop the distance-measuring device, softly alerting them. "Southeast, and also north—there are people in both directions."

"Are they together?" Holden inquired.

"No, they're scattered. It's chaotic."

"They're probably survivors, like us, looking for information," Holden analyzed coolly. With the NPA having made a public rescue declaration, no one could sit still. It made sense that Flower City's survivors would lurk nearby, waiting for any rescue teams. A few boys exchanged hushed, excited whispers. "There are so few starships here. Have they been taken away by the NPA?"

"Likely. The rescue team should arrive soon. Let's wait longer."

They waited until the sun set and the sky far in the distance became dotted with dark specks.

"Look over there. It's the rescue team!" A sharp-eyed boy exclaimed, his voice rising with excitement. People in the directions Cora had just pointed to stood up, some even taking off their clothes or hats and waving frantically towards the sky.

The group of dark dots rapidly approached them, their numbers increasing and clustering together like a migrating flock of birds.

Strangely, some seemed to fall out of formation midway, plummeting from high in the sky to the ground below.

Cora rubbed her eyes, thinking she might see things. It wasn't until someone next to her shouted in fear, "Wait! They're... falling!!"

The closest dark dot was now clear enough to see its outline. The silvery metal casing reflected an eerie, cold light, unmistakably Starships. However, these Starships appeared to have lost power high in the air, their trajectories skewed and faltering.

After struggling for a few seconds, they nosedived, plummeting straight down and crashing into the cheering crowd.

"Boom! Boom! Boom!"

The starships, out-of-control like shooting stars, collided with the ground and created massive explosions that filled the air with thick smoke. The deafening roar of the explosions left everyone temporarily stunned.

In the fiery glow, Cora saw Siegfried's face twisted in silent rage as he bellowed, "Run—!!"

The petals and buds of Starship Port were struck, and soon black smoke billowed from the burning wreckage. Countless Starships soared overhead, casting a shadow that covered everyone's vision.

Cora looked up, her pupils reflecting clear images—a few Starships were getting closer and closer, on a collision course to crash down!

Siegfried tore off a protective mesh and lifted a steel frame over ten meters long, roaring as he held it up to block the falling starship. The frame struck the Starship, momentarily halting its descent, but then it veered a few inches to the side and skimmed past the edge of the platform. The other members of the group hurried in the opposite direction.

The recoil from that impact was equally staggering. Siegfried almost instantly exhausted his strength, his left arm dislocating from the force. He stumbled back a couple of steps and struggled to regain his balance. But as he looked up, another starship was rapidly descending along a path that led directly toward the others. "No! Come back!! Don't go that way!"

The massive starship plummeted straight down, creating a deep crater in the platform. Those in the front were instantly engulfed by the flames.

Siegfried's eyes turned bloodshot, and he fell to his knees.

But the crisis was far from over. After the major wave had passed, two more Starships detached from the formation, falling from directly above them.

"You all! Get together!" Cora only had time to shove Holden before rushing toward the falling starship.

Ignoring the pain in his ankle, Holden helped up his teammate, who had been knocked aside by the shockwave, quickly making his way towards Siegfried.

Cora leaped onto the top of the platform, wielding her massive hammer to intercept the falling starship. The deep blue hammerhead stopped the metallic starship in its tracks, but it drained Cora's power in an instant.

Because of the hammer shattering, the Starship spun from the impact, causing it to careen into another starship. The two vessels collided with explosive force, creating a spectacular display of black fireworks in the sky.

The powerful shockwave sent Cora tumbling off the platform.

She rolled down, disappearing into the thick smoke and debris.

"Cora!" Holden shouted in desperation, rushing down to dig through the rubble. As he dug, two more people joined him—Siegfried, who had dislocated his arm, and another boy.

After about five minutes of digging, the pile of rubble finally moved, and Cora emerged, covered in dirt and grime. She looked severely injured, with half of her arm charred and blood flowing from her forehead down her face. She managed a cough and said, "We need to... leave this place."

Siegfried, Holden, and the other boy supported each other as they got up and moved away from where the explosion occurred.

Behind them, Starship Port was ablaze, and ahead, a massive fleet of Starships was bombarding a significant portion of Flower City, dropping along a path from the north to the southeast, with explosions and flames erupting all around.

"This can't be happening, it just can't! Those were... starships." A survivor lay on the ground, covered in ash, muttering in disbelief.

Starships were renowned not for their rare element rhenium (Re) metal hulls or their highly advanced artificial intelligence cores, but for their "Sora Wings," an innovative NPA technology that provided their power.

These alternative energy sources allowed the heavy starships to suspend themselves in the air without relying on external forces, while also achieving self-circulation, self-cleaning, and self-recycling.

From their inception, they marketed starships as "absolutely safe," touting them as the "indestructible bluebirds."

And yet, here in Flower City's Starship Port, over a hundred Starships were plummeting to the ground, as if a meteor shower of shattered faith had struck.

After leaving the Starship Port, Siegfried and the others could barely hold on, collapsing on the ground, utterly exhausted. The survivor who had narrowly escaped death sobbed uncontrollably, "What do we do now? The Starships are gone, the rescue team is gone. What do we do?"

"First, let's return to the safe zone," Holden suggested.

"But we have no signal. How do we contact Simon? How do we get in?" The survivor's expression turned despairing.

Siegfried had been silent since their escape. He had a broken arm, and his face occasionally contorted in excruciating pain.

Holden glanced at his phone. It was almost 6:00 PM. He thought for a moment and said, "I've kept a record. Our two teams usually head back between 5:00 and 7:00 PM. The earliest was 4:50 PM, and the latest was 6:40 PM. Mr. Sheridan must know by now that there's no signal. So, I assume Simon will open the gate at 7:00."

"So, before that, we have to make sure we get back."

CHAPTER 14

Weight of Despair

With only three minutes left, Siegfried and his group hastily returned to the school, racing against time.

The continuous running and their heavy injuries had drained their energy, and they slumped down against the wall, utterly spent. The surviving boy covered his face, tears streaming down without end.

Time ticked away, second by second, and the wall remained ominously quiet.

"Why isn't the door opening? Did we arrive too late? Did they already let everyone in?"

The boy repeated these questions anxiously, pacing in circles, his tone growing increasingly frantic. "Why isn't it opening? Why won't they open the door?"

"Take a deep breath and wait a little longer," Holden said, steadying him by gripping his shoulders.

He didn't want the boy to attract nearby zombies by wandering around in a panic. Despite offering reassurances, even Holden was becoming uneasy.

After about twenty minutes, the wall finally softened and collapsed, revealing the shape of a door.

"I knew you guys would make it back. They asked me to wait a little longer..." The door swung open, revealing Simon's bright smile.

However, as he looked closer at the people in front of him, the curve of his lips fell in disbelief.

Four, he counted again in astonishment. Only four.

"What's going on? Where are the others?"

Mr. Sheridan came forward from behind him, his expression unusually grave.

"Mr. Sheridan!"

Upon seeing him, the boy's psychological defenses completely crumbled.

He fell to the ground in front of Mr. Sheridan, wailing uncontrollably.

Siegfried's face grew solemn as he supported his limp left arm. Holden was limping with one leg, and Cora, though physically intact, was covered in blood, with her facial features barely recognizable. Everyone present quickly noticed the four of them.

"What happened... everything's destroyed... the Starships... the rescue team..."

"What exploded?"

"What about the rescue team? Please, tell us! We're all anxious here!"

"What exactly happened?"

The boy's emotions were too overwhelming, rendering his speech incoherent. Mr. Sheridan had him taken aside to rest. Then he calmed and dispersed the crowd, leaving behind only a few key members to gather more information.

Holden, the only one with rational speech, explained, "Allow me. Today, around three in the afternoon, the power and network throughout Flower City collapsed. When we realized, we rushed to Starship Port, hoping to meet the rescue team. However, what arrived later were large numbers of starships falling from the sky, having lost power. Others... couldn't escape the explosions. They're all... dead."

As his words sank in, shock rippled through the room. For these high school students, the idea of falling for Starships was like something out of a fantasy tale.

Mr. Sheridan pondered for a moment. "It seems it's not just the school—Flower City's entire infrastructure has shut down."

Pausing, he asked, "We didn't hear any explosions. Where did the Starships you mentioned go? How many of them?"

"Toward the southeast, probably around twenty."

"I see. The school is to the west of Flower City."

As the core members discussed, Cora walked toward a corner unnoticed by the crowd.

The commotion by the door caught the attention of several people, and Angela emerged from the restroom, visibly annoyed. "What's going on with Siegfried? He was supposed to deal with Cora. Why is he in such a sorry state?"

Irene clenched the railing with both hands, her brow furrowed. "Something doesn't seem right..."

Following Irene's gaze, Angela quickly noticed another figure in the corner. Enraged, she stamped her foot. "No way! Why is Cora still alive and kicking? This infuriates me! She promised to do something for me, but she didn't deliver. I need to settle the score with her!"

"Angie, just wait a moment!" Irene's exasperation with this foolish girl was genuine.

Was she really going to confront Siegfried in front of everyone?

All their clandestine plotting would be exposed.

Irene reached out to grab Angela.

Angela's pace was brisk, and she ended up stumbling.

Irene helplessly trailed behind her.

The two of them arrived at Mr. Sheridan's side, just in time to hear Holden speak, "Mr. Sheridan, there's one more thing. Cora is an Aberrant."

Ray, Charlotte, and others nearby were momentarily stunned. Angela, struck by the devastating news, felt her vision darken, and the world spun around her. Darkness had never felt so overwhelming.

Mr. Sheridan adjusted his glasses on his nose, his eyes glinting sharply. He maintained his calm tone, though.

"Oh? What type of Anopower does she possess?"

"The same power type as me," Siegfried, who had been silent until now, interjected. "And our levels are similar."

Holden gave him a sideways glance, recalling how Cora had effortlessly subdued him at the shop entrance. He couldn't help but be skeptical of Siegfried's swollen-faced bravado.

However, the hand that Siegfried clenched into a fist made a distinct cracking sound, revealing the immense effort he was exerting. Holden remained silent, deciding he would discuss this with Mr. Sheridan and Ray later.

"No wonder she could lift Flame with just one hand," Charlotte murmured. "She's a power-type Aberrant, just like me."

For a moment, envy, jealousy, and dissatisfaction all festered in the shadows.

The news that Cora was an Aberrant was a glimmer of solace in the dire situation. With the loss of the rescue team, their predicament had become perilous.

Were they doomed to remain in the safe zone forever? Who knew what other dangers lay ahead?

Fear and uncertainty filled the air, but the only one maintaining composure was Mr. Sheridan. He stood on the elevated platform of the courtyard, looking down at the crowd below with an authoritative presence.

"Everyone, please stay calm. Don't panic. It's not time to give up yet. Your teachers will find a solution together with you. What we need to do now is to share the situation with everyone."

Mr. Sheridan gathered everyone together, then announced the news they had brought back from outside.

The news of water shortages, power outages, internet disruptions, and the falling starships, coupled with the lost communication with the rescue team, weighed heavily on everyone.

Despite Mr. Sheridan's best efforts to console them, many succumbed to the pressure, collapsing to the ground and sobbing.

A few bold individuals, unable to bear the oppressive atmosphere, confronted Simon, making a scene.

"Staying here is a death sentence! Let me out! I want to go home!"

Simon initially tried to reason with them, but their incessant complaints eventually wore his patience thin.

He retorted, "Want to leave? Be my guest! But my Anopower is depleted. It won't recover until tomorrow morning at the earliest. So, wait!"

On the other side, Flame approached Cora cautiously. "Cora, are you okay?"

"Is there... water?" Cora's eyes were glued shut with dried blood. However, the discomfort ran deeper within her body—the searing pain that came from her depleted Anopower, throbbing in her temples.

"There's a restroom over there," Flame pointed. "Thankfully, we had stored some water earlier. You can use it."

Cora entered the restroom, scooped water from a container, and splashed it onto her face with increasing speed. The cool droplets soaked her skin, washing away the congealed blood. The persistent burning sensation seemed to ease somewhat.

But in its wake, hunger surged within her—a deep emptiness from the depths of her stomach. Cora slid down to the floor, opened her backpack, and began stuffing food into her mouth: beef jerky, crackers, ham sausages, sandwiches. She devoured half of her rations, gradually quelling the fiery sensation. Her Anopower, like a parched spring, rejuvenated, replenished itself at a remarkable pace.

After half an hour had passed, the turmoil within her subsided. Her abundant energy resumed its stable flow. Cora felt considerably better, got up, and assessed her injuries. Her earlobes, the edges of her cheeks—all bore the marks of the explosion's aftermath. Fresh wounds had joined her left arm's existing injuries.

Cora pressed a piece of gauze to her face, changed into clean clothes, and opened the restroom door. Ray was waiting for her outside.

"Holden said you were hurt. I came to check on you."

"Uh, I'm... fine."

"Your injuries should still be tended to. Shall I call Irene or Charlotte to help you?"

Irene and Charlotte stood side by side behind Ray. Charlotte waved friendly greetings, but Cora gave them a cold refusal.

"No need."

Ignoring their reactions, Cora cradled her deflated backpack and found a corner to sit cross-legged.

Ray's gaze remained fixed on her face, and suddenly, he pointed. "You've got something on your face."

Cora wiped her face casually, but there was nothing there.

"Lower."

Cora swiped her face downward.

"Not there." Ray watched her awkward movements, and an unexpected chuckle escaped him.

His laughter was unclouded and bright, his eyes like a lake shimmering with countless stars. In an instant, he kneeled down, his proximity to Cora close, his eyes intense. Swiftly, he reached out and took a crumb from the corner of her mouth.

Ray's movement was so natural that Cora, unprepared, couldn't prevent him in time.

However, she quickly took a step back, then another, until her back pressed against the wall. She stared at him, a cascade of question marks swirling in her mind. So what if there was something? It wasn't like it got on his face. Why did he care so much? Was it necessary for him to remove it with his own hand?

"Hey—!! Irene, come look!" Charlotte tugged at Irene's sleeve, excitedly whispering.

Completely absorbed in her gossip, Charlotte failed to notice her friends' emotions.

Irene, however, fixed her gaze on the ambiguous interaction between the two and her expression darkened.

Despite Cora's repeated refusals, Ray left a first aid kit behind.

Cora disliked being around people, always retreating to corners with no one. When Ray left, he turned back to look at her several times, a concerned expression on his face.

"I noticed your bandages were rather haphazard. I've had some first aid training before. When I have time later, I'll come and help you properly," Irene followed him, speaking gently, "Don't worry, I won't tell Angie."

At the mention of Angela, Ray's eyebrows furrowed involuntarily. "Yeah, I appreciate it. Seems like only you and her are on speaking terms in your class."

"Yeah, Cora... she's not the easiest person to get along with." Irene smiled.

That night, a heavy downpour engulfed Flower City. The sound of rain tapping on the skylights of the courtyard echoed like a drumbeat. Many couldn't sleep, climbing up to the windows to peer outside. All they saw was a curtain of rain stretching endlessly.

The rain continued into the next day, forcing the cancellation of any plans to venture outside. That night, Cora's dreams were filled with the sound of pouring rain.

When she woke up, she learned even worse news.

Angela had a fever.

CHAPTER 15

Sickness

Angela started running a fever after falling asleep. She had been feeling under the weather for the past couple of days, with a sore throat and a runny nose, but she was too stubborn to show any signs of discomfort. She kept running to the bathroom throughout the day to freshen up, all the while her temperature was steadily rising. It wasn't until the next morning when her classmates came to check on her they realized she was burning up and barely conscious.

With the precedent set by Ray and the others, Angela's fever was likely a sign of her imminent awakening of Anopower.

"105 degrees Fahrenheit," Mr. Sheridan announced, the temperature on the thermometer.

His expression showing concern. "We need to get her fever down with some fever-reducing medication, or else her fever might burn her out even if she awakens her Anopower."

Everyone well understood the value of an Aberrant present.

Ray, Simon, Siegfried, and even Cora were living examples.

Without Aberrants leading the way, ordinary people wouldn't dare venture out alone. Being an Aberrant came with privileges.

Despite Cora's aloofness, her refusal to take part in meetings or group activities, Mr. Sheridan's attitude toward her remained lenient.

Regardless of Angela's personality flaws, as long as she could awaken Anopower, she wouldn't be abandoned easily.

However, the issue at hand was that their hasty retreat from the school left them with limited medical supplies, and even prescription medications were absent.

They had to risk going outside to search for what they needed.

"But it's still raining outside."

"Exactly. With this kind of weather, going out would be as good as a death sentence, even without encountering zombies."

"Don't make me go out there, please..."

Ever since two days ago, the rain in Flower City had been intensifying, showing signs of flooding the entire city.

The combination of pouring rain, zombies, a sealed-off city, and loss of communication had multiplied the dangers of going outside.

In response to various doubts and hushed whispers, Mr. Sheridan stood up slowly, his piercing gaze sweeping across the room. "From the first day we established the safe zone, I've promised you all that even in the direst circumstances, I won't abandon a single one of you. That promise still holds."

His voice always carried a kind of magical persuasiveness. The room gradually fell silent as Mr. Sheridan turned to the tall figure standing beside him. "Ray, I'm asking you to lead a team to find medicine. Are you willing?"

Ray's fingers curled and then straightened. Meeting Mr. Sheridan's hopeful gaze, he reluctantly nodded. "Mr. Sheridan, I'm willing to go out, but my team members, they're not Aberrants. I don't want to force them."

Almost immediately, several other boys, including Holden, Jacky, Flame, spoke up, voicing their support. "JP, I'll go with you!" "Count me in!" "Me too, and me, the more people, the faster we can find what we need."

The courage of the young was still strong, and camaraderie was highly valued. They believed in Ray and will follow him into danger. But Mr. Sheridan's expression remained cautious, for the team still seemed too small. One Aberrant plus five or six regular people would still pose significant risks outside.

But then, unexpectedly, Siegfried, who had been sitting in the back with his head down, spoke up. "Count me in too."

His dislocated arm had been fixed, but the shadow of his helplessness persisted. He and Ray led separate teams, and they always brought their closest friends along. Ray was well-liked and had many friends, and Siegfried had his own group of brothers. However, he had witnessed his good friends perish in the explosion that day, hating his own powerlessness. Since then, he had been haunted by psychological scars, and these past few days, he had even developed a strong aversion to the idea of "going out."

Now, the girl he cared about was lying on a mat, her face pale from the high fever.

Could he back down again and only rely on others? Was that the behavior of a loyal man?

Siegfried gritted his teeth, overcoming his fear and stepping forward.

"Just me," Siegfried spoke in a hoarse voice. He didn't want to burden others any further.

Mr. Sheridan nodded solemnly, not opposing the simultaneous departure of two Aberrants this time.

"Very well. You all have my approval."

With three Aberrants on the team, one could not underestimate their strength. Even in the face of unexpected incidents, they could handle them promptly.

"Once you find the medicine, come back immediately. Don't linger outside," Mr. Sheridan advised Ray and Siegfried, who were about to depart.

Simon, seeing everyone else leaving, became restless. "Mr. Sheridan, let me go too!"

"You can't go," unexpectedly, Mr. Sheridan, usually mild-mannered, firmly denied Simon's request.

"Why not? I'm an Aberrant too, and I could go with them. It would be easier for us to come back together, rather than waiting outside."

Mr. Sheridan sighed deeply, his voice carrying an air of significance. "Yes, you're an Aberrant too..."

Simon's hope was rekindled, and his eyes lit up with excitement. "So, you're allowing me?"

"——Simon, remember, only you... only you can't go."

Everyone here could go out, except Simon. He was the cornerstone of the entire safe zone, or rather, everyone in the safe zone depended on him. If he went outside and something happened, if he didn't come back, or if he simply abandoned them and ran away, what would become of the others?

As Simon lamented in disappointment, the others quickly realized the situation and exchanged knowing glances.

With the departure time settled, Simon activated his Anopower. The moment the door swung open, torrential rain poured in, drenching everyone from head to toe. The rain was no longer just a drizzle; it felt as if someone in the sky had overturned a giant vat of water, inundating the entire city in an instant. The sky outside was dark, thunder rumbling amidst the fierce wind. They struggled to maintain their balance as they were soaked through with rain with each step they took.

Ray's team pressed on through the storm, tightly clutching their raincoats and trudging forward, cautiously navigating as they lost the guidance of their phones.

Every step required careful consideration, with frequent stops to confirm their direction.

At a fork in the road, Holden bellowed over the rain, "JP, which way do we go?"

The rain was so loud that it was difficult to hear anything.

They faced two options: continue west to the outskirts of Flower City, where a new development area lay; or turn southeast and make their way through the city center, where there were likely hospitals and pharmacies.

After a moment's thought, Ray reached a decision.

"Let's head west. I remember there's a pharmaceutical factory in the suburbs."

"Isn't that too risky in this weather?"

"And going through the city center isn't even riskier? It was just bombed recently."

"I agree! The pharmacies in the city are probably already searched, and we might not find any fever-reducing medicine."

With a simple discussion, they wiped rainwater off their faces and set off toward the outskirts of Flower City.

About forty minutes later, they indeed found the pharmaceutical factory. Ray and Siegfried worked together to deal with a few wandering zombies at the entrance and a couple hidden in the security room.

The others ran into the factory area and temporarily take shelter under the eaves.

"Let's look for the warehouse first, and if there's nothing there, we'll go to the logistics center," Ray decided quickly after studying the fire evacuation plan posted on the wall.

Since the warehouse's iron gate was tightly shut, they had to smash a window and climb over the wall to gain entry. When it was Cora's turn, she remained motionless outside the window, gazing at the rain, showing no intention of entering. Ray glanced at her but didn't stop her. The others didn't dare to boss her around, either. It was as if they had collectively turned a blind eye to her.

When Flame crawled in, he quietly asked, "Cora, why did you come out?"

"Looking... for food," Cora replied stiffly.

Flame suddenly realized, "I knew it! I heard you had a terrible relationship with Angela before. Why would you come out to find medicine for her? But at first, I thought you were afraid we might get into trouble, so you came to protect us."

Cora raised an eyebrow slightly. "Is that so?"

"Hey, I must have misunderstood," Flame chuckled. Jacky called him over, and he rushed to join him.

Cora shifted her gaze, leaning against the windowsill, staring into the distance.

The torrential rain masked many sounds and dampened ordinary people's senses.

Cora closed her eyes, establishing a connection with her Anopower. Invisible and sharp tendrils extended from her, reaching out to perceive the external world.

The world fell completely silent, and she heard Flame and the others talking. The faint sound of shelves being searched. The distant howling wind, the furious rain, the crisp sound of shattering glass, a sudden loud crash of something heavy falling, quickly swallowed by the swishing rain.

Was it an illusion?

Cora paused and cautiously turned back, wanting to investigate further. However, she suddenly sensed a powerful, surging, and chilling intent to kill. It brushed past her almost imperceptibly, a fleeting danger.

It was Anopower!

She snapped her eyes open; her gaze was sharp as she stared into the distance about a hundred meters away. The factory buildings stood there, hidden among the trees, making it impossible to discern specific locations.

Cora turned back, the high school students behind her unaware, still searching diligently.

Too close. The murderous intent of that Aberrants was so strong that she could feel it even from here. If the other person detected her, these people would be in grave danger. Cora lowered her gaze.

"F-Flame."

"Hey? Did you call me? Cora?" It was the first time Flame had heard her say his name, and he ran over eagerly, like an eager puppy.

"Over there, what is it?" Cora pointed towards the depths of the rain and mist.

"I don't know. It seems like an administrative area."

"I know, I know!" Jacky chimed in, leaning over and casually draping his arm over Flame's shoulder. "There's a big research facility over there called 'Evergreen Biotech.' My dad drove me past here once, and I inspected. Wow, the guard at the entrance glared at me!"

Cora listened quietly as he spoke, picked up her umbrella, and headed outside.

"Where are you going?"

"To... check it out."

"You can't go alone. It's too dangerous!"

Flame became anxious when he realized her intentions and tried to use his body to block the enormous umbrella.

However, Cora dragged him several meters forward while he clung to the umbrella.

"JP! JP!" Jacky noticed the commotion and quickly reported.

"What's going on?" Ray arrived promptly.

"Cora wants to go outside."

Ray hesitated for a second but swiftly put on a rain hat. "Where do you want to go? I'll go with you."

Cora shook off Flame, who had clung to the umbrella, and raised her eyes, warning coldly, "No, don't, don't follow me, and don't stop me."

Ray paused, an icy shiver running down his spine from head to toe.

He had seen this look in Cora before, three years ago. When he hurried to the third-grade classroom, she had stared at him with the same emotionless, pitch-black eyes. The next day, she dropped out of school and had never appeared again.

"Alright... I won't follow you." Ray's heart pounded. He cleared his throat and asked, "Will you come back?"

Cora opened the umbrella and jumped into the rain, vanishing from view. "We'll see."

"Why does she always act alone? She has no sense of community..." Someone had already noticed the disturbance and complained.

Cora was indeed quite willful. Even Flame didn't know how to smooth things over with her. He awkwardly explained, "Well, she's an Aberrants, you know. Aberrants are quite individualistic, and she'll come back after she's done!"

"Why is she the special one? JP and Sieg are Aberrants too, and they..."

Ray's expression turned cold, but before he could speak, Siegfried intervened, "Shut up, all of you!"

His dislocated arm was still slightly painful, but Siegfried initially didn't want to get involved. However, he couldn't help but remember the day when Cora leaped into the air to intercept the starship for them. His anger surged, urging her on, telling her to go! Hurry and go! Let her act high and mighty, let her be arrogant—she would die outside, eventually!

"If you keep jabbering, hurry and find the medicine!" He scolded impatiently. He didn't know whom he was defending, but he had become fed up with the chatter.

"Evergreen Biotech."

A discreet and elegant signpost stood in the middle of a lawn, the heavy rain adding a touch of mystery to it.

The layout of the buildings formed a shape like an inverted "V." Experimental factories and various laboratories were on both sides, with a five-story comprehensive building in the center.

They had already automated the facility and didn't find any traces of zombies along the way. However, there were a few bodies lying on the office floor, dressed in uniforms with the Evergreen Biotech logo.

Their dead bodies were strewn about, their blood solidified and cleansed by the relentless rain.

Cora's heart sank. These people had no wounds on their bodies; zombies had n't killed them. They had been murdered using some method!

The person she was about to confront was definitely not a good person. She understood this well and became even more cautious.

Amidst the fierce wind and rain, a slender figure darted between the buildings.

After surveying the area on both sides, Cora ultimately fixed her gaze on the central comprehensive building.

To avoid giving herself away prematurely, she put away the umbrella and approached stealthily in the pouring rain.

To her surprise, the front entrance of the building was made of the sturdiest steel, and her attempt to push it open was in vain. Resorting to brute force would trigger an alarm, potentially alerting the enemy.

Cora had no choice but to abandon the front entrance and look for other ways in. Eventually, she found a row of arched windows on the side of the building. However, the windows on the lower floors were still quite high above the ground. She stretched, trying to reach them, but fell short by a large margin.

Turning the umbrella upside down, Cora used the handle to hook onto the anti-theft mesh, wedging it into a gap. Then, with a swift movement, she propelled herself upward, easily clambering onto the ledge. She wiped away the water droplets on the outside of the window, revealing two figures inside, one tall and one short.

As expected, there were people inside. This must be the place.

It was a laboratory of about forty square meters. Cora cautiously peered in, her ear pressed against the glass. The voices from inside gradually became clear, sounding like a man and a woman.

Both of them had their backs to her. The woman had long curly hair, while the man was slender and wore a white lab coat.

"Where is it? I advise you to hand it over quickly!" The man interrogated harshly.

"Don't waste time talking to him. Search him directly. If you can't find it, break his leg!" The woman's voice was impatient, and she kicked forward, stepping on something. Cora heard a muffled groan.

Gripping the windowsill, Cora gradually leaned closer. She found the source of the voices, but the man was not seated at the table.

The man's eyes were a pale color, and a few strands of hair hung down on his forehead. He looked remarkably disheveled and yet exuded a heart-pounding beauty amidst the swirling rain and mist. Although he sat upright from the waist up, his right leg was softly bent, immobile, and bright red blood continued to seep out. Despite his severe injuries, a faint smile hung on his lips, an intriguing blend of fragility and contradiction.

Perhaps Cora stared for a little too long. The man suddenly lifted his head, unexpectedly making direct eye contact through the rain-drenched window. Their gazes crossed despite the wet glass, and Cora experienced a split second of distraction.

"Someone! Who's there?" The man and woman quickly noticed her and rushed towards the window.

The pen in the woman's hand slipped from her grasp, and its platinum tip gleamed coldly, an arrow-like threat aimed at Cora's throat.

Releasing one hand, Cora quickly evaded to the right, only to discover that the pen had an impressive tracking capability. It curved and continued its relentless trajectory towards her.

Cora's heart raced, and her brain's crisis of alarm sounded urgently.

Cora swiftly leaped towards the window, grabbing the iron umbrella hanging from the security net. With a somersault in mid-air, she spun around and snapped the umbrella open in a swift motion.

The massive umbrella expanded into an impenetrable shield, firmly protecting Cora from behind. It also intercepted the attacks of the test tubes and liquids coming her way.

As the two collided, the smooth surface of the umbrella seemed to corrode as if exposed to a toxic substance, emitting a pungent white smoke.

Simultaneously, the surface of the shield lit up with a brilliant blue glow, casting its radiance even onto the walls. After a moment, the glow subsided, and the residue from the liquids was shrouded.

Yara, who had been watching from the sidelines, turned pale, her voice sharp and urgent.

"Kill her quickly! She's an Aberrant!"

Having shouted, Yara's expression contorted as she extended her hand, summoning the pen-like weapon once again.

Meanwhile, the three of them engaged in a fierce battle. The man in the corner seemed detached, as if he were an outsider, calmly observing. Despite being surrounded by blood, he appeared unfazed, like he was on a holiday retreat. He even leisurely tapped his fingers on his knee, creating a tune.

While the attackers' methods were peculiar, their combat skills were inferior to Cora's. Coupled with the confined space of the laboratory, their control over the pen and test tubes was lacking.

Cora swung her umbrella-turned-giant-mace, blocking and striking, while using her helpful height to target their joints and vulnerabilities.

After a few rounds, the two assailants were left dazed, covered in bruises, lying on the ground, groaning in pain.

Cora leaped down from the lab table and glanced once again towards the corner.

Throughout the entire battle, the man had shown no signs of surprise.

Whether it was the rare attack methods of the two assailants or Cora's unconventional umbrella-shaped Ethereal Artifact, he remained emotionally unaffected.

Locking eyes with her at that moment, the man's lips curled into a smirk. "Not dealing with them? That could lead to endless trouble."

Cora furrowed her brows.

Almost as soon as he finished speaking, a barrage of test tubes flew towards her from behind. Not this again. Cora quickly deflected the attack with a reverse swing of her umbrella. Her vision was briefly obstructed, but as soon as she moved the umbrella aside, she realized the woman was no longer there. A faint noise came from behind, and in a life-or-death moment, Cora swiftly turned around. Yara, her hair disheveled, lunged at her with a vicious pen thrust aimed straight for Cora's eyes, screaming, "Die!"

Cora's eyes remained calm and composed. Without a hint of panic, she drew a short sword from the handle of her umbrella.

She lifted the short sword, blocking the pen's attack and sending it flying. The pen spun in mid-air and crashed into the wall, shattering into pieces.

Then, Cora countered!

The swift sword energy struck Yara, and in the next instant, the short sword pierced through her sternum, pinning her ruthlessly against the wall.

With Yara dealt with, Cora turned around, flinging the iron umbrella in her hand. The umbrella, weighing hundreds of pounds, crashed down on the frail figure of Bob, rendering him immobile. He spat out blood and fell unconscious on the spot.

In less than a minute, the battle came to a complete halt. Cora looked towards the man in the corner for the third time. He had withdrawn his smile and was now applauding slowly. "Impressive, easily taking down two C-grade Aberrants like that."

"Is your Anopower the umbrella? A weapon-type? No, it seems it can transform..."

The man's dark eyelashes fluttered, his soliloquy turning into analysis.

Gradually, his eyes seemed to understand. "Ah, I see now. It's of the Gold element."

Cora was at first puzzled, her expression one of confusion.

Then came disbelief.

Followed by astonishment.

Appearances can deceive, and Cora's seemingly emotionless demeanor concealed a storm of emotions within her.

How could this man know about her Anopower, something even she was unaware of?

Observing the mix of shock and confusion in her eyes, the man's expression held a hint of surprise. "Huh? You really know nothing, do you?"

A girl who understood nothing, yet had navigated the post-apocalyptic world unscathed. Confronted with a stormy downpour like this, she dared to venture outside? Perhaps... it wasn't just extreme luck, but an immense strength that knew no fear.

Based on her recent performance, she most likely fell into the latter category.

A solitary, powerful, and naïve top-tier Aberrant? Well, well...

She certainly looked like an easy pawn to manipulate.

The man's gaze shifted, his expression growing pensive.

Cora snapped back to reality and glanced at him with caution. She silently picked up the iron umbrella that had been pressing down on Bob and was ready to leave.

Her grandfather had once said that he had a friend who lived to a ripe old age, and the key to surviving in this chaotic world was to avoid meddling in others' affairs. After the apocalypse, Cora felt like she had aged several years because of various unexpected situations. This man seemed like trouble, and her rational mind reminded her it would be best—no, it was crucial—not to get involved.

After all, they had eliminated the immediate danger. She needed to return to Flame and the others quickly to regroup.

"Hey," the man's voice called out from behind her.

Cora turned her head to look at him, maintaining her guard.

"You forgot your sword."

Cora's expression tightened, but she instinctively caught the short sword he tossed to her. Then, in one fluid motion, he approached Bob, who lay on the ground, and ruthlessly thrust the sword back into Yara's heart!

Yara trembled all over, her breath fading within seconds. The man withdrew the sword and then turned to stab Bob, splattering his handsome profile with warm blood, adding a cruel touch to his already distinguished appearance.

Cora's heart chilled, and she stared at him with frosty eyes.

The man raised his head, a weak smile on his face as he playfully explained to her, "What? Do you think I'm ruthless? But between me and them, only one can survive. If I don't kill them, I'll be the one to die. Trust me, the feeling of being at the mercy of others is not pleasant..."

Cora wasn't unsettled by his act of killing, but...

This man, who could kill without remorse and still smile afterward, was difficult to read. He displayed almost no empathy, making him one of the most indifferent individuals Cora had ever encountered.

The man tossed the short sword back to her, and Cora caught it reflexively. He then leisurely pulled out a handkerchief from his pocket and wiped away the bloodstains, all the while keeping a watchful eye on Cora.

Outside, the heavy rain poured down, creating a cacophony as it beat against the windows. The two of them stood there, one by the window and the other against the wall, silently facing each other.

Impressive, she thought.

He's quite composed. His psychological resilience is remarkable.

The man abandoned his probing intentions, his lips curving into a teasing smile. "Little girl, you saved my life, and I have nothing substantial to repay you with. So, how about I become your lapdog?"

Cora fixed him with a look that could turn people into stone, slowly drawing her sword. "Are you insane? Do you want to die?"

Finally, her emotions flared, and her stuttering intensified, fully exposing her agitation.

"Hehe..." The man's laughter was that of a wicked evildoer, his dark pants soaked with blood, yet he showed no sign of embarrassment. Instead, he seemed to glow with an aura of elegance, like a nobleman. He stared intently at Cora, confidently stating, "You won't kill me."

Indeed, Cora thought, she wouldn't... Frustrated, she sheathed her sword and turned to leave, one foot already stepping onto the windowsill.

"Hey," the man called out from behind her.

Cora didn't stop, but she popped open the umbrella and prepared to leap into the rain.

"I'm a researcher from Arashi Research."

Arashi Research.

Cora recognized the name she had heard it on the TV in the martial arts gym.

It was said to be the most elite and mysterious research institution under the NPA, and each of its achievements was internationally renowned and highly esteemed.

"Aren't you curious? About the apocalypse, about your Anopower, and even... about the origin of this rainstorm in Flower City—no one has told you any of these things, have they?"

Cora's back stiffened, and she stubbornly retorted, "I'm... not curious."

"If you truly weren't curious, you wouldn't be here today."

Blood loss had paled the man's lips, yet he remained unaware, continuing to entice her.

"I know the entire truth you want to unravel."

"Or perhaps... I know even more than you can imagine."

"So, how about we make a little trade?"

Three sentences brought Cora's footsteps to a halt. Wedged by the windowsill, she listened to the rain's cacophony as her heart churned.

What Cora desperately needed now was the truth. She hailed from District F, secluded from the world since childhood, always feeling out of place, and her knowledge of this world was minimal at best. This man seemed to have grasped her thoughts and was skillfully manipulating her, seizing control over her choices.

If there truly was someone who knew all the secrets about the apocalypse and would share them with her, she had no way of refusing.

"How... how can you prove it?" Cora's resolve wavered.

The man smiled and pulled out an ID card from his pocket. It bore the name of Arashi Research and featured a photograph of the man.

Cora glanced at it briefly, thinking he looked less appealing in person.

"How would you like to conduct this trade?"

"If I'm not mistaken, you have companions, right? Transfer me to a safe location, and then help me find a healing-type Aberrant."

"Agreed."

A safe place was available—the sports arena was an option. As for finding a healing-type Aberrant, though Cora had never encountered one, it was a reasonable request from the man.

Cora withdrew her leg from outside the window and hopped back inside. The deal was struck, and the man seemed to exhale a sigh of relief. He slumped down, asking, "Do you have any first aid supplies?"

Cora rummaged through her backpack, producing some bandages and antiseptics, and pushed them toward him. The man nonchalantly began a rudimentary job of stopping his own bleeding. When he stood up, he wavered.

Jumping out of the window with such an injured man was obviously out of the question. Cora had no choice but to head towards the door. The man followed behind in silence. Cora walked about ten meters when she turned around. The man had only moved about two meters.

This was a real problem—such a big problem indeed.

Cora took a deep breath, turned around, and strode back to him. She scrutinized him from head to toe, then reached out and grabbed his waistband.

"What are you doing?!" From the moment he entered the room, the man's grace disappeared, replaced by a cold, imperious expression. Cora paid no heed, her other hand gripping his collar. With a little effort, she lifted him off the ground, his heels dangling about two inches above the floor.

"You're too... slow!"

The man grabbed her wrist, his forehead veins throbbing faintly. "Take a left after leaving the building's main entrance. It's the second building. There's a medical support equipment production line there. You can find a wheelchair."

"Downstairs, the door's locked," Cora reminded him.

While she could come and go freely through the window, a wheelchair was too large to fit. Going through the front door would mean having to spend time and effort dismantling the lock. It was much easier to carry him directly.

The man took a couple of steps forward, rummaged through a drawer, and produced a silvery access card. "Here, use this to unlock it."

Cora went to the designated location and, just as he said, found a variety of finished wheelchairs, each with its own unique design. They all appeared to be top-of-the-line, equipped with a multitude of complex buttons. Cora picked up two with her hands and hurried back to the main building.

Inside the laboratory, the man sat himself in a wheelchair, his forehead beaded with cold sweat.

"Can we... go now?" Cora urged.

"Just a moment."

Before leaving, he maneuvered the wheelchair beside the bodies of Yara and Bob. Bending down, he didn't even avoid Cora as his hands explored their corpses. Finally, he removed a valuable watch from Bob's wrist and a string of a pearl necklace from Yara's body.

Cora's eyes widened in disbelief.

What kind of person was he? Even in a situation like this, he was still focused on taking things?

Meeting her incredulous gaze, the man chuckled helplessly. His chest vibrated with laughter. "It's not what you think."

Cora half-heartedly responded with a couple of "uh-huhs," unable to meet his gaze. She questioned whether her impulsive decision was the right one.

He's even looting from the dead. Maybe... I should just leave him here and go by myself?

Casting a slightly guilty glance at the man, she saw him with his loot in hand. After ransacking the two corpses, he calmly rested his hands on his knees, smiling at her.

Cora. "..."

This is bad. I can't escape now.

She sighed inwardly, accepted her fate, and walked towards the man.

Evergreen Biotech's entrance stood tall and unwavering, a testament to the violence and hardship it had witnessed.

Cora opened her umbrella, shielding both of them thoroughly. She used one hand to push the wheelchair as they ventured into the boundless curtain of rain.

Hot gusts of wind greeted them, drenching the man's knees and

Cora's back in an instant.

Their figures were slowly engulfed by the torrential rain, leaving behind fragments of their conversation that were faint and elusive.

"I forgot to ask earlier. What's your name?"

"Co... Co..."

"Coco? Well... that's cute."

"N-no! It's Co-Ra!"

"Alright, alright. Cora it is. Hey, move the umbrella over here a bit. Don't forget about me."

"Oh, and I'm Onyx. Onyx de Montclair."

CHAPTER 16

An Unwelcomed Guest

"JP, someone's coming." Holden's eyes were locked on the window as he relayed the message to Ray.

Having completed counting the medicine supplies, Ray gazed at the rain falling outside.

The weather remained fierce, with thunderstorms raging outside. A pair of figures drew near, coming from the hazy border between sky and earth—a slender girl clutching a massive iron umbrella, using it to withstand the wind and rain.

She pushed a wheelchair with a young man on it.

Squinting, the group tried to identify the newcomers. Before they could make out who they were, Ray had already opened the warehouse door and rushed into the rain. "You're back?" He reached Cora in a few strides, his eyes fixed on her. "Are you hurt?"

"No."

"That's good. Come inside, it's pouring outside."

Despite only being out for a short while, his hair and clothes were soaked. Ray didn't seem to mind; in fact, he looked quite pleased. Of course, he was happy because this time Cora didn't disappear—she had come back.

Cora nodded, closed the enormous umbrella, and followed him

into the warehouse.

"We found the fever-reducing medicine. Just in case, we're also taking some of the other prescription drugs back," Ray explained the current situation to her.

Even as Ray was explaining the current situation to her, his attention remained fixed on Cora until he unexpectedly caught sight of the man in the wheelchair.

"Who's this?"

"Um, he..." Cora hesitated for a moment.

Primarily because she wasn't very eloquent, and the situation with Onyx was quite complex. She didn't know where to begin.

Cora's quick trip outside with a stranger in tow had already attracted attention.

However, since the others had interacted with Cora several times, their curiosity wasn't malicious.

They discreetly stole glances, still huddled together, trying to find out what was happening.

Facing the onlookers, Onyx cleared his throat and spoke weakly, "Hello, everyone. I'm Onyx de Montclair, a pharmaceutical researcher from the neighboring Evergreen Biotech. I had been conducting closed experiments there before the apocalypse, but alas... I've been trapped in the research facility for several days now. Luckily, Miss. Thornton came to my rescue."

He let out a sigh of relief, as if he had narrowly escaped disaster. "I'm truly grateful. If it weren't for Miss. Thornton, I doubt I would have made it out."

Cora. "..."

Well, she didn't need to explain; he had already come up with an elaborate story.

He was portraying himself as thankful and genuine, shifting the focus away from his true identity.

What pharmaceutical researcher? What closed experiments? In those experiments, you'd be poking people's eyes with pens and splashing sulfuric acid on their faces, wouldn't you?

Cora grumbled internally, although outwardly she maintained her composure and didn't expose him.

Ray noticed Cora's subtle expressions and beckoned her over. She followed him a few steps away, away from the crowd.

"Is this guy really someone you rescued from Evergreen Biotech?"

"Yes."

While the details were different, the result was indeed as Ray had guessed.

"Are you planning to take him back to the safe zone?"

"Yes."

Ray's eyebrows furrowed.

"Is it not a good idea?" Cora countered.

"It's not that it's not a good idea, it's just..." Ray disliked gossiping about others behind their backs, so he had to hint at the situation.

"In the safe zone, Mr. Sheridan ensures everyone contributes their fair share. In a situation like his, with limited mobility and no unique Anopower to shine, he might not receive any supplies or food."

Indeed, someone reliant on a wheelchair, physically weak, without the ability to venture out to gather resources or exhibit a unique Anopower, would hold little value to Mr. Sheridan.

The two fell into silence. Unable to resist, Cora looked back. Onyx, posing as a pharmaceutical researcher from Evergreen Biotech, had become the center of attention. He held a pile of medicine boxes with long and complex names, explaining to everyone. Catching Cora's gaze, he turned his head slightly, his eyes curved as he smiled at her.

"Could not receive... then, he just won't receive," his affected smile momentarily blinded Cora's eyes.

She glanced away. Cora wasn't surprised at all by what the situation Ray had described. She had expected this outcome when she brought him back.

For Cora, whether she could stay in the safe zone wasn't as important as Ray thought, and it was even less important than the meaning Onyx brought to her. If she wasn't wanted here, she could just leave.

"The person I saved, I'll be the one to deal with him."

Ray's breathing suddenly became labored.

There was still some time left until we had to return, as agreed. After tidying up a bit, they planned to search the nearby area again.

The Flower City suburbs were vast and sparsely populated, making it extremely challenging to find supplies. They had explored several places in succession, but the results were disappointing.

After a few days since the apocalypse had begun, the number of active individuals outside had been decreasing.

The locals either fled to higher-tier cities or hoarded supplies in their homes.

As productivity remains limited and resources continue to deplete, there will eventually be a day when everything runs out.

Jacky muttered in confusion as he walked, "Why do I feel like there are fewer zombies lately? Is it just my imagination?"

Holden replied, "It's not your imagination. The frequency of zombie appearances is indeed decreasing."

"Really? Zombies are afraid of rain?"

"I don't know, logically they shouldn't be."

"Damn! Where did all the zombies go?"

The boys were discussing this up front, while Cora held an umbrella for Onyx, walking slowly behind them.

With so many people around, it was difficult for them to have a private conversation. There wasn't time for hushed discussions along the way.

Finally, finding a canned food factory after much searching, Cora seized the opportunity while the group was busy loading supplies.

She rolled Onyx's wheelchair to a corner of the wall. "Can you, can you answer my questions now?"

Onyx leaned against his chin, powerless to resist as Cora pushed him. After a moment of contemplation, he nodded slightly. "Well, I can, but let's make it clear—only three questions a day."

"Why?" Cora was shocked. He hadn't mentioned this condition when negotiating the deal!

Onyx pointed at the wheelchair and smiled leisurely.

"You see, I'm a disabled person now. Shouldn't I be cautious? What if you ask all your questions, realize I'm not useful, and decide to get rid of me?"

Cora. "..."

Ridiculous, this guy was just shameless! She felt her cheeks puffing up with anger. Fortunately, she had double-checked with him earlier. "How, how can I be sure you're telling the truth?"

Onyx looked genuinely hurt by the suspicion in her eyes.

"We're strangers. What benefit do I have in lying to you?"

That logic seemed a bit twisted. Well, she had saved him, after all. Whatever, she'd trust him for now.

Cora quickly fired her first question.

"So, I want to ask... who were those two people just now? Why did they want to kill you?"

Onyx replied, "You mean Yara and Bob? I had a research result that they cared a lot about. Oh, don't give me that look—me or them did not steal it. Strictly speaking, it belongs to Arashi. However, those two had coveted this achievement for a while. I refused to hand it over, so they got angry and came to kill me."

"What kind of achievement?" Cora asked.

She couldn't completely trust Onyx.

His background and appearance were too suspicious.

Also, what kind of research result would drive two Aberrants to kill, even if it meant eliminating any loose ends?

Onyx lifted his gaze, smiled, and countered, "Are you sure you want to know? Explaining this achievement will take more than a few days, and this counts as your second question."

"No, it doesn't!" Cora was frustrated. This guy was just too shameless!

Unable to argue with him and outwitted by his cunning, Cora was close to losing her mind. She twisted the wheelchair a few times, pretending to lose control, and aimed it at the gate. Then she lifted her feet off the ground, ready to let go of the handles.

"Miss. Thornton, let's talk, don't resort to violence!" Onyx's wheelchair lifted slightly. If he dared to trick her, Cora was ready to send him tumbling into the rain.

Regaining control, Cora let out a breath of frustration. She asked her second question with a commanding presence, "What exactly is my Anopower?"

Onyx appeared to have solved the puzzle - Cora's heart was tough, and she didn't trust him. She would make him reveal some information before letting him go any further, or else she might actually leave him halfway on the road.

He pondered for a moment. "Can you manipulate the form of objects?"

Cora remained silent, yet she grabbed an empty can of pineapple next to her.

In an instant, the can transformed into a shiny dagger, and she swung it gently, a dim blue radiance flickering.

Onyx nodded.

"For now, known Anopowers can be roughly divided into three categories: Mental, Physical, and Mystical. Mental Anopowers primarily involve controlling elements and psychic abilities. For example, the Gold category is recognized for its strong offensive capabilities. From what I can see, your Gold-based Anopower is impressive. However, your ability to materialize weapons shows a clear capacity for manifestation, making you more formidable than other Aberrants of the same level."

He gestured to the dagger in Cora's hand, "Like this..."

"Ethereal Artifacts," Cora interjected.

"Ethereal Artifacts. Although it looks like a knife and feels like a knife, it doesn't have the same existence as an actual knife. It's an externalization of your Gold-based Anopower. I'm guessing you can manipulate it freely, right?"

Cora turned her palm over, causing the dagger to vanish, leaving no trace behind.

Onyx paused, and Cora's mastery over her Anopower, especially her fluid weapon changes, was becoming more clear.

She realized her initial encounters with various Aberrants, like Wind, Damian (Ice), Vincent (Lightning), and even Ray (Fire), were all examples of elemental Anopowers.

Siegfried's enhanced strength and Jeremy's teleportation fell into the physical category, while the mystical Anopowers, like Yara's tracking pen and Bob's sulfuric acid vials, proved to be unpredictable and dangerous.

"The strength of Aberrants ranges from E to A, with E being the lowest. E-level individuals have heightened senses. A-level Aberrants are the most powerful, with Anopower intensities reaching up to about 83% of the human body's tolerance. However..." Onyx paused and smiled ambiguously, "If one were to surpass this threshold and awaken more latent potential, there might be S-level Aberrants that transcend these levels."

Onyx was almost certain that Cora's Anopower level wasn't low.

She not only could externalize her Anopower, but her physical attributes also surpassed those of ordinary physical-type Aberrants. Her precise and aggressive combat skills, as seen during the battle at Evergreen Biotech, confirmed her strength.

This was why Onyx had allied with her.

"You easily defeated two C-level Aberrants, so your level is likely B or higher. It's even possible that you're A-level. However, Anopower responses can be quite fluctuating. To get the most accurate data, you'd need access to authoritative detection equipment."

Cora recalled something, "Detection? Is it that... black box with lots of wires?"

"Have you seen it?" Onyx was slightly surprised.

"That sounds like the most basic Anopower tester, an outdated and ineffective model. It can only determine whether the subject has Anopower fluctuations; it doesn't serve any other purpose."

"I'm curious. Where have you seen it?" Onyx's interest was piqued.

The most advanced R-type Anopower tester was developed by Arashi and was only controlled by the regional authorities. Portable versions were mostly owned by the military.

If Cora had undergone Anopower testing, would they have let her leave easily?

"I've seen it, but... it exploded." Cora remembered it with frustration, briefly recounting her evacuation from District F199, omitting the part where she saved someone and the "objective fact" that the tester exploded because of her interference.

"Too bad," Onyx sighed after hearing her story. "Unfortunately, it's a pity for those people."

Onyx glanced outside at the pouring rain, his gaze growing distant. "The Aruzes, huh? It's been a while since I heard about them. Once the most glorious fighting force in the Alliance, and now they're resorting to recruiting Aberrants from civilians. Can't really help but call it a pity, can we?"

With only one question opportunity left, Cora found herself overwhelmed by curiosity, unable to decide what to ask.

Faced with a choice of paralysis, she postponed her questions and ponder them once they returned to the safety zone.

With her own supplies running low and now an extra mouth to feed, she joined Ray and the others in raiding the canned food factory, amassing a haul of strawberry, peach, and orange-flavored cans.

Throughout the trip, Onyx sat silently in his wheelchair. Cora inexplicably felt that he wasn't as bothersome as when he was quiet.

Almost half an hour early, the group returned to Flower City Central High, waiting for Simon to open the door. As the appointed time arrived, the wall recessed, and the Anopower door opened on schedule.

Simon appeared, eager to ask, "Did you find the medicine? Angela woke up, but her fever hasn't subsided."

"We found it," Ray nodded.

Simon breathed a sigh of relief. "That's good. She awakened her Anopower."

Angela's awakening had already been a foregone conclusion before Ray and the others had returned. There was a subtle magnetic interaction among Aberrants.

This morning, Simon sensed the energy fluctuations in Angela. He reported it immediately to Mr. Sheridan.

However, because of her high fever and weakened state, she couldn't speak until Ray and the others returned with the life-saving medicine.

Mr. Sheridan took the medicine box, thoroughly examined it, and had Irene administer it to Angela.

"Angie, how are you feeling now?"

Angela weakly leaned against Irene, lifting her eyelids slightly.

She was the center of attention now, everyone looking at her expectantly.

Only Ray's gaze seemed to wander, not aligning with everyone else's.

Feeling the attention, Angela's mood turned sour. Disregarding the situation, she played the temperamental card. "Not good. My throat hurts, my head hurts, and my whole body hurts."

Everyone exchanged glances. Mr. Sheridan didn't indulge her drama and asked bluntly, "Do you know what kind of Anopower you awakened?"

"What Anopower I awakened is none of your d--" Angela was in a huff, about to retort with a foul word, but when she saw who was asking, she swallowed it back, looking down and then answering honestly, "I've always been afraid of getting hurt since I was a kid. I am worried about scars. When I just awakened, I could vaguely feel a connection to wounds."

"Wounds..." Mr. Sheridan's eyes lit up. He called over a young man who had gone out with Siegfried last time. Despite narrowly escaping the explosion of the Starship, he had not properly treated his arm and leg wounds, causing them to fester.

Angela stared at the gruesome wounds, visibly disgusted for quite a few minutes. Then, under Mr. Sheridan's guidance, she put her hands over the wounds through the gauze. About ten minutes later, sweat formed on her forehead, and she slowly withdrew her hands. The young man eagerly removed the gauze to reveal that the wounds had completely healed. Not a single scar remained! He excitedly jumped in place, his actions no different from an ordinary person's.

Witnessing this miracle, the atmosphere in the safe zone ignited like wildfire, erupting in cheers.

"It's a Healing-type Anopower!"

"Really? You're not joking, are you?"

"That's amazing! We won't have to worry about getting hurt anymore!"

"Come on, let's be realistic. Do you think Miss Chou would kindly heal your injuries?"

"Well... you're right. Celebrating for nothing."

Mr. Sheridan smiled gently, instructing Angela to take her medicine on time and rest more. As he got up to attend to other matters, Ray approached him and whispered, "Mr. Sheridan, Cora brought someone back."

"Oh? Who's the person?" Mr. Sheridan's pleasant expression hadn't faded yet, and he nodded casually, "I'll go look."

As the others crowded around Angela, Cora remained motionless, and Onyx, self-proclaimed as the "crippled" one, stayed put as well. He observed the bustling crowd with a calm expression. "Your classmate seems to have awakened. Aren't you interested in seeing the commotion?"

"I'm not going. It's boring."

"Oh? You're not curious about the commotion, or are you disagreeing with someone?"

"Is this guy a mind reader? How does he know everything?" Cora was at a loss for words, poking at the wheelchair's wheel with her toe, causing it to spin in all directions.

Affected by Cora's actions, Onyx's viewpoint spun around, forced to change directions several times. However, he remained unperturbed, maintaining his amused smile, and continued to tease her. "Really? Did I hit the mark? Do you really have a grudge against someone?"

Cora became more irritated, speeding up her poking of the wheel.

During their playful banter, Mr. Sheridan and Ray stopped in front of them.

"Cora, I heard you brought a stranger back."

Cora's movement halted, and the subtle expressions that had been present moments ago vanished completely. In an awkward silence, she suddenly remembered Ray's mention of the "to each according to their contribution" system. She opened her mouth stiffly. "I'll... handle his supplies. No need for you guys."

Mr. Sheridan's expression darkened, and he scolded her in a low voice, "What do you think this place is?!"

The girl before him kept her eyes lowered, exhibiting a defiant resistance. She was just like this before, and she remained the same now. Mr. Sheridan had taught for many years, and while Cora wasn't the most troublesome student he had encountered, she was certainly the most stubborn. She never learned to be obedient.

He suppressed his impatience and intensified his tone a bit.

"The safe zone results from everyone's effort. We will take you in because of the bond between teacher and student, not to let you act recklessly. If you randomly bring someone back today and save someone else tomorrow, how can the teacher manage it?"

Cora's mind went blank, automatically activating the "I don't care about your bullshit" mode. She allowed her thoughts to drift, letting Mr. Sheridan's words enter her left ear and slide out of her right, as light as they came.

Unfortunately, her play-dead appearance was seen through by another person.

"Aha, haha!" A magnetic and low laugh suddenly rang out, interrupting Mr. Sheridan's words. Onyx, who had been likened to a "cat or dog," seemed to have a better grasp of self-awareness than Cora. Realizing his own rudeness, he quickly apologized, "I'm sorry, I couldn't help it. Carry on, carry on."

Mr. Sheridan's lenses glinted, a trace of cold light crossing his eyes. In the safe zone, no one could challenge his authority.

He composed his expression, glancing down at the wheelchair. The man seated there looked languid, his handsome face glowing, every feature exquisite. He seemed like a masterpiece meticulously crafted by Artemis herself.

Surprised, their gazes met.

Onyx raised an eyebrow, maintaining his smile. In contrast, Mr. Sheridan seemed struck by lightning, his face filled with shock! He touched his temples and stumbled back a few steps. Thankfully, Ray was nearby, quick to support him.

Cora, who had been daydreaming, jumped at his sudden movement, her shoulders trembling.

Mr. Sheridan stopped in his tracks, raised his head suddenly, his face filled with disbelief. His gaze was complex, even fearful, as he stared at Onyx. Onyx looked innocent and puzzled.

"Um, Mr. Sheridan? Are you okay?"

Mr. Sheridan stared at him for a while, finding no abnormalities, and let out a suppressed sigh. "I'm fine."

Turning his gaze to Cora, his expression turned stony. "Cora, you brought this person here. We have no obligation to take care of him. You're responsible for him."

"And this is the last time."

Ray left with a hasty "I'll find you later" before following Mr. Sheridan.

As they walked away, Cora asked in confusion, "What's... what's wrong with him?"

He collapsed while speaking so calmly. It's kind of scary.

"Maybe... he suddenly fell ill?" Onyx glanced at Mr. Sheridan's departing figure, chuckling.

CHAPTER 17

The Crazy Gambler

Cora stared at his smile, a chill running down her spine and goosebumps forming on her arms.

She remembered the Anime from the ancient civilizations that Ben loved. In her free time, she used to catch glimpses of them occasionally.

Onyx's smile bore an uncanny resemblance to the handsome and devious villains in those shows.

As the others walked away, the corner where they stood regained its quietness. Onyx's smile faded, and his expression seemed to return to a bit of normalcy. "While we have some time, why don't you tell me about how things work here?"

"About... what?"

Cora was bewildered.

"The organization structure, the management system here. You can't know anything, right? After all, you were the one who brought me to the safe zone."

Of course, she couldn't be clueless. On her first day inside, she cleverly asked Flame for information. Cora raised her head confidently. "You can ask. Go ahead."

"What's the organizational structure here? Who are the principal leaders? How do they allocate Aberrants as rare resources?"

Cora paused for two seconds, hesitating before shaking her head.

"How are personnel assignments and defenses arranged? Are there rules? Taboos? Also, have you noticed anything unusual?"

"Assignments? Unusual?"

Cora continued, shaking her head.

She didn't understand.

"..."

After a brief pause, he rubbed his temples in frustration.

"Cora, can I ask, what do you do every day?"

"Eat, sleep, kill zombies."

"... Just acting on instinct, right? Well, that's fine. Perfectly reasonable. I can't find any faults."

Onyx sighed inwardly.

Cora glanced at Onyx's expressionless face and guiltily gestured with her fingers. She turned her head and called out, "Flame!"

It's okay if she can't explain; someone else can.

With his sharp ears, Flame heard her call from afar and dashed over energetically, asking, "Hey, what's up?"

Cora pointed at Onyx. "Can you explain about the safe zone to him?"

Flame had been curious about Onyx for a while. He had wanted to get closer to him outside, but didn't dare. Now that he had the opportunity, he enthusiastically approached.

"Onyx, can I call you that? After all, Cora saved you. We're practically bonded for life now! What do you want to know? I'll tell you everything."

Onyx keenly caught the word "bonded" in his words and leisurely cast a glance at Cora. Oh, so the girl's into wholesale rescues now?

Cora finally felt at ease after passing along the metaphorical hot potato.

Oblivious to his gaze, she bent down and rifled through her backpack.

Onyx stopped looking at her.

"I want to understand the personnel structure here. How about starting from the beginning? How did you all end up here?"

Flame responded with an "Oh" and began recounting the origins of the safe zone. He delved into the apocalypse's arrival, the outbreak of the first zombie wave, Mr. Sheridan leading a hasty retreat, and continued up to the present situation.

Onyx occasionally interrupted, posing questions that concerned him.

Flame didn't have all the answers, but after thinking and talking for quite a while, he provided a lot of information.

Beside them, Cora found it dull. With one hand, she tapped and twisted open a can of oranges, burying her head in the bottle. She sniffed the fruity aroma greedily, then fished out a spoon from her bag. She gleefully filled her mouth, swiftly finishing a can.

"So, the number of Aberrants among you isn't high?" After listening to Flame's narrative, Onyx quickly honed in on the key issue.

"Yeah, excluding Cora, there are only four of us now: Ray, Simon, Siegfried, oh, and Angela."

"Four?" Onyx's expression twitched slightly. "But Mr. Sheridan, didn't you say he's in charge? So, he's just a regular guy?"

Flame scratched his head. "Um... Mr. Sheridan is a normal person. He used to teach 11th grade, and he's the only teacher left in the safe zone. So, everyone listens to him willingly. Without him leading us these days, we might not have survived."

It was understandable for high school students sixteen or seventeen years old to trust and respect teachers inherently.

Onyx didn't comment, and nonchalantly tapped the metal wheelchair joints.

"You mentioned he's the 'only' teacher left?"

"Yes, at first, there were Mr. Wong, Mrs. Keller, and Vice Principal Lincoln. But they had accidents... and only Mr. Sheridan remained."

Accidents? That word deserved some thought.

Onyx smiled faintly.

"Is he a selfless teacher or a supposedly benevolent dictator? Perhaps we can only find out by peeling back that layer of hypocrisy."

His cryptic words left the only two listeners puzzled.

Cora placed down an empty can, letting out a small belch. She promptly opened another can, a distinct flavor this time. Gobbling it up, she remained unbothered by whether she understood. Eating was her primary focus.

After talking for nearly half an hour, Onyx had a basic

understanding of the safe zone's operational mode.

Before leaving, Flame received a call from Jacky in the distance, reminding him to hurry and collect today's supplies. Just before he departed, he remembered something.

"Oh, by the way, you probably don't know yet. Angela awakened as a healing-type Anopower."

Cora froze with a canned peach halfway to her mouth. The fruit slid off the spoon and hit the ground with a soft splat. She didn't have time to feel sorry for it; her reflexes kicked in, and she turned her gaze towards Onyx's legs.

Chin resting on his palm, Onyx sighed softly. "Hmm, lucky me."

Both conditions of the deal, bringing him back to the safe zone and finding healing-type Aberrants, were accomplished so quickly.

It was undoubtedly good luck. However, Cora didn't feel the slightest bit happy about it.

Her emotional shift was too apparent, and Onyx noticed it. Combined with her solitude in the corner earlier, he realized something and asked, as if catching on, "You don't want to ask for help, do you?"

Cora didn't respond, and after a while, she reluctantly nodded, her face showing understandable reluctance.

Onyx fell silent, gazing down at his own knees. Perhaps because of blood loss, his complexion had become even paler than when they first met.

Hanging on till now was a display of his utmost strength. At this moment, it was as if he stood on the gambling table of fate.

Cora clearly didn't want to ask for help; would she just give up on this opportunity?

He didn't know if he could hold out for the next healing-type; should he venture out alone to find that Aberrant, whose level was unknown?

It might save his life, but it would undoubtedly offend this new ally.

The prospects were rather grim.

Onyx needed a high-stakes gamble, an all-in, even if the cost was his own life.

Unfortunately, he was always the most audacious gambler.

However, wise gamblers often employ confusing tactics before placing their bets. As he opened his mouth once more, Onyx's emotions were stable, and his voice gentle. "If you don't want to, you don't have to find her."

Cora's moist eyes blinked, showing a hint of guilt. "Your... leg."

Onyx didn't hesitate to harvest her sympathy at this moment.

He spoke softly and kindly, "Don't worry, it's been bandaged. It's not that serious."

Cora felt relieved and saw him in a better light. She thought for a moment, then reached into her backpack and retrieved a beautifully packaged small cake, handing it to him. "Please, have some."

"What?"

"Cake."

"Why cake?" Onyx gestured towards the pile of empty cans on the ground. "I thought you might treat me to canned food?"

"Because... today is... my birthday." Cora smiled subtly, and the small dimples on her cheeks became more pronounced. This was the last piece of cake she had saved, the best looking one with strawberry tips. She had been reluctant to eat it, wanting to reward herself on her birthday.

Onyx prodded the cake with a plastic spoon. The small amount of cream on top had oxidized to a pale yellow. It was the lowest-quality vegetable fat cream, the type he would never try in the past. It was classified as "junk zone specialty," junk food that was subpar. However, his expression didn't change, and he scooped a tiny piece, placing it in his mouth. He then smiled with his eyes crinkled. "Thank you, it's delicious. Cora, happy birthday."

Cora's eyes widened slightly.

From the time she could remember, this seemed to be the first time someone had specially told her "happy birthday" aside from her grandfather. It wasn't the existence that was optional in District F199, nor was it an accessory that came with Felix from the Yue Mountain Martial School. It was a complete, single wish for her birthday.

Cora felt somewhat lost. She fiddled with the strap of her backpack and awkwardly pushed two unopened cans toward him, saying, "You can have these too."

Couldn't get supplies? No problem! She had them! She could

manage him during this time.

The wind and rain field outside was quiet in the early morning.

Cora tossed and turned, unable to sleep. She felt like she had forgotten something until a "ding" in her mind. She suddenly remembered that she still had one more opportunity to ask questions. One day, three questions–she was running low on these. How could she waste them?

Cora swiftly turned over and moved towards the side in the dark. Onyx slept quietly, his hands neatly resting on his abdomen, even his breaths light.

Cora gave him a push, but he didn't respond. She tugged at his sleeve, only to find his hand cold and clammy.

Cora froze, squatting down to inspect him.

The nighttime lighting wasn't great, but her night vision was excellent. She soon saw his face clearly.

Cold sweat covered Onyx's face, making it pale as paper. His jet-black hair clung to his forehead, and he looked terrible.

Having been rained on during the day, he hadn't changed clothes, and he spent the entire night cold and wet. Now, his wound had worsened rapidly, and he had lost consciousness.

Cora gently rolled up his pant leg.

The vibrant bloom of a transcendence flower stained the white bandage with a vivid red. She tried to press gently on the broken leg.

The fragmented bones shifted, lacking any trace of support, far from what he said was "not that serious."

The injury was even worse than she had imagined.

"On... Onyx!" Cora called out his name anxiously, slapping his face.

She used too much force and accidentally knocked his head sideways. His handsome face lost all vitality as it tilted slowly to the other side. No way... Cora was taken aback, quickly righting his head. She leaned close to his chest, her ear against it. Thankfully, there was still a heartbeat.

Anxious, Cora pinched her fingers. What to do? If she disregarded his words, he probably wouldn't last through the night. But to save him, the only option left... She looked in another direction, where darkness stretched out, faint signs of vitality flickering.

Should she seek that person? Even if the person was willing, getting them to intervene wouldn't be so easy. What bargaining chips did she have to exchange? And what price would she need to pay?

A voice deep inside her kept advising her: Give up, forget about it. You've only known him for less than a day. Leaving him behind isn't a big deal. Surely, more than one person knows the truth about the apocalypse. Worst-case scenario, she could go outside and capture another researcher.

Maybe she should just give up... Maybe...

However, Onyx's voice kept echoing in her mind. He had said to her, "Cora, happy birthday."

Cora closed her eyes, and when she opened them again, she stood up with a sharp movement. She picked up Onyx and placed him in the wheelchair.

Hasty and disordered footsteps, the harsh friction of the wheelchair against the ground—these noises abruptly woke up many people who had been sleeping soundly.

"Who's there? Why the heck are you making noise in the middle of the night?"

"Is something wrong? Did zombies get in?"

"Who? Who got in?"

Flashlights flickered, revealing the concerned faces of a group of people in the central area of the safe zone.

Cora pushed Onyx's wheelchair and stopped right in front of Angela. "Save him."

Angela, feeling groggy, was surprised by the pale appearance of the person in the wheelchair.

When she heard Cora's words, she looked up at her in disbelief. "Are you out of your mind?"

"You're a healing-type Aberrant. Please, please save him."

"Why should I? I'm not saving him!"

Fate had turned the tables. Cora hadn't expected that she would also have to beg Angela at some point. Angela was probably lighting fireworks to celebrate, let alone expecting her to save someone. It was beyond outrageous!

With her arms crossed, Angela looked down at Cora from her higher position, staring harshly.

She scoffed. "I've said it before. You're a disaster. Anyone who comes into contact with you is unlucky. It serves them right to die. Let's see who else you can deceive in the future!"

Resentment and malice were clear in Angela's eyes.

Cora knew it was useless to continue arguing with her. She changed the direction of the wheelchair and turned to the person who could actually decide: Mr. Sheridan.

"Save him."

Mr. Sheridan, wearing a coat, stood at the center of the inner circle, half of his face obscured by darkness. He remained silent.

Cora had considered that Mr. Sheridan might not agree unconditionally. She looked around, surveying the bewildered and lost faces in the dark. They were all helplessly watching the confrontation. This included Flame, Charlotte, Jacky, and others. Whispers spread, "What happened to him? Why does he look so bad...?"

"Can Angela just change her temper a bit and help?"

"Um, Cora, are you okay?" Flame looked at her with concern.

Cora didn't respond. She was contemplating the fact that Simon's Anopower had usage limits. The earliest they could open the door would be in the morning. They were trapped in the safe zone and couldn't get out. Could she wait? Could Onyx afford to wait?

Cora raised her gaze and counted the number of survivors. There were fewer of them these days, now just a little over a hundred. A little over a hundred ordinary students, defenseless. Going out to face zombie's head-on did not differ from courting death. She thought about her bargaining chip.

Carefully analyzing her mental abilities, Cora tightened her fist.

In the chaotic night, her right hand glided rapidly over the back of the wheelchair. Then she opened her palm. A blue-glowing Cleaver Knife materialized, its blade serrated and sharp, exuding an intimidating aura.

"One hundred weapons. Ex-exchange for saving him."

The blinking blue light illuminated a circle of astonished faces. Soon, a wave of shock echoed, "What the hell! Jesus! One hundred weapons?"

"How did that knife just appear? Did anyone see it clearly?"

"Am I dreaming? I must not be fully awake... someone pinch me!"

"Cora? This knife... how did you..."

Charlotte, a girl with a round face, exclaimed in disbelief and almost lost her ability to speak.

"Anopower," Cora responded slowly, enunciating each word clearly.

There was a brief moment of calm amidst the commotion.

"So you're not even a power-type Aberrant!" A boy who had been treated by Angela pointed at her and shouted, "We went out before, and you used a giant hammer to break down the door. And the strange iron umbrella last time, they were all created by your Anopower!"

"Mr. Sheridan kindly took you in. Why did you lie to us?"

"It's not really a lie. Cora never admitted to being a power-type. It's just that everyone assumed..."

Flame weakly spoke up on her behalf.

The sudden appearance of powerful weapons, combined with Cora's conditions, left the people in the safe zone dumbfounded.

A hundred weapons—they all couldn't help but feel tempted.

It could almost equip every person, fully arming their one-hundred-person team.

People were uncertain and began discussing amongst themselves.

While others were distracted, Irene's expression changed subtly.

Leaning towards Angela, she whispered something in her ear.

Mr. Sheridan took the Ethereal Artifacts Cleaver Knife from Cora's hand. He examined it for a moment and then, without warning, swung it at the volleyball pole nearby.

"Crack!" The solid steel column snapped, and the volleyball net fell to the ground.

He weighed the hilt of the knife, and his expression lost its calm. Suddenly, he looked up at Cora.

"Weapons of equivalent quality. Are you sure you can provide a hundred of them?"

"I can."

"When can you deliver?"

"Half... an hour."

Trading Ethereal Artifacts for Onyx's life was the only valuable exchange condition Cora could think of.

Through her observations over the past few days, she realized that what the safe zone lacked most wasn't food, but weapons.

With weapons, they could increase the size of the exploration teams and have a way to handle emergencies.

After all, the situation during the apocalypse was ever-changing.

Zombies surrounded the school.

It was just a temporary buffer zone, and how long the safe zone could remain "safe" was uncertain. No one could guarantee it.

Mr. Sheridan adjusted his glasses, and his certainty wavered. He didn't directly say yes or no; he seemed to wait for something.

"I don't agree. Why should I save him?" Angela, who had been ignored for a while, burst out discontentedly.

Mr. Sheridan glanced at her lightly. His eyes behind the lenses were cold and devoid of warmth. "Why don't you agree?"

"Anopower is mine; I may decide!" Angela spoke, but her voice suddenly faltered for a moment, replaced by a fleeting sense of fear. She lowered her voice and her teeth chattered, but she still stubbornly yelled, "If you want me to save him, you can. But I have one condition."

In the dim light, Mr. Sheridan's tone seemed subtly suggestive. "You're right. So, what's your condition?"

As Angela's fear subsided and her courage grew, all eyes were fixed on her.

She quickly uttered her condition, "I hate Cora. If you want me to save him, she has to kneel and apologize to me, then get out of here!"

Irene closed her eyes, her nails digging deeply into her palms. Angela, you fool! You absolute fool! I explained it to her so clearly. The top priority is to get Cora out of the safe zone. Why on earth is she adding to the drama?

"Angela!" Ray's stern voice cut her off. "It's late. Can you please not go crazy now?"

"That's going too far! Cora has saved us before! And she's a rare Aberrant!" Holden's face was serious as he spoke.

"What if she's an Aberrant? I'm a healing-type Aberrant too. She's just capable of conjuring some junk, and is that more important than me? If you're not satisfied, then you guys can go save him yourselves! Don't come begging me!"

Mr. Sheridan remained silent. He glanced at Cora and then looked at the unconscious man in the wheelchair, lost in thought. One disobedient chess piece, one disabled figure whose bottom line wasn't clear—how much benefit did they still bring to him at this point? Angela's demand seemed unreasonable and overbearing, but upon closer inspection, it might not be a terrible choice after all.

"Angela, that's enough. Humiliating a fellow student is unacceptable," Mr. Sheridan advised.

His words were calm and measured. Deciphering his true intentions was even more challenging.

Surprisingly, he seemed to have handed over the decision-making power to Angela?

With all the power now in her hands, Angela did not understand the concept of stopping while ahead. She looked triumphantly at Cora, a cruel innocence clear on her pretty face. "So, what do you say? Either watch him die or kneel and apologize to me, then get out of here!"

In the tense standoff, Ray suddenly spoke up in a calm tone, "If Cora leaves, I'll go with her."

"JP! Don't be impulsive!"

"Ray, what are you doing, going crazy again?"

One stone creates a thousand ripples.

Cora leaving and Ray leaving meant entirely different things. Cora, the lone wolf who kept to herself and hadn't been here for long, wouldn't be a significant loss if she actually left.

But Ray was different. He was the backbone of the safe zone, strong and well-liked. His departure would inevitably shake the morale, and losing two Aberrants at once, especially one of Ray's caliber, would be a heavy blow to the entire safe zone.

Angela's eyes reddened with anger, and she screamed hysterically. "Ray, you're like this again! You're always like this!"

Seeing the situation about to spiral out of control, Mr. Sheridan stared at Ray for a couple of seconds and then called him aside. "I'll give you some time. Calm down and think things through. There's room for negotiation in everything. Don't be so impulsive."

Behind him, Angela continued to yell and throw things. The

others kept their distance, avoiding her outburst. Amid the uncertain glances of people like Holden, Ray returned to his spot and started packing his bag. Suddenly, a slender hand pressed against his movements.

"Why?" Cora asked.

"You don't need to worry about this burden. I'm doing this willingly," Ray replied.

"Why, willingly?"

Cora's gaze was innocent, filled with curiosity about why he made this decision.

Ray looked into her eyes, his lips moving, and finally, he summoned the resolve to say, "Cora, I was wrong before. I apologize to you. There was something I couldn't tell you back then... Actually, I..."

"No need for this," Cora pulled back her hand, her brow slightly furrowed. "No need for apologies. The past is behind us."

The experiences that had once embarrassed her, she could now accept.

Reconciliation with Angela and the others was not her priority, given Onyx's troublesome nature, so she didn't need Ray's compensation or apology.

She didn't need another liability.

"I understand," she emphasized. "there's no need for this."

As expected... she was rejected.

Ray looked down at the hand she had pulled away, and couldn't help but smile wryly. "You don't know, you never know."

You don't know that during that summer, when the shade was at its thickest, a boy once had feelings for you.

Yet he couldn't bring himself to say, "I like you."

Because of every wrong choice he made, he gradually drifted away from you, unable to get any closer.

Cora squatted in front of him, tilting her head as she looked for a couple of seconds before realizing, and patted his shoulder.

"Don't worry, I'm strong."

She stood up, her slim shoulder blades stretching as she moved. She walked ahead on her own, facing Angela and the others.

Angela gnashed her teeth, her expression filled with the desire to devour Cora. "Cora, are you satisfied now? Are you feeling proud? Let me tell you, I'll never help you save him. I want all of you to die..."

A faint blue light pierced through the darkness, passing close to Angela's temple, cutting through her fallen bangs.

"Clang!" The platform behind Angela split in two with a deafening explosion, debris filling the air.

"Save him, and I'll leave this place."

Cora held the pose of her thrown blade.

It circled the area once before landing safely back in her palm.

Angela's legs gave way as her pupils constricted in shock, leaving her too scared to utter a word.

Cora's mentor had once said that when reasoning falls short, rely on your fists to determine the outcome.

Well, it worked.

A feeling of contentment came over Cora.

CHAPTER 18

An Eye for An Eye

The assortment of objects piled into small hills filled the entire equipment room. Cora had simply asked for materials, the more the better, without specifying their exact types. As a result, apart from heavy objects used to block the door, everyone had brought in anything they could carry.

Jacky set down the last basketball storage basket and moved in closer to Flame.

Just as they got in front of Cora, before they could even say anything, he gestured with a thumbs up.

"This is so cool! Even though it's kind of bullying Princess Chou, I still want to say damn good!"

Flame was being choked by his arm around his neck, limbs flailing in the air, unable to break free. He stomped on Jacky's foot with his heel, causing Jacky to release his grip, clutching his foot and hopping around, resembling a lively flamingo.

Despite their constant fighting and fooling around, their relationship was truly strong.

"Hey Cora, Little Fire wanted me to ask you, what were those swooshing things that were flying around earlier? So awesome!"

"Jacky, it was you who wanted to ask. Why are you blaming me?"

Flame retorted with annoyance.

"Oh, come on, is it any different if I ask or if you ask?" Jacky said with a mischievous grin, leaning in close to Flame's ear and whispering, "You two are pretty close, huh!"

Cora didn't keep it a secret and took out the object from her pocket. It was a blade as thin as paper, about seven inches long, shaped like a willow leaf, with a bright red silk tied at the end. In the dimly lit room, the blade's surface had a faint blue glow.

Jacky let out a low whistle, his eyes lighting up.

"It's for you." Cora handed him the flying knife since he seemed to like it, and she did so generously.

"Really? Well, I won't refuse then!"

Jacky exclaimed with excitement, accepting it without hesitation.

Who was kidding? Refuse what? This was no ordinary flying knife; it was the legendary Anopower flying knife! It could cut through iron like mud, and every shot would hit the mark. Even if Jacky didn't know how to use it, it would still be great to have it for warding off evil spirits.

"Cora, are you really leaving?" Flame asked quietly from the side.

"Yeah, I'll leave once Onyx is better."

Flame let out a reluctant "Oh." He wasn't talkative within the safety zone. And he hadn't convinced Cora to stay, especially with Mr. Sheridan's tacit approval.

Cora's departure was inevitable.

Once Jacky and Flame finished moving everything, they departed after closing the door. Cora only occupied the massive equipment room.

Facing the pile of equipment on the floor, Cora focused her attention. She placed her hand on the nearest metal rack, and within moments, a nearly two-meter-high metal rack disappeared in place, transformed into three brand-new entrenching shovels. This was followed by the second and third items...

Like a well-ordered assembly line, Cora arranged many standardized weapons in a row, revealing their formidable might.

She connected to over a hundred Ethereal Artifacts, hastening the depletion of her Anopower.

Gradually, her immense Anopower field faltered, unable to

sustain itself. With a single thought, Cora severed her connection to that portion of Anopower.

Almost instantly, Cora felt herself losing connection to these Ethereal Artifacts.

This was the first time she had attempted to sever her Anopower connection. Cora looked at the entrenching shovel in her hand and contemplated for a moment. Releasing Anopower once again after a few seconds, she saw the recently formed Ethereal Artifacts destroyed and dispersed. However, the Anopower within them didn't return to her.

Did severing the connection turn Anopower into a one-way existence that couldn't be retrieved?

By doing so, these Ethereal Artifacts no longer required her constant maintenance.

Though their power might diminish, they would be easier to distribute.

Cora left a subtle mark on the handles of each Ethereal Artifact.

According to the rate of natural consumption, the energy within this batch of Ethereal Artifacts would last around 2-3 years before being exhausted and shattered.

One hundred weapons, not quite her limit, but the massive consumption of Anopower in such a brief span had placed a significant burden on her.

Cora tallied the shimmering Ethereal Artifacts strewn across the ground, paused to hydrate and recuperate, and revitalized her exhausted mental fortitude.

With people stationed outside the equipment room, as soon as Cora emerged, several core members of the safety zone immediately approached her to count the weapons.

Cora remained motionless. One hundred weapons, not more or less. She had already handed them over.

They considered the distribution of weapons as an internal matter.

The male student in charge of counting the quantity came out and nodded to Mr. Sheridan, who was standing nearby. "Mr. Sheridan, everything is in order."

With the transaction completed, Cora didn't bother to engage in insincere conversation with them. She took a folding chair from the equipment room and sat down in front of it. She stared at it for a while, then suddenly grabbed Angela's wrist without warning. Angela instinctively tried to shake her off, but Cora's grip was too strong, like steel claws, unyielding.

Having just been intimidated by Cora's display of force, Angela still trembled with fear of the violent girl. Even though she didn't want to, she didn't dare to provoke her at this moment. She could only speak forcefully, "What... what do you want?!"

Cora's demeanor became cold, and she directed her attention towards Onyx in the wheelchair.

Despite his pale complexion, the man's features remained superior, even in such circumstances. However, from the knee down, a distorted lower leg destroyed this perfection.

"Why... why is it like this?"

Perhaps her eyes were too terrifying; Angela's teeth chattered as she continued, "I've already stopped the bleeding and tried to help the wound heal. His leg... his leg... it can only be like this. If you ask me, it's already good enough if he survives!"

On the surface, the wound on Onyx's right leg had indeed healed. On closer examination, it became evident that it was frail and fragile, with protruding broken bones in a disorderly manner. This resulted in his entire lower leg being forced to maintain a curled posture.

"Did you... did you do this on purpose?"

Angela brushed aside her fear and stood up angrily, "Cora! Spare me your accusations! This has nothing to do with me. His leg is broken like shattered ice. I'm not a doctor; how would I know how to mend it? Besides, my Anopower automatically absorbed as soon as I touched him. I can't control—"

Instantly, she felt remorse for revealing too much in her outburst. She bit her lip in frustration, unable to control her own Anopower.

Cora grasped the crucial point with keen insight. She concluded Angela was simply insufficient for her abilities and didn't deliberately tamper with the treatment.

There was no use in staying here any longer. Cora adjusted Onyx's pants and prepared to leave while pushing his wheelchair.

Angela timidly asked from behind, "I saved his life, so when are you... leaving?"

"Tomorrow, give him another check-up."

"Why?"

Cora looked at her expressionlessly.

In the unnoticeable space, Anopower rushed forth like a tide.

Angela's body prickled with sweat, and she compromised before Cora's overwhelming force, "Fine, fine, I got it!"

Onyx felt as if he were moving through a cold mist, surrounded by countless nuclear faces. They stared at him ominously, slowly drawing closer, eager to reach out with hands that pulled at his legs, gripped his throat, covered his mouth, dragging him into an endless swamp to sink. Just before he suffocated, he abruptly opened his eyes —His vision gradually focused, and Cora held a tissue a couple of inches from his nose.

A frosty look came into Onyx's eyes. Reflexively, he wanted to wave her hand away but realized this action didn't fit his current "persona." He hesitated, and the tension in his gaze softened, forming a weak yet handsome smile.

The subtle change in his expression went unnoticed by Cora, as she didn't mind. Seeing he was awake, she tossed the tissue to him, "Angela already treated you. How are you feeling now?"

Onyx lowered his head to look at his leg. The same oppressive feeling, like a bone-deep sore, returned. He quickly realized something was wrong. Onyx noticed a problem when his entire right leg, from ankle to knee, started feeling as if it had been injected with a subpar anesthetic. The nerve cells were completely dead, the meridians paralyzed, devoid of any sensation, stiff as if they were poorly crafted prosthetic scraps.

Onyx's eyelashes fluttered. He braced himself on the wheelchair's handles and attempted to stand up. "Clang—" Having lost one leg, his body couldn't maintain its balance. He leaned off-center and lashed to the ground.

Worthless.

With his fists clenched, he forcefully uttered the word in his thoughts.

After enduring the day with his injured leg, Onyx knew well that his condition was grim and required immediate treatment. Though he had taken a dangerous gamble, staking his life on it, he was fairly confident Cora would save him. And he was right.

However, he had overestimated Angela's abilities.

This newly awakened Aberrant in the healing class probably didn't even possess D-tier Anopower.

That would have been forgivable, but she turned out to be an utter medical ignoramus, focusing solely on stitching up the skin's surface without considering the flesh and bones underneath.

As a result, he had truly become disabled!

Worthless.

He clutched the wheelchair's handle tightly, repeating the word in his mind. He didn't know if he was cursing Angela or himself.

Cora didn't offer him any help. Onyx lowered his head, the veins on the back of his hand straining. She couldn't see his expression clearly at this moment.

"Angela's Anopower is for stopping bleeding and healing wounds, but her control is very poor, and she doesn't know how to set bones."

Cora pursed her lips and revealed her further plans. "She'll examine you again tomorrow, and then we'll leave this place."

"What? Is this the condition for saving me?" Onyx propped himself back into the wheelchair, responding with detachment.

He was naturally clever and quickly inferred the hidden implications in Cora's words.

"Yeah." Cora briefly explained the cause and effect of the Ethereal Artifacts exchange.

She admitted to forcefully coercing Angela in front of Mr. Sheridan, which had led to a complete breakdown in relations with the safety zone. Staying here any longer might pose hidden dangers. Even if Angela didn't make any demands, Cora intended to leave on her own.

The reason she came here originally was to collect information on the Aberrants. Upon meeting Onyx, she effortlessly answered these questions.

"Before we leave... let's take them out." After listening, Onyx lightly said.

His face held a half-smile that didn't quite reach his eyes, a similar expression to when they first met, when he casually killed two people.

"Taking them out will save you from a lot of trouble. You can go wherever you want with no one commanding you."

Without uttering a single word, Cora stared at him.

Their gazes locked, neither willing to look away first. Seconds ticked by, and Onyx gradually suppressed his smile.

"Just kidding."

He leaned back in his wheelchair, resuming his casual demeanor.

Those sharp jabs of hostility faded as quickly as they'd appeared, concealed with remarkable subtlety.

"I just didn't expect you to be so unpopular."

This person's emotions shifted too quickly for Cora to determine. She couldn't tell if, in that instant, he had truly harbored murderous intent.

After a few seconds of standing still, she couldn't discern anything unusual. Cora retrieved a brand-new blanket from her bag and draped it over his legs.

"I'll heal your leg," she said firmly.

Onyx glanced at her and allowed her to proceed.

"It's not that simple. Healing-type Aberrants are already rare, and given my current condition, I'm not even certain about achieving A-rank."

He wasn't intentionally making things difficult for Cora.

In order to fully recover, he would have to break the displaced bones and meridians again, then use Anopower to realign them properly.

This process required precision akin to a top-notch surgical procedure, far beyond what a regular healing-type Aberrant could achieve.

"I will heal it," Cora stubbornly repeated. She rarely made promises, but when she did, she intended to keep them.

No words were exchanged between them for a while. The surrounding noise—the clamor of people and the patter of rain—filled the air, but in their corner, there was an unusual silence.

Cora felt a sense of guilt, along with an overwhelming sadness. This person was someone she had taken in, someone she had vowed to be responsible for. Yet, she had messed up. Not only had she failed to heal Onyx's leg, but she also dragged him into another round of turmoil.

"Sorry," she clutched her backpack, curling up in disappointment.

After a while, Onyx finally spoke in a calm voice, "No need to apologize. It's not your fault."

Cora shook her head, her mood still low.

"You didn't say wrong; they all... they all dislike me."

Onyx's gaze shifted towards the corner. Cora was crouched there, rain falling on her head, looking quite pitiable, far from her usual spirited self.

"All of them? What did you do? Offend so many people in one go?" He shifted into a more comfortable position, his interest piqued. "I remember D District still employs... collective education, right? Did you blow up a school? Or set fire to the dormitory? With your personality, I doubt you beat everyone up, did you?"

Cora's eyes widened. Why did he guess that?

She weakly defended herself. "No, no, not everyone. Just... maybe a few dozen."

"Just—" Onyx dragged out the word, emphasizing it slowly. "A few dozen."

"You're quite the fighter."

"I am...?"

In the prolonged silence, Onyx's light laughter broke the awkward atmosphere. He rotated his wheelchair, gazing at Cora at his leisure, "So, these few dozen people, why did you have to beat them up?"

Cora clutched her backpack strap tightly, her gaze downcast. Her voice grew softer and softer until it trailed off.

Not waiting for an answer after a while, Onyx remained patient. His slender fingers tapped rhythmically on the wheelchair, his gaze dropping and then lifting.

In an instant, his face changed, and he quipped, "Let me guess, it's those people's fault because Miss Thornton is just too kind-hearted. Am I right?"

Cora suddenly looked up, revealing two eyes full of regret from behind her backpack, staring straight at him.

Onyx smiled knowingly, his gaze confident, an expression that completely trusted her. The tight knot of tension in Cora's heart seemed to relax a little. After thinking about it, there wasn't much she couldn't say, so she spoke slowly, "I used to... go to school here."

It was the first time she voluntarily talked about that experience with someone else. Perhaps because so much time had passed, the feelings from back then had become distant. When Cora spoke again, her mood was surprisingly calm.

Six years ago.

The NPA implemented a new mandatory education law that merges middle and high school into a five-year program and redistributes teaching resources across regions.

Old Thornton was already on his deathbed but he held on, using Old Cheung's connections to secure Cora a spot at school, giving her a chance to study.

Having lived away from society for most of her life, "going to school" was an entirely novel experience for Cora. With great enthusiasm, she came to Flower City.

Flower City (D56 District) was a D-rank, prestigious city, and this school had the most enrollment under the new system. Coming from the F199 District, Cora was like a tiny drop of water merging into the vast ocean, hardly drawing anyone's attention.

She was inconspicuous in her class, maintaining consistently poor exam scores—always within the bottom five.

Because of her inherent stutter and slow speech, coupled with her lack of communication with classmates, Cora was content with this kind of life.

She attended school in Flower City during the week and took the cheapest public route to Mountain Yue (E104 District) to practice martial arts on weekends.

Unlike between F and D districts, travel between D and E districts was relatively normal and inexpensive.

So, by the end of the first semester, Cora's calm life was disrupted.

At the end of June, on a hot summer afternoon, Cora finished her meal and, passing by the outdoor basketball court, was drawn by the deafening cheers and shouts coming from within. Unable to resist, she turned her head to look.

Just at that moment, a nimble figure darted past her, running, turning, dribbling the ball with dazzling moves, then leaping high into the air—slam dunk! The boy wore an oversized white basketball jersey, akin to a soaring seagull with outstretched wings. He hung on the rim with one hand for several seconds before landing effortlessly, exuding a bold attitude.

"Ah," Cora murmured to herself, her mouth agape.

The idea of people fighting over a ball seemed unfathomable to her until she had a sudden revelation about the boy's intricate footwork.

Such flashy footwork was probably what Master Zhang often referred to as "martial artists dying from unnecessary movements," right?

It looked good, but in reality, it was riddled with holes.

She was confident she could find 100 ways to counter it in an actual fight.

Without realizing it, she suddenly stopped walking, unable to tear her eyes away from the basketball court.

A basketball rolled to her feet. The boy in white stood beneath the hoop, backlit by the sun. He shouted from a distance, "Hey! Classmate, could you throw the ball back?"

Cora held the basketball in her hands, looking at the boy, then at the hoop above his head. She assumed the boy wanted her to do what he had just done—toss the ball into the hoop. So, with a languid push of her wrist from nearly thirty meters away, she responded with a nonchalant, "Okay."

The basketball traced a perfect parabolic arc through the air, swishing perfectly into the net.

The boys on the court, who had been casually talking and making adjustments to their wristbands, were completely surprised.

Some even spit out their water, exclaiming, "WTF?"

The boy in white was also momentarily stunned. Then he jogged over, tossing another ball to Cora. "Classmate, want to try again?"

Utterly baffled, Cora stood there. Yet, in front of him, she threw the ball once more. The basketball swished through the net again, eliciting gasps of amazement.

Everyone was shocked.

Intense and inviting, the boy's eyes called her over.

"You've got a good aim. We're short one person; how about joining us?"

Cora shook her head rapidly, "I can't... I can't play."

Amused by her dazed expression, the boy's brows relaxed, and a bright smile spread from the corners of his eyes, revealing a row of white teeth. "No worries, I can teach you. I'm Ray."

Guided by Ray, Cora returned to the court and joined a 3V3 game. While Cora had excellent accuracy with her shots, she was utterly clueless about the other rules, to the point of being infuriatingly naïve.

Ray patiently explained the rules again and again, feeding her the ball as he jogged backward. The vibrant sunlight generously shone upon him, and even the sweat seemed to favor the boy, streaming down his body in abandon.

Cora's skills drastically improved throughout the match, enabling her to shoot accurately from beyond half the court. Their opponents lay scattered on the ground, panting and begging for mercy.

Ray stood radiant at the center of the crowd, spinning the ball in one hand, his arched eyebrows and sparkling eyes exuding a triumphant air.

Idle and unaffected, Cora stood on the sidelines without even breaking a sweat. She thought the matter would end there. She didn't even remember Ray's name.

But the next day, during a break, just as the teacher left the classroom, someone brazenly rapped on her desk through the window.

Cora looked up.

Ray had placed his hands on the windowsill. His animated eyebrows seemed even more vivid. "Hey, junior, want to play ball this weekend?"

Cora shook her head, "No, I can't. I have... something to do."

"Alright then, time. Well, see you later," Ray wasn't hung up about it, giving her a casual wave.

However, before departing, he reached his arm through the window and left a cold bottle of milk on her desk. "Here, have this."

"What's the point of being so short? You can't even touch the hoop."

Cora wiped her name, which had been smudged by the moisture, her expression annoyed. She didn't notice that the girls in the back of the classroom, who had been enthusiastically discussing cosmetics, had all fallen silent.

Onyx, who had been quietly listening, seemed to sense something. He frowned and muttered, "Tsk, school can be troublesome."

Puzzled, Cora ceased speaking and glanced at him.

Onyx raised his chin, gesturing for her to look the other way.

The dawn had just arrived, and there was a lot of commotion happening.

Ray held a shovel, instructing people on how to use it. His adoring fans nearly engulfed his tall figure.

Amidst this bustling scene, the corner where they stood felt even lonelier and more abandoned, devoid of attention.

"You and him are not on the same path. The closer you get, the more trouble you'll face."

Ray was like a luminous, heat-emitting star, naturally attracting all celestial bodies within his gravitational pull to orbit him.

Those wandering celestial bodies that mistakenly entered his orbit would be mercilessly burned.

Cora thought of the trouble that had happened later on and nodded in agreement, "Yeah, troublesome."

Meeting Ray became the beginning of Cora's calamity.

For the girls at school (and perhaps some boys), Ray was the unattainable North Star, the little prince of the rose star, an elusive presence.

And Cora, who had the misfortune of catching his attention a few times, turned into a patch of filthy mud at the feet of the deities.

As a new week started, Cora felt the malice closing in from all directions. Cora found her desk stuffed with dead snakes and mice. Someone splattered ink on her assignments inexplicably. Her backpack, left at her seat one moment, vanished the next, only to reappear in the washroom sink.

Though the NPA's campus anti-bullying law had been in place for years, in the remote D-grade city of Flower City, it was almost non-existent.

Cora did not know what "bullying" entailed, let alone how much harm intensified "malicious pranks" could cause.

During that period, Old Thornton couldn't overcome his illness and passed away. Cora became an orphan. With no one to confide in about her grievances and no one to help her find clarity, she couldn't understand why she was being treated this way.

Old Thornton had once warned her to stay low in Flower City, to avoid acting impulsively, and not to lay a hand on ordinary people.

So Cora merely discarded the withered animal carcasses from her drawer, retrieved her backpack, and silently returned to her messy seat—she had lost her desk partner since the beginning of these pranks.

However, these bullies misread her attitude as tolerance and acquiescence, giving rise to a cascade of maltreatment.

Angela, the most stunning girl in school, the proud peacock, intercepted Cora in the cafeteria, dumping her food from top to bottom, drenching Cora's neck.

Even though there were plenty of students eating and two patrolling teachers witnessed the act, no one stepped in to stop it. Some saw but remained silent, while others pretended not to notice.

The viscous liquid flowed down her spine, trickling all the way to her heels. Cora caught a whiff of the damp and fishy odor mingled with mud. Slowly wiping the liquid from her face, she belatedly realized, "Ah... so it's not soup."

It wasn't soup, and it wasn't an accident. It was yet another malicious prank that had been happening to her day after day.

"Hey, stutterer, can't even speak properly, but you already know how to seduce men?" Angela sneered, arrogantly tossing her tray aside, pinching her nose in disgust, "I heard you came from District F. No wonder you smell like fish from a mile away."

"Hey! Come over here and smell her. Is she stinking or what?"

"Stinks, really stinks! Hahaha!"

"Ugh, I'm going to puke."

At the table behind her, Irene set her phone down. She had just taken a photo. She stared at Ray's back, her fingers quickly gliding through her contacts until she found Angela's name, then sent the picture.

The eruption day came swiftly.

It was Cora's turn to be on duty. The boys in the class lingered, intentionally making loud noises, banging tables and chairs. By the time she realized something was wrong, they had formed a "concave" formation with tables and cornered her against the wall. Her classmates, using the water hose from the restroom cleaning bucket, drenched her from head to toe.

Someone got a bit too enthusiastic, swinging an iron bucket.

"Clang!" It hit Cora's head.

The classroom fell silent for an instant, only for the nonchalant laughter to resume as if nothing had happened.

The high-pressure water jet left Cora unable to open her eyes and fully awakened her from her patience, making her increasingly alert.

Grandpa had said that she should get along well with her classmates in school. She had tried, but unfortunately, she had failed. But Master Zhang had also taught her the principle of "an eye for an eye." If someone hit her, she had to hit back. And that was something she could do.

So Cora kicked over the desk in front of her.

Cora didn't think she was going too far. She was just giving back what others had done to her—equal exchange. But when she poured the dirty water onto Angela and Irene, the group of boys seemed possessed, rushing towards her with distorted expressions. Cora raised the mop with her toes and thrust the grimy cloth into their faces, smearing them vigorously.

Cora acted with caution, ensuring she did not break anyone's limbs. Yet, these fourteen or fifteen-year-old adolescents lacked physical training. It wasn't clear to Cora why, after doing the same thing that was done to her, these perpetrators were now writhing on the ground, wailing and crying.

Did they never consider that others might feel as miserable as they did?

The brawl caused such a ruckus that people from other floors came running to watch, crowding around the front door, back door, and corridor.

Cheers, taunts, gossip—rumors took flight like wings, circulating everywhere. Ray was the first to get wind of the news. He rushed over anxiously.

But upon entering, the sight of bodies strewn all over the floor took aback him.

Angela lay in a pile of trash, her uniform skirt covered in paper scraps and filth. She called his name while sobbing uncontrollably.

Irene's braids also came undone, and she timidly hid behind Ray, gently tugging at the hem of his school uniform.

"Ray, you need to stop Cora, please. She's hurt so many students. Angie's dad has already informed the principal. If this continues... she'll be expelled."

Ray's full attention was on someone else; he paid no attention to Irene's gestures. He walked past her and approached Cora, his face taut with tension. "Stop," he commanded.

Ray held the mop that was still dripping with dirty water, his expression frosty. "Cora? What's gotten into you? This isn't the person I know you to be!"

Cora stubbornly glared at him, neither nodding nor shaking her head.

Ray felt his headache intensify, and he lowered his voice. "... You've hurt people. Apologize first."

With two teary eyes, Cora clenched her teeth. "No."

Suddenly, startled cries echoed from outside. "Mr. Sheridan's here!" "The principal and vice principal are here too!"

Ray grew even more anxious. He exerted force to snatch the mop from Cora's hand. "Listen to me. No matter the reason, when the teachers arrive, you apologize first, and then we—"

Cora's eyes turned bloodshot, and she pushed forward.

Ray was unprepared. He, along with the mop, was shoved several meters away, and the back of his head struck the wall with force. The hook hanging from the mop hit his brow, creating a gash that bled profusely.

Time seemed to stand still. The surroundings fell silent, so quiet it was as if one could hear the drip of blood. Irene's face turned pale, and she disregarded the fallen Angela. She rushed to Ray's side, frantically trying to stem the bleeding with tissues.

Amid the chaos, the stern-faced vice principal burst into the room, gasping for air as he bellowed, "Stop this right now!"

Following him was the displeased Mr. Sheridan, the grade

director. Observing the entire scene, he realized that his chances for a bonus this year had been thoroughly obliterated. His gaze fixed on Cora, the only one standing. It was icy and sharp as a blade.

Ray felt dizzy and disoriented. Various screams and exclamations filled his ears. In his blurry vision, stained with blood, he saw Cora's lips move. She whispered something so softly that only he could hear.

Then she flipped over a windowsill, leaped from the second floor, and ran out of the school amidst the stupefied gazes of the entire student body.

Before making her escape through the window, she had told Ray, whose ears were still ringing, something.

"You're the same."

After listening to her story, Onyx fell unusually silent for a moment. He knew Cora wasn't sharing these details out of resentment or seeking comfort. This tough girl, physically strong and somewhat simple-minded, probably thought that since he was disabled, she needed to offer him a more tragic story to console him.

"And then you just ran away like that?" he finally asked.

Cora nodded.

From that day on, Cora returned to Zone F199. She refused to leave after that, though it was strange that neither Angela nor the school's board of directors seemed to trouble her.

"It might have felt good to give them a beating," Onyx sighed softly, "but the governance in Zone D is mixed at best. You don't have any backing, and even if you're right, it won't matter. Even if you took this to the police station, there wouldn't be much they could do."

Cora shook her head. Throughout the entire ordeal, she never considered fairness or justice. Mr. Sheridan said she was wrong, that she shouldn't have stirred things up, and Ray said she was wrong, that she shouldn't have assaulted her classmates. Everyone seemed to believe she was wrong.

Onyx snorted lightly, "Wrong? So if you did nothing, would this have blown over?"

If Cora hadn't fought back against Angela, the bullying from other students would have continued unabated. She couldn't endure such days for even a moment.

Onyx's eyes narrowed slightly, concealing the destructive impulse lurking beneath.

"You hit them because they deserved it. Even if you were wrong, what difference would it make?"

"Some people spend their entire lives doing 'right' things and die without ever being recognized as saints."

He reached out and ruffled Cora's hair. "Still a kid, huh?"

"—Remember, in this world, right and wrong don't matter. What matters is living freely."

It was twisted reasoning, but Cora couldn't argue.

This person's perspective differed completely from the philosophy of her grandfather had taught her. Grandpa had said to integrate into society, to be friendly with others as much as possible. But Onyx seemed to care about nothing. Others' lives or deaths were irrelevant to him, as long as he found enjoyment and happiness.

"If it were you, what would you do?" Cora asked.

"What would I do? Haven't you already seen?" Onyx rubbed his chin, revealing that characteristic grin of a classic antagonist.

Cora thought of Yara and Bob's fate, feeling a pang of sorrow.

Unbeknownst to them, time passed quickly. The sky outside gradually lightened, and a new day began. The atmosphere in the safe zone had changed too. High school students equipped with new weapons became more daring, and a large exploration team assembled.

Cora stood up. "I'm going out to scavenge for supplies. You rest."

They were leaving today. Cora planned to scope out the route beforehand so that when Simon opened the door again at night, she could take Onyx with her.

Before leaving, she poked Onyx's leg, and this time, he didn't evade her.

"Remember, check one more time."

Onyx promised nothing. Instead, he stared straight at Cora with a gaze full of plaintiveness.

"What's the matter?"

"I was just wondering if you'd leave me here all alone."

"You think you'd sneak off while I'm scouting the route? You think you'd abandon me?"...

Cora rolled her eyes inwardly, thinking that only he could come up with such a thing. "I'll be back to get you!"

Onyx saw her off all the way to the exit, leaning on his wheelchair. He waved with a cheerful smile. "Remember to come back early. I'll be waiting for you."

Cora. "..."

She couldn't quite put her finger on what was odd.

With a mighty formation, the group departed.

And as usual, Cora lagged at the end, isolating herself from the others. She had also brought along the massive Ethereal Artifacts umbrella.

After everyone had left, Onyx returned to his corner. He pulled out Bob's wristwatch from his pocket, gazing at it for a moment. His fingers moved slightly, and with no visible motion, a clean set of clothes appeared in his hand out of thin air.

After changing into the new clothes, he checked the watch and necklace once more. Bob had left only clothes and food on the watch — nothing out of the ordinary. However, within Yara's necklace, Onyx found something unexpected.

A small, silver-colored, miniature smart terminal, far beyond Zone D's technological capabilities.

Onyx casually operated it, destroying the tracking device within.

CHAPTER 19

Liars

The wristwatch Bob left behind was, in fact, a storage space crafted by Anopower.

It wasn't very spacious, around twenty square meters.

The creators of this space, the Aberrants, may not have had the authority to set access restrictions, allowing any user with a hint of psychic energy to unlock it.

It was an unexpected boon for Onyx.

Before the New Dawn arrived, the military had a monopoly on Aberrants' resources.

These portable spaces were only distributed among the military, and obtaining one illegally would be quite expensive.

Even in the current chaotic situation, as more ordinary people awakened their Anopower, these items remained rare and precious.

Onyx was slightly taller than Bob, but their builds weren't vastly different. He selected a brand-new set of black casual clothes from the space and also retrieved a large bucket of purified water.

After giving himself a thorough cleaning from head to toe, he put on the fresh clothes. He looked clean and youthful, as if he were a young college student just starting out.

With Cora absent, the overly familiar young man, Flame, had also left with the dominant group. Onyx didn't recognize anyone left behind, yet he displayed no signs of unease. He strolled around the safe zone as if he were on a vacation, controlling his wheelchair with an air of leisure.

From his perspective, this place was not meant for a long stay. Although there was still some water left in the washroom, at the current rate of consumption, it would run out in less than three days. That wasn't the biggest issue, however. The safe zone had a fatal flaw —the abundance of "wasters."

"Wasters" referred to those who lacked the courage to explore the outside world and were unwilling to use their brains to find solutions. They spent their days sobbing in corners and yet consumed significant amounts of resources. Of course, this category included Onyx himself, the "disabled" one, as he self-deprecatingly thought.

He didn't believe that "Mr. Sheridan" was being so kind-hearted. At least he had noticed no radiant halo over the man's head. Mr. Sheridan will keep these wasters around, so there must be his own motives.

The metal wheelchair effortlessly moved across the surface and entered the safe zone's inner circle.

Hearing the commotion, Angela and Irene both looked up and clearly froze.

Angela was the one to judge people by appearances. Previously, in the dim morning light and aggravated by Cora's actions, she hadn't really looked at Onyx, the "crippled" one, but now that Onyx had cleaned himself up and was facing her with a smiling gaze, she realized that this man was rather handsome.

It's a shame, Angela thought and pursed her lips. Cora brought this person.

Irene waved her hand gently, giving him a bright smile. "Hey, how are you?"

"Hello," Onyx replied with a calm expression.

Miss Caldaro seemed genuinely concerned about him. "You're awake. How's your leg? Both Angie and I were worried about you. We were just discussing visiting you. After all, you're someone we worked hard to rescue."

Onyx ran his slender fingers across the blanket on his knee, his lips slightly curving but remaining silent.

Irene sensed his reaction and sighed softly after a moment. "Cora is a bit careless, usually. You need to take care of yourself. By the way, have you known each other for a long time?"

She had stayed behind to take care of Angela yesterday and didn't join Ray's group. She had only heard that Cora was the one who discovered him and brought him back, heavily injured. However, as the exact nature of their relationship remained unclear, she carefully chose her words when asking the question.

Onyx smiled wordlessly and replied in line with her intention, "No, we only met yesterday. We're not close."

"I see," Irene said thoughtfully, adjusting her hair. "There's something I don't know if I should say…"

"Please go ahead."

"You might not know, but Cora offended Mr. Sheridan yesterday, which is why she was kicked out. If she hadn't caused so much trouble and implicated you, maybe you could have stayed here to recover."

"Oh…" Irene pretended to have just realized her slip of the tongue and bit her lip in chagrin. "I didn't mean to speak ill of Cora. I just thought you had the right to know the truth. She might have her reasons. Just don't get into a fight with her!"

"Oh dear, I shouldn't have said anything. I just felt that this wasn't quite right…"

Onyx observed the person in front of him quietly, appreciating her poor acting skills. Although his pillar, Cora Thornton, might be simple-minded, she had a pure heart. As for Irene, who appeared helpful on the surface, she was far from a good person.

Onyx tapped his wheelchair lightly, and his deep, magnetic voice carried a meaningful tone. "So that's how it is. No wonder you've been treating me so well. You're kind. I thought maybe you…"

His expression was full of accusations, his beautiful peach blossom eyes lowered, and he placed a hand over his heart sorrowfully. "You didn't need to tell me, but now that I know the truth, can you bear to watch me go to my death? How can you claim to care for me while refusing to take responsibility? I find you quite frightening."

Irene. "…"

What was the Chinese ancient saying Simon Liu told her? Lift a stone only to drop it on one's own foot? Trying to steal chickens only to lose the rice?

She had just wanted to sow discord between this guy and Cora, making Cora uneasy after she left. But this man turned out to be such a peculiar breed.

How had she gotten wrapped up in his twisted reasoning, making her seem like a heinous criminal?

If you want to blame someone, blame Cora for leaving. Why did I end up in this mess?

Irene rarely found herself at a loss for words. She quickly tugged on the sleeve of the person beside her, attempting to change the subject. "An, Angie, you still need to help him with his check-up, right? Maybe now is a good time."

During the emotional intelligence showdown, Angela remained silent by the side, holding her head in discomfort. When Irene called out to her, Angela responded weakly, "I know. Let's get on with it. I'm not feeling great."

Finishing her words, Angela stood up impatiently and reached out to touch Onyx's leg.

Onyx swiftly maneuvered his wheelchair, evading Angela's touch.

His left-hand finger joints twitched nervously, a hint of icy hostility flickered in the air.

"No need," he said with a disdainful expression.

His abrupt evasion and the obvious disgust on his face caught Angela's attention.

Nevertheless, Irene failed to detect any abnormalities.

Angela took a few unsteady steps forward before turning pale and fainting.

"Angie? Angie!"

The treatment-type Aberrants were highly valued, and someone rushed forward immediately, calling out to Mr. Sheridan for help.

Someone pushed Onyx aside to the outer circle.

He lazily leaned against the back of the wheelchair, looking towards the crowd surrounding Angela. He arched an eyebrow in surprise. While others might not have understood the situation, he certainly did.

When Aberrants were subjected to external psychic energy

shocks, their energy fields could become disrupted and imbalanced. If their personal strength wasn't strong enough to withstand the shock, they could lose consciousness and fall into a coma.

Mental impairment can occur when their neural pathways are damaged in more severe cases.

He knew Cora had used psychic energy to frighten Angela before.

Angela had been fine until later in the day when she suddenly lost consciousness.

It didn't seem like an impact that had occurred recently. Rather, it resembled an explosion resulting from the accumulation of psychic pressure.

This is interesting, Onyx thought with a cold smirk.

In this safe zone, aside from Cora, who else would have been "oppressing" Angela with psychic energy for a "long" period?

Finally, Angela woke up in a daze after a long and difficult struggle.

She seemed devoid of energy and could barely gather the motivation to speak following the incident.

The others didn't understand the cause, attributing the incident to the aftereffects of her awakened Anopower.

At exactly 7 o'clock in the evening, Simon stood up promptly.

"It's time. I need to prepare to open the door."

This time, the exploration team was large, with everyone hoping for unexpected gains. They gathered at the door, ready to welcome those returning.

Onyx's wheelchair was parked in the shadows further away. With nothing to bring, he only awaited the door opening so he could follow Cora out.

Simon placed his hands against the wall and began releasing Anopower. Soon, the outline of a door became clear and solidified. He wiped the sweat off his forehead and let out a sigh of relief, a more relaxed expression on his face. He smiled as he pulled the door handle, and the wind and rain outside poured in like a deluge.

It hit them like a barrage, making it hard to keep their eyes open. The others hadn't yet seen what was happening—when the unexpected occurred!

A burst of crimson flames shot up into the sky, sweeping sideways and forcing those inside the door to step back. The next second, a strange burned protein smell reached their noses, followed by a chilling, scraping sound that sent shivers down their spines.

Ray's shout came amidst the raging storm, "The door's open! Hurry inside!"

"—Everyone, back off!"

A thunderous roar from the sky illuminated a vast, open area outside the door. Simon, the closest to the door, had a dazed expression as he saw the boundless, black, pressing tide and countless pairs of gray-white, eerie pupils.

One by one, messy figures entered, one after the other.

Siegfried, Holden, Ray… and last, Cora leading the group.

She held the Ethereal Artifacts umbrella fully open, its spikes protruding menacingly.

The sound of impacts resounded, and the umbrella surface continued to bear weight—bearing, bearing, and bearing again.

This noise wasn't the sound of rain; it was the sound of thousands of creatures striking the umbrella.

Some trapped fish sneaked in through the door's gap, moving quickly to crawl inside. Ray used his whip to knock down a group of them, but a few slipped through and dash into the crowd.

"Ah—!!" Fearful screams echoed one after another.

Luckily, Holden and others had entered safely, armed with weapons.

Working together, they finally killed those creatures.

Cora wedged the umbrella handle against the wall, performed a rolling motion from where she stood, and slammed the door shut with a loud "clang."

Siegfried's arms bulged with veins as he held the door's surface firmly. However, the outside entities grew in number, and the sound of impacts intensified. The others realized what was happening and rushed to help support the door panels and walls.

They persisted for over ten seconds until the Anopower door slowly disappeared beyond its time limit. At least for the time being, they prevented the intruders from entering.

"What... what are these things?"

Within the spooky stillness, someone crumpled to the floor, pointing at it in sheer terror.

Ten minutes ago, Ray's team had returned to the gym's side wall.

With a larger group this time, they had ventured further. Heading east, they approached the city's outer ring. Resources outside grew scarcer, and the living conditions turned harsher. If they remained in one spot, they wouldn't make any progress.

Fortunately, they hadn't encountered hordes of zombies over the past day and today. The torrential rain seemed to have driven them away, making the outside safer to explore.

Team members, clad in raincoats, leaned against the wall, resting in various positions.

Some were chatting while others waited for Simon to open the door.

A few guys had especially positive attitudes, vlogging around the corner.

They intended to post the content on social media for an exorbitant amount of views after they were safe.

The heavy Ethereal Artifacts umbrella mostly hid Cora's tall figure. She held a pen in her mouth, staring at the spread-out city map in confusion.

Her geography skills had always been poor, and now, apart from the cardinal directions and few circular traffic routes, she couldn't make heads or tails of anything.

Ray approached her quietly, whispering, "Before the network went down, I saved the locations of nearby safe zones. Shall I share them with you?"

"No need," Cora declined.

She didn't plan on taking Onyx to crowded places, and she didn't have a phone, anyway.

"Thanks."

Ray fell silent. His wet hair and face resembled a half-soaked dog —pitiful and stubborn. Cora glanced at him, adjusting the angle of the umbrella to shield his head.

A few minutes later, she paused and suddenly looked up. "Did you hear that... that sound?"

"What sound?" Ray asked, puzzled.

Cora furrowed her brow, struggling to describe it. It sounded like the buzzing of wings in motion and the friction of many feet walking on the ground. Her eardrums pulsed due to the rapid and dense frequency.

Cora raised her gaze, observing where the distant mountains met the horizon. Besides a dark line separating them, there was nothing else. She shifted her focus, scanning left and right, but found nothing.

The next moment, Cora abruptly turned back. She hadn't been mistaken—she saw it clearly! The separating line was moving!

The rustling sound grew nearer, almost at arm's length. Cora held her breath, and her intense expression prompted the surrounding people to stop talking and become alert as well.

The grass in front of them swayed gently, and suddenly, a massive insect leaped out. Its black wings vibrated rapidly behind it, humming and buzzing as it flew toward them.

Siegfried was closest to the insect and reacted swiftly. The insect met its demise as his biceps flexed and his machete sliced it in half from the belly. The two parts fell apart, and black pus oozed out, creating a foul-smelling mess in the puddle.

Before the others could even catch their breath, the second, third, and countless more insects emerged. It wasn't a rapidly moving horizon; it was an overwhelming tide of bugs!

Several guys recording videos took positions forward and hesitated for a moment.

In an instant, the swarm of insects overwhelmed them. Layers upon layers of bugs quickly covered their legs, arms, and faces.

Their agonizing screams filled the air as they flailed and swatted at themselves, but their movements became slower.

Ultimately, they fell, leaving behind fragmented, gore-covered skeletons.

"Stay close together!" Ray's ring emitted a red glow, and a massive fire whip shot up, pushing back the vanguard of insects. The remaining people quickly raised their weapons, ready to defend themselves.

After the insects devoured the flesh, countless compound eyes trembled slightly. They turned their attention towards Ray's group, locking onto their next prey.

The disturbance outside the door gradually diminished, creating a deadly silence in the safe area.

"What… what on earth are these things?"

The broken bodies of insects littered the ground, their size comparable to that of a volleyball. Oval-shaped, dark brown, with two long antennae protruding from their heads, and their compound eyes cloudy and grayish. They resembled the mutated zombies to an uncanny degree. Just looking at them sent shivers down one's spine.

"These are cockroaches," Onyx, in his wheelchair, suddenly spoke up.

Most of the people looked puzzled.

"Flat bodies, blackish-brown color, medium size, long filamentous antennae, well-developed compound eyes, membranous wings both in the front and back...According to the records of the ancient civilization's biological data, these are cockroaches, commonly known as roaches."

Yet, one individual, known for his deep fascination with prehistoric creatures, remembered something.

"But didn't roaches go extinct a long time ago?"

He often studied ancient life forms and remembered from his books.

"According to the Alliance records, roaches went extinct in the 4th year of the new calendar. Besides, how can there possibly be… roaches this large!?"

Normal roaches were just a few centimeters long, whereas these in front of them were almost the size of volleyballs!

Onyx wrapped a stick with tissue paper and turned over the bodies on the ground.

"Because these are mutated roaches, or you can think of them as zombie roaches. They share similarities with zombies, feasting on carrion, while also possessing the characteristics of roaches. They reproduce quickly, move fast, and gather in groups."

"Reproducing rapidly, gathering in groups." This piece of information led to a sense of despair for many.

Could there be news even worse than this? Dealing with zombie humans was already a challenge, and now there were zombie roaches.

Would they be able to make it out alive? Was there any hope left for the next Alliance rescue?

"Don't lose heart, everyone!"

Charlotte's voice quivered, but she mustered the courage to console them.

"These... zombie roaches aren't that frightening. We've killed some, haven't we?"

Others quickly chimed in. "Yeah, they're dead, aren't they?" "We have weapons. We can just chop them up!"

"Exactly, one by one, ten by ten, a hundred by a hundred. Let JP burn the hell out of them!"

The young boys and girls became excited, each one louder than the last.

"We have weapons, and JP is still here! What's there to be afraid of?"

Ray's expression, however, wasn't as optimistic.

Fire-based Anopower would have been perfect to deal with these creatures, but the persistent rain significantly reduced his Anopower's effectiveness.

He could only unleash about forty percent of his true power.

He had no chance of winning when faced with an overwhelming number of zombie roaches alone.

Amid the clamor, Mr. Sheridan made a gesture to silence everyone.

He pushed up his glasses, his expression unusually grave.

"You're right, we can kill one, two, ten, or a hundred, but what about a thousand, or even ten thousand?"

"Just based on us, who among you is confident you can take down ten thousand zombie roaches outside?"

Cora frowned, recollecting the immense gathering of black insects. She found it a challenging prospect.

No one could answer the question. The hope that had just ignited had now plummeted to the freezing point. The prospect of ten thousand zombie roaches felt like an insurmountable mountain, shattering everyone's determination.

The boy who had escaped death at the Starship Harbor suddenly broke down. He angrily raised the knife in his hand and stabbed it into the abdomen of a zombie roach repeatedly.

"I don't believe it. It's all fake, it's all fake! There are no zombies, no apocalypse!!"

Holden held him back, but it was too late. Someone couldn't bear the oppressive atmosphere any longer and burst into tears. A somber haze quickly took over the safe zone as fear and dread became contagious.

"Unfortunately… there might be even over ten thousand," it was Onyx who spoke at this bleak moment.

"When you spot a roach in the sunlight, it means the dark corners are already too crowded."

Everyone. "…"

CHAPTER 20

Underneath Dangers

Cora sat on the ground, wiping her lance.

Her Ethereal Artifacts umbrella, previously used to fend off the insect tide, had been left outside the door. The iron umbrella itself was too bulky and not helpful for dealing with these small creatures. So, she had conjured a lance, entirely blue and about three to four feet long. She carefully wiped the tip of the lance.

"Sorry, I should have taken you out earlier in the morning," she said.

Onyx shook his head. "It doesn't matter. With the quantity so large, we would have encountered them eventually when we went outside." His gaze drifted towards the distance. "This safe zone won't hold for much longer. Be cautious tonight."

"You just..."

"Hmm? What's wrong?"

Cora paused, her lance-wiping, swallowing the latter part of her sentence.

When she looked at him, Onyx was still smiling, as if he had no recollection of what had sparked outrage earlier.

She had now realized that this guy had a knack for driving people crazy. With just a casual sentence, he could make over a hundred people in the safe zone want to grab weapons and attack him.

If she hadn't made the quick decision to push him away, someone would probably have fought him.

Troublesome. Seriously troublesome.

Cora sighed inwardly and decided not to continue the conversation.

Instead, she leaned in a bit and begged, "The roaches, the mutations — are they related to the apocalypse?"

"They are," Onyx nodded. "You're probably wondering about the truth of the apocalypse and how Anopower and zombies came about, right?"

Cora nodded eagerly. These were her biggest questions.

Onyx looked slightly troubled as he teased her, "Well, that's already two questions~"

"?" Cora suddenly looked bewildered.

Cora bit her lip, her annoyance clear.

Cora raised her lance.

Onyx cleared his throat and, seeing that things were escalating, he said, "Um... calm down first, lower your lance, and I'll explain."

"Contrary to what many people believe, this apocalypse wasn't caused by a virus."

"It's radiation."

Onyx's expression finally turned serious.

"Have you ever wondered why the mutations among the zombies are happening so rapidly? Why, in different places, people are awakening Anopower at the same time... It's because a pathogenic strain did not cause this apocalypse, nor is there any kind of transmission chain. Every one of us was stark exposed to the air, and the real culprit is radiation."

"Because of frequent solar wind eruptions, the current radiation levels have exceeded normal values by five times. The Earth's strong magnetic field is in chaos, unable to resist the surge of radiation. High-speed particles and cosmic rays are recklessly entering the ground and the air. The continuous radiation energy is fusing into the cells of our bodies, causing genetic mutations. Under these conditions, some people have 'evolved' successfully, upgrading into Aberrants, experiencing an explosive growth in strength. Others couldn't withstand the excess radiation and had their cells rapidly degenerate, mutating into zombies. However, most people have maintained a fragile balance, becoming 'ordinary people' somewhere in between."

"People can mutate into zombies, and animals naturally can too. Animals that turn into zombies often possess even greater aggressiveness."

Onyx's gaze turned somewhat cold.

"The NPA hasn't held back from doing some less-than-ethical animal experiments. A swarm like today's, whether it's an act of fate or manipulation... it's hard to say."

Zombies don't possess consciousness, and it's likely the same for zombie roaches. Cora recalled the strange bird she had seen at the martial arts school. She had an inkling that there was something different about it.

That bird... didn't seem to have a strong desire? Perhaps she was just lucky? Maybe the gigantic bird was full at the time? Didn't fancy her, this little bean sprout?

Cora shook her head, casting aside these baseless speculations, and continued, "If a zombie bites someone, will they turn into one?"

"Based on the outcome, the answer to that question is 'yes.'"

Cora was puzzled. "What do you mean?"

Onyx explained, "As I mentioned earlier, the cause of the apocalypse is radiation. So, when someone is bitten by a zombie, it's like experiencing a radiation bombardment once again. But this time, it's contaminated radiation. Most people can't withstand this impact, their internal magnetic field goes haywire, and they transform into zombies."

"Most people?" Cora keenly caught on to the key point. Did this mean of survival too?

"Since it's a magnetic field imbalance, there's also an extremely small probability of passive awakening, evolving into Aberrants."

Cora squeezed her palm, which had become moist without her realizing. Her lips pursed. "What if the one bitten is already an Aberrant?"

Onyx squinted. "What, were you bitten?"

Cora's hair stood on end. "N-No, not at all!"

Fooling Onyx was difficult.

To show her innocence, Cora promptly offered her arm for inspection.

The bandages were removed, and there wasn't a trace of a scar left.

Not only her arms, but the wounds on her back, abdomen, and lower back were also completely gone. It had only been a short week since the battle at the martial arts school, and her body's healing ability was so fast that even she found it hard to believe.

Onyx lowered his gaze, his scrutinizing eyes seemingly capable of penetrating her.

Cora had just been caught in the rain and had taken off her jacket. She was now wearing only a thin T-shirt and knee-length shorts.

Onyx's gaze traveled from her slender neck to her wrists, down to her ankles. With her shoulder-length damp hair and round, startled eyes that resembled those of a frightened little animal, she anxiously shifted her gaze around.

There was a piece of gauze stuck to her cheek. With her slender arms and legs, she appeared, based solely on her appearance, to belong to the category of "completely harmless."

"If Aberrants mutates into zombies, the consequences are unimaginable. Therefore, if discovered, even if there's a one-in-a-million chance of self-healing, their fate has only one outcome."

"What... what is it?"

"Execution."

A chilling smile played at the corner of Onyx's mouth.

"The NPA can accept many casualties because of radiation, but it absolutely won't allow Anopower-equipped zombies to exist."

With a tight-lipped expression, Cora experienced a shiver down her spine.

No one will sleep tonight.

To conserve power, only a few flashlights illuminated the vast safety zone.

Accompanied by the raging wind and pouring rain outside, survivors kept their eyes wide open, huddling together and shivering.

An emergency meeting was called by Mr. Sheridan, leading to some heated arguments because of divergent opinions.

"Let's charge out!"

"Are you out of your mind? There are not only zombies out there but also tens of thousands... maybe even more cockroaches! Are you rushing out to die?"

"Staying here is just waiting to die!"

Ray and Holden, the radicals, believed that they should charge out while the situation wasn't worse. Near to the safety zone was the middle school's parking lot. Holden had scouted it and found several buses. They could safely drive out of there.

However, the plan was high-risk. Even if they took the nearest route, they had to pass two dormitory buildings, meaning they'd have to navigate through thousands of zombies to cover around 100 meters before reaching the parking lot.

The opposing group supported a more conservative strategy.

Simon, for instance, insisted that staying within the safety zone was the wiser choice.

This gymnasium's exterior walls were constructed with the latest NPA materials, rendering it an impregnable fortress. As long as they guarded the entrances on both sides, the people inside would be safe.

But when would the rain stop? Would the insect tide recede?

Simon had no certainty.

The two factions clashed in argument, while Cora and Onyx in the corner remained unaffected. Cora gestured left and right by Onyx's wheelchair, focusing on her psychic energy. A faint blue light formed the shape of a bow and crossbow on his wheelchair, providing him with a means of defense in case of emergency.

Then she picked up a piece of cake she had scavenged from a convenience store. As she slowly nibbled on it, she observed Onyx.

Onyx quickly adapted to the complicated commands of the wheelchair's control panel. He quickly got the hang of it.

After becoming familiar with it, Onyx brandished the Ethereal Artifacts crossbow, a weapon known for its rapid-fire capabilities and lightweight design.

Its intricate internal structure was paired with arrows about eight inches long. It could shoot ten at a time, making it nearly invincible for close-range crowd control.

Onyx's fingertip whisked the arrowhead, and it immediately left a cut, blood flowing profusely.

"Is this what you call a 'crossbow'? How was it made? The NPA doesn't have weapons like this."

"Artifacts from the old civilization?" He quickly dismissed his own conclusion.

"No, right? The old civilization lost this kind of repeating crossbow," he quickly dismissed his own conclusion.

Cora's eyes dimmed, and her cake suddenly lost its flavor.

"Master drew for me it."

Onyx had heard Cora mention that her master and fellow disciples had all turned into zombies. He understood she wasn't in a good mood and didn't press further.

He played with the crossbow bolts for a moment, then smiled and asked, "Miss. Thornton, how about teaching this crippled researcher how to use it?"

"Sure." Cora swallowed the cake in one bite, wiped her mouth, and approached to instruct him.

Meanwhile, the argument over whether to "charge out" or "stay put" had escalated to a heated level.

"Enough bickering! Let's listen to Mr. Sheridan and let him decide!"

Siegfried, whose eardrums had suffered enough, shouted in exasperation.

After his forceful shout, the voices of those attending the meeting instantly quieted down. Siegfried was taken aback—when did his words become so effective?

He soon realized that it wasn't his words that were effective, but everyone's expressions had transformed. They stared anxiously at the floor.

"Squeak, squeak..."

"Crack, crack..."

Something was moving beneath the floor!

Simon's words were only half right—while the gymnasium's exterior walls were indeed impenetrable, the ground underneath wasn't.

Sounds of stone being chewed echoed continuously. In just a few seconds, the floor suddenly cracked open, revealing a large hole about two meters wide. Like a hornet's nest being poked, countless zombie cockroaches flew out from below and crawled out...

Unbelievable! They could actually tunnel!

The three Aberrants in the area, Ray, Siegfried, and Cora, sprang into action. Ray cracked his fire whip, pushing back the first wave.

Siegfried's veins bulged as he hoisted a piece of a door, slamming it into the gap. Cora, like an agile cheetah, leaped off the ground, lance in hand, piercing the zombie cockroaches emerging from the hole one by one.

"Turn on the lights! It's too dark!" Siegfried bellowed.

The flashlight beams flickered intermittently, barely illuminating more than half of the safety zone.

However, dark shadows still darted around the dim corners.

Some people wielded their weapons to fight back, while others found their hands and feet trembling, unable to muster the strength to attack.

Frightened, the swarming zombie cockroaches that gradually surrounded and overwhelmed them, gnawing at their toes, shins, chests, heads... within seconds, only bloody skeletons remained.

The light from above suddenly dimmed, and everyone looked up in panic. Zombie cockroaches densely packed the skylight from above, their countless pairs of gray-white compound eyes coldly staring down at their prey and blocking the last faint glimmer of moonlight.

Mr. Sheridan saw the worsening situation and immediately decided.

"Let's go according to plan one! Get ready, I'll open the east gate!"

Cora rolled back to Onyx's side, strapping her backpack on. "We need to run."

Onyx quickly adjusted the wheelchair's direction. "Yes, I'm ready."

Siegfried cleared the obstacles behind the gate, while Mr. Sheridan dashed over to enter the password. The control panel of the long-sealed door slowly opened again. People rushed out in a mad scramble.

Those caught in the back couldn't break through. Someone shouted to Simon, "Simon! Open another door!"

Simon attempted to gather Anopower, but the weak light cluster dissipated before taking shape. He shook his head at the person.

"I can't. This worthless Anopower doesn't work when it matters most. I can't release it!"

The person who had just spoken stared at him in horror. "Bugs! Bugs!!"

The skylight couldn't bear the weight of the zombie cockroaches. It shattered, and glass fragments rained down alongside the pouring black insects.

They covered Simon from head to toe and also swallowed up a few people who hadn't escaped.

"Aaaah!"

Heart-rending screams came from behind.

The male student, who was at the forefront, had a look of survival on his face. He turned back excitedly to his companions. "Haha, we're out! You filthy bugs..."

A gaunt figure in a school uniform pounced on him, cutting his words short and biting into his neck: a zombie.

The students halted their steps, afraid to advance.

Below the dim dormitory, hundreds of zombies turned their heads in unison, their hollow pupils fixated on the group.

Flames erupted as Ray's whip cut through the air, severing five or six zombie heads. Ray dashed ahead. "Stick close to me, and get ready to charge through!"

Cora's lance flew out like a string of candied haws, piercing through one zombie cockroach after another. Soon, a long chain of them hung from her lance. Ray's flames followed closely, burning a path through the encircling horde.

Onyx followed behind Cora, dodging with agility. It was unclear how he managed it, but the zombies and cockroaches that came near him were notably fewer. Around him, it was almost a vacuum.

Two powerful Aberrants led the way.

The students, agile and robust, successfully navigated through the first dormitory building, with the distant parking lot in sight.

Flame lagged the group, running while wiping tears from his eyes. He didn't dare cry out loud. He had almost failed to make it out of the gymnasium. "Jacky, wh-what do we do... Can we make it out?"

Running at a slower pace, Flame relied on Jacky, who was pulling on his collar to provide him with some physical acceleration. "It's okay, we're following Mr. Sheridan."

"With Mr. Sheridan here, everything will be fine. He'll lead us out!"

The two boys were just a few meters behind Mr. Sheridan, who wasn't running fast either. Several girls and frail boys were beside him.

This small group of them had terrible athletic coordination. Despite pushing themselves to their limits, they were falling behind. Slowly, they lost connection with the larger group ahead.

Suddenly, a window on the first floor of a nearby dormitory opened. Several zombies jumped out, catching them by surprise and colliding with their group. Jacky and Flame tumbled, crashing onto the ground. Several boys cried out in terror as zombies attacked, trying to bite them.

Mr. Sheridan also got knocked down, rolling into a heap of zombies. He could see a zombie opening its jaw, ready to pounce on him. Its foul saliva had already dripped onto his glasses. Mr. Sheridan's pupils contracted.

Two girls beside him anxiously called out, "Mr. Sheridan!"

Suddenly, their voices stopped abruptly.

As if an invisible hand was choking them, their expressions twisted, and their bodies convulsed violently. Gradually, their movements slowed, and their bodies eerily fell backward. Seizing the opportunity, Mr. Sheridan grabbed them and pushed them into the mouths of the zombies. Using the recoil, he struggled to climb to his feet and continued running forward, desperately catching up with the front of the group.

Midway through the escape, Mr. Sheridan seemed to sense something, and he turned his head back for a quick glance.

The zombies had savaged the two girls, their faces unrecognizable.

Not far behind them, Jacky instinctively pushed Flame's head down, making him lie face down on the ground. Jacky shielded him with his own body.

Jacky lifted his head and locked eyes with Mr. Sheridan. There was no warmth in those eyes behind the glasses.

Jacky became motionless as his heart almost ceased beating.

CHAPTER 21

Withering Blossoms

Cora and Ray guarded the entrance to the parking lot.

Behind them, the bus's engine roared, and the headlights blinked, casting a hazy light in the pouring rain. People continued to rush towards them, climbing onto the bus with all their might. They collapsed onto the seats, gasping for air, some even collapsing directly in the aisle.

In the life-or-death moment, no one cared about their appearances.

Saving their own lives was the only concern.

Cora and Ray waited for a full five minutes, but very few people reached their location.

"No one else is coming, let's go," Ray muttered in a low voice, exhaustion clear.

Because of the sudden attack of zombie cockroaches, their escape had been hasty, resulting in far more casualties than expected.

They had to escape hastily because of the sudden attack of zombie cockroaches, resulting in the group being reduced to less than fifty from over a hundred.

Ray's grip on the flame whip tightened as he vividly realized he couldn't rescue everyone.

Any sound or movement in the rainy night reverberated endlessly. From their position, a faint light pierced through the darkness and caught the attention of dark creatures. Hundreds of meters away on the playground, thousands of zombies raised their heads, their hollow eyes fixed on that direction as they converged.

"Quick, get on! We're closing the doors!" Holden leaned halfway out of the driver's window, shouting at them.

"Wait!" Cora pressed her palm against the bus door.

She had seen Jacky and Flame stumbling towards them. A few horrifying zombies followed closely behind them, along with the rustling and chittering mass of cockroaches.

With a slight motion of her wrist, Cora's lance shot out like lightning. She dashed forward, using a tornado-like move to create a powerful air wave that knocked down the pursuing zombies and cockroaches, providing a momentary buffer.

Jacky and Flame rolled and crawled their way onto the bus.

"Let's go!"

Holden roared, starting the engine. In the midst of a rainy night, the bus veered and increased its speed, smashing through the zombies and cockroaches obstructing its path. It charged through the gap in the iron fence and headed towards the road. After ten minutes, they finally shook off the densely packed pursuers.

The bus was an older hybrid model with manual control capabilities, even if the automated driving system failed.

Recently, automated driving had become popular in the NPA, and fewer people bothered to get regular driver's licenses.

Holden was a repeat student, two years older than the others.

As a joke, he had gained a driver's license last year, never expecting this seemingly frivolous skill to become a lifesaver.

In normal situations, it would require approximately two hours to drive from First Middle School to the downtown area of Flower City.

However, with rain falling and visibility poor at night, zombies and insect swarms could appear at any moment. Holden couldn't afford to let his guard down, so he slowed down and drove cautiously.

Three hours later, as the bus neared Flower City's downtown area, Holden was the first to sense that something was off. It was nearly 5 AM, yet the highway was still congested. There were many private cars on the road, all heading in the same direction as them.

They were running away from zombies and the insect tide. Why were these people heading back to the city at this hour?

"Bang, bang, bang!" A series of loud thumps broke the silence, causing everyone inside the bus to startle and look outside.

Weaving recklessly through the traffic, the young woman pressed herself against the side of their bus. Her shoes were nowhere to be found and her toes were stained with blood.

She ran while desperately pounding on the bus door. From her lip movements, they could vaguely make out her cries for help.

This behavior was incredibly dangerous.

Charlotte's face showed a mixture of pity and reluctance.

"Should we... save her?"

Angela suddenly stood up, her voice shrill.

"Don't open the door!"

Her sudden scream startled the others. No one dared to speak, let alone move. They all sat frozen in their seats, acting as if the woman outside didn't exist.

Seeing that the bus door wasn't opening, the light in the woman's eyes gradually dimmed.

Eventually, her expression turned into one of despair.

The individuals on the bus averted their eyes from her.

Several fierce zombies leaped onto the roof of the bus from the other side and tackled the young woman. Looking from the rear window, they saw her outstretched hand slowly fall.

"Look! She got bitten! We can't let her on!" Angela's voice sounded jittery and erratic. "We can't let her on..."

At the back of the bus, Cora was observing the surroundings. Upon hearing the commotion, she turned around. Onyx had moved closer to her, and his voice was barely a whisper. "Don't you think she's too noisy?"

Cora was momentarily surprised. After giving it some thought, she realized it was true.

Angela's emotions were becoming harder to control ever since she awakened her Anopower.

She either screamed at the top of her lungs or rambled

incoherently, leaving everyone puzzled.

"Someone is manipulating her using psychic abilities."

"Angela has an E-level Anopower. She can subtly influence her behavior and personality. The other person is probably a C-level psychic Aberrants."

"Care to guess who's the puppeteer behind the scenes?"

Onyx's breath was close to her, and the warm air tickled her ear. When did he get so close?

Cora extended two fingers and pushed him away with a disgusted expression. After a brief pause, she provided the answer.

"Mr. Sheridan."

Memories of the peculiar feeling she experienced upon locking eyes with Mr. Sheridan on their arrival to the safe zone resurfaced.

Mr. Sheridan had likely attempted to use his psychic abilities to manipulate her, but he had failed.

This led to his suspicions about her being an Aberrants.

Subsequently, numerous attempts were made to test and manipulate her, resulting in his determination to remove her from the safe zone once he realized she was difficult to manage.

"Bingo!" Onyx snapped his fingers.

"He can control even E-level Aberrants. Naturally, he wouldn't spare ordinary people. To him, these people are all his puppets, expendable pawns he can easily discard in dire times. No wonder he's willing to keep so many 'useless people' around."

"This Mr. Sheridan is truly a hypocrite."

At Onyx's comment, Cora glanced at Mr. Sheridan.

Seated at the front of the bus, he had set aside his frameless glasses that had visible cracks. He was currently wiping his face with a towel, his expression obscured from view.

Onyx followed her gaze.

"Are you thinking of exposing his true nature? Don't forget, we're Outcasts; they won't believe your accusations."

"Don't worry. Mr. Sheridan's tricks are just a show for you guys... He's willing to manipulate those naïve high school students. If they're all safe and sound, his ugly intentions won't surface. The more dire the situation, the more his twisted thoughts will be revealed."

At 5:40 in the morning, the bus entered Flower City's inner ring. It seemed like the sky never really brightened up, staying overcast. Chaos enveloped the city, with collapsed buildings and scattered starship debris. The deafening air raid sirens resounded throughout the streets and alleys.

"This is a Level First Alert." Jacky stood up, gripping the back of the seat, his expression grave.

"My dad was a designer for the defense array. He once mentioned that a Level One Alert only sounds in Flower City during the most severe natural disasters."

Charlotte's face turned pale as she added, "I took part in safety drills in Flower City. I remember that during a Level One Alert, the highest priority order is to enter the defense array."

"Exactly. The defense array is Flower City's last line of defense. Once activated, it means the outer perimeter of Flower City has been abandoned."

Flower City had a natural basin-like terrain, with the center at a lower elevation and concentric traffic networks descending layer by layer until reaching the central core of the defense array.

This core was a floating shopping mall, also the most iconic landmark of Flower City. It was adorned with lights, shimmering and bustling day and night.

Flower City had a plan for when a disaster struck - sealing the eight entrances and sinking the defense array to create an underground shelter.

Jacky listened intently to the frequency of the alarms, his expression growing anxious. "Quick, Holden! Drive faster! The entrance is about to close!"

In the distant sky, the floating mall was descending slowly. The alarms intensified as the ground cracked open in multiple directions, making way for its descent.

Holden pressed the gas pedal frantically, pushing the bus forward.

People were running in all directions on the chaotic streets, with different vehicles and zombies chasing after them.

Survivors who had previously hidden in their homes were now pouring out, sprinting towards various entrances of the defense array.

The entire Flower City was falling.

The cracks in the ground grew deeper, skyscrapers and circular sky bridges lost their support, swaying and collapsing onto the ground.

Suddenly, a steel rod pierced through the bus window, shattering the glass like a spiderweb. Roaming zombies climbed through the broken window, grabbing Charlotte's arm and trying to pull her out. She didn't even have time to scream before being yanked out of the bus. The other passengers inside stared blankly, unsure whether they should help. Cora had already followed right behind, leaping out.

"Holden, slow down!" Ray suddenly stood up.

Holden, sweating profusely from nervousness, clenched his teeth and hit the brakes.

Midair, Cora had already flung her lance. With a move resembling a striking snake, the lance's sharp tip penetrated the zombie's skull, pinning it fiercely to the ground. Cora swiftly picked up Charlotte, ran, and grabbed the window to vault back into the bus.

Charlotte clung tightly to Cora's arm, trembling uncontrollably. Fortunately, she was dressed in long sleeves, pants, and a thick raincoat. Other than a few scrapes from the fall, the zombies had n't bitten her.

But in the delay, the cracks had reached the bus's wheels.

"Ah—!"

Holden slammed the gas pedal to the floor.

The bus lost control, careening forward at an angle, the intense acceleration causing passengers to feel dizzy.

Amid the chaos inside the bus, Jacky grabbed Flame's shoulder.

"Little Fire, Flame, listen to me!"

"After entering the defense array, there's a hidden door inside. It's located right below the main control room. This is the escape route of the defense array. My dad was involved in its core design. It's not marked on the map. I'm going to tell you the route and code now; remember it!"

Flame had a sinking feeling.

"Jacky, why are you telling me this... You should remember it. I'll follow you."

Jacky fell silent. After a few seconds, he rolled up his pant leg.

"I was bitten by a zombie."

Flame widened his eyes in disbelief and looked down. The next second, tears overflowed.

On Jacky's calf, there was a conspicuous tear wound. A few hours had passed, and the surrounding veins had turned a murky black, his leg already swollen and festering.

"How is this possible? When did it happen?"

Flame suddenly lost his voice, recalling the incident outside the dormitory.

Jacky had accidentally collided with a zombie while shielding him from Mr. Sheridan.

Could it be... Could it have happened then?

Redness filled Jacky's eyes.

"At the cafeteria, I didn't intentionally leave you behind and run away first. I didn't react in time."

"Jacky, I'm not that ungrateful. Besides, you're my best friend."

Flame gripped his sleeve.

"Jacky, let's find a solution. There must be a way!"

Jacky managed a smile uglier than tears.

"There's no solution, my Little Fire. I feel terrible. Look, my hand isn't responding anymore."

Veins in his eyes turned bloodshot, while a grayish-white hue appeared under his fingernails.

His fingers spasmed uncontrollably.

"I want to live too. I want to be human. I don't want to become a zombie..."

Jacky's laughter was even more pitiful than tears. "Little Fire, you must live on."

CHAPTER 22

Necessary Sacrifice

On the fractured ground, a bus wobbled and slid forward.

At the center of the floating mall, there were eight glass sky bridges, each linking to one of the eight entrances.

The nearest entrance was the "South-West Gate."

Holden tightly gripped the steering wheel, aiming the bus towards the sky bridge.

Right before they reached the last fifty meters, an unforeseen event took place.

A high-rise office building suddenly crumbled and collapsed in their path.

Holden slammed on the brakes, but the bus was going too fast, already out of control.

It started a 180-degree sideways drift, spinning wildly. The passengers' vision whirled around them. Their insides felt like they were shifting.

"Boom—"

Tons of steel and concrete crashed down, landing squarely on the bus's midsection, splitting it in half. The tons of falling steel and concrete instantly crushed into pulp several people sitting in the middle.

Angela and Irene were in the rear seats among those people.

Siegfried acted swiftly, covering Angela's eyes, but Irene wasn't as fortunate. She faced death head-on, witnessing people she knew turned into mush, blood, and gore. A suffocating fear surged through her, leaving her mind blank.

The bus was severed and its two parts skidded in opposite directions due to a strong impact.

The front portion, occupied by Mr. Sheridan and Holden, carried on rolling towards the South-West Gate. The back half of the severed bus, with Cora, Ray, and Onyx inside, skidded towards the North-East Gate because of the immense force.

South-West Gate.

Holden's forehead hit the steering wheel, blood soaking into his eye sockets. Amid the continuous ringing in his ears, he faintly heard urgent cries from a distance.

"Holden, wake up! Wake up!"

Holden found the voice annoying, struggling to lift his head. The lingering effects of a concussion were clear. He couldn't help but feel nauseous. After a moment, he opened his eyes and saw Flame, who had been shouting his name all along.

The door trapped flame's foot, lying on the ground while tugging at Holden's pants, trying to rouse him. Jacky was beside them, exerting all his strength to push at the door panel, but his efforts alone weren't enough.

Holden supported his head, his head swimming as he stood up.

"Don't move, let me help you all…"

Flame's throat was hoarse, tears streaming down his face as he yelled, "Forget about me, Holden, run!"

Holden squatted down and, along with Jacky, put all their strength into it. They finally lifted the door, but the movement, crouching and standing up, worsened Holden's dizziness. He had to clutch the windshield and pant heavily.

"What about the others? What happened to you all?" Holden's words were cut short as he suddenly widened his eyes, his gaze fixed on something beyond the glass.

What he saw left him speechless, bewildered by the bizarre scene before him.

The floating mall ahead had descended below ground level. The sky bridge of the South-West Gate was gradually retreating. However, at the gap between the ground and the sky bridge, there was a path made from human bodies!

A small group comprised the native residents rushing toward the entrance. The majority, though, were survivors from their bus—former companions. At this moment, though, their eyes were vacant, their expressions dull as they moved forward, using their bodies to create an escape ladder.

Behind this group stood Mr. Sheridan, standing there incongruously, looking as if he was a scavenger.

People within the safety zone, who Mr. Sheridan had manipulated to varying degrees, were easier to control.

But it seemed his psychic strain was reaching its limits, let alone controlling ordinary people on top of that.

No, he absolutely couldn't die here.

It was so close. More, just a bit more.

Just one more person would be enough. Mr. Sheridan grew increasingly impatient, scanning the surroundings.

Then he saw the three people in the driver's seat.

Holden, trying to process what had just happened, suddenly felt a tremor in his pupils. His thoughts disappeared from his mind, leaving him empty. He moved stiffly out of the bus, taking hesitant steps towards the wall of people.

Flame's body swayed, his mind becoming increasingly muddled.

Suddenly, his utility knife escaped his pocket and soared uncontrollably.

Its indigo glow drifting before his eyes.

In a brief daze, Flame's mind cleared again.

"Holden! Don't go over there!"

"Jacky! Holden seems to be controlled!"

Jacky was already half-zombified, black veins spreading to his right jaw, making him look sinister and horrifying.

However, these zombie characteristics made it hard for Mr. Sheridan to control him right away.

Jacky shook his head, fully aware that his human reasoning was fading slowly. Summoning his last ounce of strength, he lurched forward, fiercely striking Holden from behind.

The blow intensified Holden's pain, as his head was already injured.

His vision went black, freeing him from Mr. Sheridan's mental grip. Jacky gave him a push towards Flame and yelled his last words.

"Run, quickly!!!"

Tears streamed down Flame's face as he rushed over to help Holden. He then ran towards the North-East Gate, where the back half of the bus was located.

Mr. Sheridan was powerless to divide his attention. He stared at the progress of the human ladder, struggling to find a chance to look towards the bus. He saw the approaching figure, and his brow immediately furrowed.

What was happening?

He was clearly focusing on controlling Holden.

Why was it Jacky who was approaching?

Well, Mr. Sheridan consoled himself. They were roughly the same height. As long as he could catch the last section of the human ladder, he could reach the eye and devise his plans from inside. He could continue cultivating his puppets.

Jacky's steps were sluggish as he got closer to Mr. Sheridan. His eyes held a hint of an abnormal white glow, his hands extending stiffly. He leaned over the person in front of him, his arms just long enough to reach the descending sky bridge passage.

Mr. Sheridan's heart loosened. He was in the clear now!

With his own hands, he built a human ladder and ruthlessly stepped onto those people's backs, resulting in a gory sight. Eagerly, he rushed forward, getting closer and closer to the entrance of the South-West Gate.

Almost, they were almost there.

Suddenly, he felt an intense pain in his shoulder. Mr. Sheridan turned back in disbelief, his gaze meeting Jacky's grim expression. Jacky had fiercely bitten him.

Mr. Sheridan's pupils contracted in shock. He stumbled back, climbing onto the platform. He shoved Jacky away, and Jacky's arms slipped from the sky bridge. With the string of human bodies, he fell.

Trembling, Mr. Sheridan unbuttoned his collar. There was a

blood-stained, clear bite mark on his shoulder.

North-East Gate.

The situation at the North-East Gate was even worse. This used to be the main street of a bustling commercial district, bustling day and night before doomsday hit.

Now, it had gathered the largest number of zombies. Adding to that, zombies had torn away most of the sky bridge, leaving a steep cliff of broken terrain. The usual methods were useless to cross.

"We're out of time," Angela murmured, her face ashen.

Siegfried glanced at her profile, gritting his teeth.

"We still have time!"

Like a gust of wind sweeping fallen leaves, he searched the surroundings and actually found a trailer's iron chain, as thick as a thigh. He picked it up and dashed towards the cliff's edge.

Cora gave him a hand as he passed by, fortifying the end of the chain with her blue-glowing palm. Siegfried shouted, throwing the chain, which hooked onto the entrance of the sky bridge.

"Angie, you all go first. Don't worry, I'll hold on to you!"

Angela stared at him, as if truly seeing him for the first time.

Her mind was in a haze for the past few days, making it difficult to differentiate between reality and illusion. Sometimes, she even forgot things she had said or done.

But at this moment, the torrential rain seemed to wash away the water that had flooded her mind. Her thoughts broke free from their shackles, and she had never felt so clear-headed.

"Angie, let's go!" Irene tugged at her sleeve urgently.

Anyone who had survived until now, even the girls, had extraordinary physical stamina and determination.

Otherwise, they would have died when they fled the school.

There were no complaints among the girls in the group. They gripped the iron chain with all their might, slowly climbing through the air.

After landing safely, Angela, Charlotte, and the other girls turned back anxiously, looking at their companions on the other side.

An altercation seemed to unfold over there. Some survivors who were also running towards the North-East Gate had noticed the escape route and attempted to cut in line.

Ray, with a stern face, stopped them.

"Let our people go first."

Some who were unwilling tried to push past Ray directly. They leaped to grab the hanging iron chain, but they overestimated themselves.

Maybe it was fear of heights or the overwhelming clamor from all directions that shook their resolve. Their hands let go after only a couple of pulls, and they fell into the abyss, devoured by thousands of zombies below.

Holden and Flame arrived after enduring their journey.

"JP!" Seeing Ray at this moment felt like encountering a savior.

Ray patted the backs of the two without time for many words. "Can you hold on? Get over here quickly!"

Holden gritted his teeth. "I can!"

At such a life-or-death moment, he had to be able, even if he thought he couldn't.

Because of the ground's collapse, a massive chasm had formed beneath the eye, teeming with countless zombies that crawled upwards. The fastest among them were almost reaching the end of the iron chain.

On the other side, their companions were still slowly moving, a distance away from the entrance of the sky bridge.

Suddenly, Irene pushed past Angela, crazily trying to dislodge the iron hook caught on the sky bridge.

Her movements were swift and fierce, and she caught everyone off guard—everyone had initially planned to fend off the climbing zombies together.

In just a few moves, the steel claw loosened and fell from the edge of the sky bridge.

Siegfried had one foot on the edge of the cliff, sliding forward. He barely steadied himself when the support point on the other side vanished. He lost his footing and fell directly off the cliff.

Angela's hand reached out in futility as she stared with wide eyes. "Siegfried!!"

It wasn't just Siegfried.

The individuals hanging on the iron chain, namely Holden, Tian, and Ray, also descended.

Anger consumed Angela and rushed forward, slapping Irene hard. "What have you done? Do you know you've killed people?"

Despite her swollen cheekbone, Irene covered her face and sneered.

"Idiot. The zombies are climbing up. Can't you see? They're coming up, and we'll die. If you want to die, go ahead by yourself. Don't drag me with you."

Irene was terrified. She feared being crushed like those on the bus and being bitten by zombies.

She knew Ray hadn't come yet, but she was in danger too, right? Who could save her?

She was only sixteen. Her promising life hadn't even started. She could only save herself.

In that instant, extreme selfishness overrode everything, and she didn't regret it.

Irene didn't spare a glance for her former companions, turning and running into the North-East Gate.

At the moment of falling, Ray's fiery whip shot out, coiling around the steel beam of the sky bridge.

However, with the support gone from both sides, the iron chain swung uncontrollably downwards.

Ray's feet were only a few meters above the countless zombies below, roaring up at them.

"Siegfried!" Ray yelled in heart-wrenching anguish.

Siegfried had completely vanished after falling into the abyss.

"F**K! F**K!!!" Ray's eyes were bloodshot, cursing with profanity. He couldn't believe that classmates, including Irene, could be so heartless as to disregard their lives.

The fiery whip couldn't bear the weight of so many people anymore and slid downwards. Ray's strength wasn't enough, either. His arms trembled, and he was about to lose his grip.

A slender figure jumped over in his vision, which was gradually becoming blurry.

Like a swiftly flying falcon, Cora moved rapidly in the air. In one move, she jumped onto a slanted lamp post, and in the next, she grabbed a protruding rock in the cliff's middle, maintaining an upright posture as she moved like walking on a tightrope.

Her lance had transformed into a nine-section whip in her hand.

Using the power of her entire arm, she spun the whip rapidly and then swung it, one end pulling upwards and hooking onto the sky bridge, the other end extending towards Ray.

"Catch!"

Ray reached out, the scorching hot fiery whip and the cerulean nine-section whip entwined tightly, indistinguishable from each other. Cora exerted force from her waist, pulling back, and the people hanging on the iron chain were lifted again, back into the air.

Next, she executed a whip toss that could only be described as a textbook.

Cora grabbed the iron chain with her right hand, another whip materializing in her left. With a quick swing, she coiled the whip around those hanging on the iron chain, then flung it upwards. It landed precisely, and with a splash, they tumbled into the North-East Gate.

Angela and Charlotte, who were still on the platform, rushed forward to help them.

Cora retracted her whip and swung it again. The whip threw several more people over, one after another. The last one was Ray. He used the intertwined whip cords to swing like on a swing and flew over, rolling as he landed. The next second, he hastily stood up, running ahead.

But it was too late. The entrance to the North-East Gate was slowly closing, and the eye was rapidly descending, plunging into the abyss swarmed by thousands of zombies.

"Cora!!!" Ray shouted in heartbreak.

By the edge of the abyss, Cora and Onyx watched as the Bagua Formation collapsed.

Onyx clapped slowly, with a touch of amusement in his eyes.

"Heroes, sacrificing themselves for others, truly touching."

Cora didn't want to engage with his cryptic remarks. She turned to him with a direct gaze.

"Why didn't you—didn't you go just now?"

When Siegfried threw the iron chain, Cora had suggested that Onyx could carry him across, but Onyx had refused.

Onyx didn't answer. He spread his palms, catching the falling raindrops.

"Look, the rain is getting lighter."

He smiled.

"Since the rain has stopped, everything should be over now."

Cora's eyebrows furrowed.

She couldn't fathom what Onyx was thinking, but she also didn't believe that he would give up his life willingly and wait to die. Why did he always speak in riddles? Why couldn't he just speak clearly?

"Annoying," Cora muttered irritably.

Onyx took slight offense at her snark. "I'm not annoying. They are."

As they turned their heads, a sea of black insects was converging from all directions, surrounding them.

CHAPTER 23

Cockroaches

Flower City's surface had become ruins as the eye descended into the abyss in the center of the formation.

With a swift maneuver, Cora propelled Onyx to the top of a skyscraper.

Among the nearby buildings, it was the only tall one still standing and the highest point around.

The elevated terrain gave them a moment to catch their breath. Looking down from the city's peak, in the east, south, west, and north directions, an unending sea of insects formed a black expanse.

The suffocating and horrifying scene made Cora deeply question the earlier words of the top student.

Weren't the cockroaches supposed to be extinct? Then what were these? And where were they coming from?

Ah!!

The rain continued to fall from the sky, shifting from a heavy downpour to a gentle drizzle, with no indication of ceasing.

The damp rainwater trickled down Cora's hair, splashing small droplets at her feet. Dressed in combat gear, she stood tall like a lance.

She had zipped up her jacket all the way to her chin, keeping her chin tucked in.

Perhaps this was the most dire situation she had encountered since the apocalypse began, Cora thought solemnly.

Even though Aberrants possessed extraordinary abilities, human strength and mental power had their limits. She could hold off the endless tide of insects for a while, but there would come a time when fatigue would set in, and her mental strength might wane.

It was likely that she wouldn't return if that happened.

However, hiding here wouldn't save her, either.

Eventually, they would be overwhelmed by the relentless swarm of zombie cockroaches that had taken over the entire city.

She would not sit around waiting to die. If hiding wasn't an option, then she would fight!

Cora raised her hands and formed a martial arts gesture.

Then she pressed her index and middle fingers together, with her index finger's tip pressing on the middle finger's knuckle.

Her little finger extended out, and she rapidly performed a series of intricate hand signs.

This was the ancient Daoist secret technique called the "Golden Blade Seal," representing a divine sword for slaying ghosts and spirits.

Cora was that divine sword.

Of course, her mastery of the technique wasn't perfect. She couldn't use it in combat like Master Zhang and Felix could. At best, it was a formality to boost her confidence, but that was a rule of Mountain Yue Dojo, and more importantly, a rule set by Master Zhang. Cora was always obedient.

Different hand signs held different meanings in formal combat, dueling, and challenges. The hand signs she formed now meant one thing—fight to the death. Fight, and don't retreat. With determination, she was about to take that step forward.

"Wait." Onyx grabbed her cap, causing Cora to freeze mid-step. Onyx looked at her with a slightly exasperated expression. "Don't be so reckless. There are alternatives."

"Alternative?" Cora's round eyes widened.

If there was an alternative, why didn't he say so sooner?

"I only just confirmed it." Onyx adjusted his expression and spoke seriously. "Among this wave of insects, there's a 'king'."

"I've had suspicions from the start. This outbreak of insects isn't purely natural. Remember how the zombie cockroaches first appeared in the western mountains? Then they followed you to the safe zone and pursued you all the way here. Their movements have a logical pattern, which fully supports my theory."

"Just like the hierarchy of drones, worker bees, and queen bees in a bee colony, the 'king' among the zombie cockroaches also has commanding authority. It can command and control all its kind. So, if we take down their 'king,' the remaining cockroaches will lose their leader and disintegrate."

Arashi Research had once carried out a secret bio-experiment under NPA, codenamed "Plan Eternity."

Onyx had perused the classified information on this project, which contained records of arthropod test subjects.

Many of which could be considered monsters.

Cora blinked, questioning, "But how do we find, find this 'king'?"

With tens of thousands of zombie cockroaches swarming below, finding the 'king' sounded like a pipe dream.

"Don't worry."

Onyx rubbed his temples.

"I'll figure something out."

The relentless black tide had taken over Flower City's surface and was crawling upward along the broken walls.

If they didn't stop it soon, in another ten minutes, the relentless black tide would corner them with no escape route, and it would consume them completely.

Onyx's beautiful peach blossom eyes deepened as he scanned the area.

The countless zombie cockroaches below turned into grayish-white figures in his vision, like silent film footage.

His gaze darted rapidly, searching north...nothing. East... nothing. South... wait!

In a certain corner to the southeast, a repugnant, chaotic black aura clung together. That was it!

Onyx swiftly decided and deduced the direction from residual marks on the ground. He gestured twice with his hand.

Cora tilted her head, puzzled.

Onyx's brow furrowed as he looked at her.

They exchanged perplexed glances.

Two seconds later, Onyx cleared his throat and said, "Head east until you reach the end, then turn southeast for about 200 meters."

Cora was once again confused.

East? Where's east? And where's southeast?

Onyx, exasperated.

Had D District's collective education really deteriorated to this extent?

At this moment, he had profound concerns about NPA's future among its youth.

He sighed, touching his forehead.

Switching tactics, he tried a third way of explaining, "Head to the 3 o'clock direction, go to the end, then take a right to the 5 o'clock direction, and walk approximately 200 meters... The 'king' will emit a strong radiation, so be aware of energy fluctuations around you."

Cora's expression remained unchanged.

"Okay."

Should've said it that way from the beginning.

Should he be glad Cora could at least read a clock?

Cora, cautiously, rotated 90 degrees to face east, then glanced back at Onyx uncertainly.

Onyx nodded with a blank expression.

Having received confirmation, Cora tightly gripped her lance.

"I'll go... and take it down."

She leaped off the elevated platform. Her tiny figure plunged into the ground, and the swarm of insects instantly swallowed her.

However, in the next moment, the lance burst forth from the ground, unstoppable in its momentum. The tip of the lance surged forward, flipping over the cockroaches that were encircling it.

With a surge of energy, it swept through the tide of insects, scattering them like fragments in the wind. The insects were sent tumbling, their six legs flailing as the gust of wind overwhelmed them.

Cora supported herself with one hand, flipped mid-air, and kicked her lance. The frigid lance kept pushing forward, its blue light creating a streak resembling an afterglow. The cockroaches that encountered it disintegrated like shards, vanishing into the air, and in the face of just one person, thousands of enemies scattered.

Cora wasn't lingering in the battle. She broke free with her fastest speed, determined to break through the swarm. Her goal was to find the cockroach king.

Near the South-East Gate, the magnetic field fluctuations twisted chaotically.

Cora abruptly halted her steps, closed her eyes, and let her mental energy spread out. Quickly sensing something was amiss, she snapped her eyes open and looked straight ahead.

In the midst of the horde of zombie cockroaches, a uniquely patterned one with a basketball-shaped body and a small badminton-sized head was squeaking in a frenzy.

She had found it. A joyful smile crept onto Cora's face. Releasing her lance, it shot forward like lightning towards its target. The cockroach king's compound eyes showed a hint of fear, and it attempted to turn and flee.

With a sharp sound, the lance embedded itself in the cockroach's back. The shell there was unusually tough; the lance didn't pierce through but left a deep dent. A dark ooze sprayed out immediately.

The cockroach king flapped its wings and narrowly dodged the second strike. Its panicked squeaks grew more urgent as it fled towards the nearest drain, attempting to burrow underground.

Cora couldn't let it escape. Anopower surged within her as she struck again. A blue light imbued with the force of thunder cleaved forward.

"Shh—"

This time, the lance pierced through the cockroach king's tiny head. It finally collapsed at the entrance of the drain, its antennae shattered.

Cora retrieved her lance and struck another blow, making sure it was truly dead this time.

Instead of scattering following the king's demise, the swarm surrounding Cora intensified, converging on her from every direction.

The never-ending fight engulfed her in chaos before she had a chance to be amazed.

All she could do was curse inwardly, "Onyx, you idiot!!!"

High above on the skyscraper, Onyx quickly realized something was amiss.

Why?

Regular zombie cockroaches lacked self-awareness.

So why, when the cockroach king died, did the swarm not retreat and instead become more aggressively inclined?

Suddenly, a dreadful suspicion arose within him.

Unless... a nest with dual kings.

Not just one "king."

In bee colonies, lucky larvae could inhabit queen cells and enjoy royal jelly throughout their lives, ultimately maturing into queen bees.

However, there wasn't just one queen cell.

In the event that two queens appeared at the same time, they would inevitably fight until one emerged as the winner.

What if these two cockroach kings were in a life-or-death struggle?

Onyx was lost in thought. If he were one of those kings, he wouldn't foolishly expose himself. His plan was to stay hidden and manipulate the humans to get rid of his rival. And he will eliminate humans with no hesitation.

Using others to do your dirty work? Perhaps the "king" Cora killed was just bait. The true commander of this swarm, the one calling the shots, was still alive.

Amidst the light patter of raindrops, faint sounds seemed to reach his ears. Onyx spun around abruptly, and at the edge of the rooftop behind him, cockroaches had already ascended!

So soon?

They had taken over the rooftop around seven to eight minutes earlier than expected.

However, not all the zombie cockroaches had arrived, just a few thousand of them acting as an assault force.

When had he been exposed?

These zombie cockroaches were clearly more ferocious.

Their grayish-white compound eyes fixated intently on him, contemplating where to strike.

At this distance, Cora wouldn't be able to save him.

Releasing his mental energy, Onyx quickly assessed the massive army of cockroaches before him.

None of this batch of zombie cockroaches rushing at him had the energy signature of a king. How was that possible?

But Onyx was Onyx after all. Though he was astonished for less than a second, he immediately devised a plan. How could he let a low-intelligence creature play tricks on him?

Raising the crossbow, he turned his wheelchair half a circle and deliberately pretended to be unskilled as he shot towards the left. He exposed his back as though in a vulnerable position, but the cockroach swarm on that side continued charging blindly forward.

So, not on the right side...

Feigning weakness, he turned the wheelchair to the right with a clumsy motion, appearing as if he were trying to escape.

The swarm behind him suddenly erupted, changing direction and converging towards his back.

It's on the left!

Onyx's fingers flew over the control panel, inputting a series of commands.

The wheelchair shot forward uncontrollably, and just as it was about to plummet off the rooftop, he abruptly made a sharp turn.

He looked back.

Amid the chaotic swarm, one smaller figure stood out.

It remained stationary, antennae high, and wings spread open and shut.

It appeared to come to a sudden halt, except for the antennae rapidly emitting high-pitched vibrations, constantly issuing commands.

Got you, you little thing. A bitter smile played on Onyx's lips.

His killing intent condensed into a thin line that shot towards the "king" at lightning speed.

Telekinetic thrust!

The tiny, hard-to-find ruler of cockroaches seemed to be suspended by an unseen string in the dark.

It was suspended in mid-air, its short six legs swaying as it hung helplessly.

The intense, high-frequency impact of telekinesis caused its antennae to tremble violently.

Finally, it exploded with a resounding "pop," its parts shattering and oozing a foul-smelling slime.

With the true king's demise, the remaining cockroaches lost their direction, becoming a motley crew of low-tier zombies without intelligence.

Unable to deal with them using mental energy, Onyx grabbed the rapid-fire crossbow in his wheelchair. He took aim and shot out several fierce Anopower arrows, clearing the area in no time.

Onyx directed his wheelchair towards the southeast and looked down as the battle ended.

The fearsome horde of cockroaches was rapidly retreating. Standing amidst the boundless sea of moving darkness was a slender figure. Clinging to a lethal lance covered in a mysterious black substance, this person stood on a broken piece of stone. Covered in grime, she looked like she'd been fished out of the mud, except for her eyes, which glowed in the rain.

Separated by a hundred meters, they couldn't discern each other's expressions.

A mysterious bond appeared to develop through their locked gazes.

Unbeknownst to himself, a smile spread across Onyx's face.

CHAPTER 24

Identities

Too far away, Cora couldn't make out Onyx's expression clearly. But she vaguely saw him waving.

Is he signaling her to come over?

After the sudden riot of the roach swarm just now, Cora had prepared for a desperate fight. However, to her surprise, the surrounding insect tide had inexplicably retreated.

It was all too strange. She went over and ask Onyx what exactly was going on.

Putting away her gun, Cora hopped off the rock and walked forward with brisk steps.

The wind had picked up, and raindrops spun down like dancers. Distant rumbling thunder grew closer.

Cora's footsteps slowed as she spun around, sensing a powerful psychic wave. In a matter of seconds, a vision emerged.

Rolling dark clouds filled the sky, and thousands of purple lightning bolts struck down. The ground became obscured by sand and dust as mounds of earth resembling old tents rose from the ground, trapping the scattering roach swarm.

Following closely, a blizzard descended, and a deluge of ice spikes followed suit. Countless roaches were frozen in place.

The roach horde, first struck by lightning, then buried in earth, and finally frozen, couldn't withstand the onslaught of natural disasters. They fell in waves, like harvested wheat.

Aberrants could only orchestrate this kind of phenomenon.

Mysterious Aberrants arrived, not only cleaning up the roaches but also setting up some sort of advanced mobile artillery.

"Humming—" Deep red super-particle shells fired in unison, slamming into the swarm of zombies in the pit. The bombardment persisted, the smoke and dust refusing to disperse. For over ten minutes, the pit echoed with explosions until the howling ceased.

Cora stood there with her mouth agape, forgetting even to blink.

Finally, descending from the rooftop, Onyx found his golden opportunity and, upon first sight, discovered Cora's provincial appearance.

He smiled. "Looks like reinforcements are here."

In a slightly rear section of the inner loop, four or five individuals were slowly pushing a colossal terminal.

"How's the road clearing going?" A slender man with a buzz cut approached, inquiring about the busy team members.

Payne Onathaqua, an Earth-aligned Aberrants member, replied.

"The main roads are almost reduced to rubble. We cleared a few smaller paths, but there were quite several zombies and bugs around. Is this some sort of bug infestation? I've feared these things since I was little. They're creepy."

As he spoke, Payne rubbed his arms where goosebumps had appeared.

"Should I go help Strong and the others clear out the zombies?"

Kiwamu Maeda, the buzz-cut man, whispered.

"They're just mutated low-level bugs. Clear them out quickly. Don't let the Captain see you like this."

Thinking of their Captain's haughty demeanor, Payne suddenly gained a burst of energy.

"Yes, I'll complete the mission!"

He earnestly continued sweeping away the insect horde. After a while, he craned his neck and exclaimed, "Looks like there's someone ahead?"

Before anyone else could react, they burst into laughter.

"Fix your nearsightedness, Payne. Are you mistaking zombies for people?"

Payne spat, "Get lost! I might be nearsighted, but I'm not blind!"

Vincent had just returned from the front and snapped his fingers upon hearing Payne's words, purple lightning crackling, "All the living people should have gone underground. How could there be regular people here?"

He puzzledly stroked his chin, "Could they be Aberrants?"

Vincent stretched his long legs over piles of roach corpses and looked in the direction Payne had mentioned. Sure enough, he spotted two tiny figures, one seated and one standing, engaged in conversation.

"Hey, there really are people," he beckoned the man behind him, "Captain, what do you think?"

"Let's go look," Jeremy said calmly, "and verify their identities."

Cora and Onyx hadn't exchanged many words when the group of Aberrants spotted them and started walking towards them.

A group of tall individuals around 6 feet tall closed in, certainly exuding an imposing aura.

Amid these tall figures, however, was a short boy, his steps much smaller, hilariously contrasting with the others.

As they drew closer, one man with clear eyes and eyebrows spoke, "Please show us your identification."

Cora didn't move.

Identification? What was that?

She didn't know.

She was an unregistered individual, and besides, they never required such things in Area F.

Onyx also remained motionless, his gaze shifting over the silver emblems on their shoulder patches, lost in thought.

Vincent furrowed his brows, thinking they might not have heard him clearly, so he repeated louder, "Please show us your identification... Hey? Little miss, you look quite familiar. Have we met somewhere?"

Although his words sounded like a rogue's pickup line, Vincent's face showed no trace of roguishness or flippancy. Instead, it bore an earnest expression of contemplation.

"Aren't you... the one from the docks? Captain, do you remember?" Vincent quickly recalled and reminded Jeremy of a booming voice.

Oh no, why was it them?

Cora tightened her grip on the lance in her hand and timidly moved behind Onyx.

Her disheveled appearance was a clear sign she had just experienced combat, and the hostility still lingered on her weapon. Even a fool could tell that she was an Aberrants member.

The problem was, she had adamantly denied being an Aberrants member the last time they encountered these people.

Now, she had been caught red-handed.

Grandpa was right. People should never lie.

"It's you." Jeremy stepped forward.

His movements deliberate.

However, with each step, an overwhelming pressure surged towards Cora.

"Engaging with mutants illegally. Concealing your Aberrants identity. Fleeing a safe zone without authorization. Your actions make up a severe endangerment in public safety. And according to Article 45, Section 11 of the NPA Emergency Regulations, I have the authority to detain you."

Onyx glanced at Cora and she emanated an impressively intense psychic pressure. Yet, she showed no reaction. Her eyelids drooped slightly, and her cheeks puffed up. Oh? Was she displeased?

Well, given how badly she had been treated and how she couldn't stand up for herself, she was probably feeling quite frustrated.

Onyx inwardly chuckled and crawled his wheelchair forward, standing in front of Cora. "Wait a minute, Captain. I think there might be a misunderstanding."

Jeremy gave him a sidelong glance.

"Misunderstanding? Do you have any objections?"

Onyx's face didn't turn red, nor did his heart race as he skillfully wove his lie.

"Captain, my friend here awakened as an Aberrants member just last night. We didn't have time to report it, so how could this be considered concealment?"

Cora stayed silent.

Even though she had already been aware of Onyx's ability to spin stories, his boldness never failed to amaze her whenever she witnessed it.

Jeremy's gaze was sharp as a knife, and his icy expression seemed to convey: Do you think I'll believe you?

"As for fleeing the safe zone without authorization... oh dear! That's just a misunderstanding. We were evacuating with the dominant force but got caught in the crowd, unable to make it into the shelter. That's why we were unlucky enough to be stranded outside."

"And... engaging with mutants illegally," Onyx raised an eyebrow.

His tone is casual and unhurried.

"Which law has she violated? The NPA has issued none legislation concerning mutants. Or are you applying the internal regulations of Azures in a civilian?"

Jeremy fixed his gaze on Onyx. "Who are you?"

Onyx's grin grew wider.

"I'm a researcher from Arashi Research. Here's my ID." He looked as innocent and respectable as one could get.

He was just a step away from having "I'm a good citizen" written on his forehead.

Jeremy silently accepted his work ID and glanced down at it, then instructed the team behind him, "Go verify."

"Yes, Captain."

Onyx timely reminded, "Captain, we've shown you our IDs. It wouldn't be reasonable for you to still arrest us, would it?"

Jeremy didn't answer, still looking at Cora. "Where's her ID?"

Cora's face puffed up even more.

Onyx raised an eyebrow. "My friend is from Area F."

Jeremy said flatly, "So?"

"Dear officers, high and mighty in the military. It's understandable that you're not familiar with civilian matters. People from Area F don't have identification. Isn't that a normal thing? Besides, strictly speaking, isn't civil registration outside your military jurisdiction?"

Onyx spoke with veiled sarcasm, targeting Jeremy at every turn.

The members behind Jeremy showed their indignation, struggling to contain their irritable tempers.

Unbothered, Jeremy restrained his subordinates from moving forward.

"Indeed, it's not under military jurisdiction. But I need to confirm whether she poses a threat."

"Captain, you're stretching your authority too far. My friend and I are just law-abiding citizens."

Cora obediently nodded in agreement.

"Captain, verification is complete. The IDs are genuine."

The team member who had gone to verify returned to Jeremy's side, adding in a hushed voice, "But his clearance is very high, and we can't access specific information."

After hearing his subordinate's report, Jeremy didn't react outwardly. He calmly glanced once again at the ID in his hand—the young man in the photo was gaunt, with a cold pallor and prominent dark circles under his eyes.

Even though he was good-looking, there was a lingering sense of sadness that seemed to surround him.

Then Jeremy looked at Onyx. He sat in the wheelchair, his words dripping with honeyed deceit. He didn't seem like a researcher. Rather, he exuded the entitled demeanor Jeremy had encountered in the privileged young men of Area B, accustomed to giving orders and having their every whim catered to.

"Are you really a researcher?"

"Without a doubt."

"What kind of researcher?"

Onyx wiped away a droplet of water that had splashed onto the wheelchair armrest, answering earnestly, "I'm a senior maintenance technician for the Weather Mimicry System."

She was so shocked she almost bit her tongue.

Hold on a second.

Weren't you a pharmaceutical researcher two days ago?

CHAPTER 25

The Weather Mimicry System

"I'm a senior maintenance technician for the Weather Mimicry System."

As those words were uttered, several members of the Azures team displayed expressions of doubt and caution.

The deputy captain, Maeda, reacted more directly. Emitting a cold snort, he muttered incomprehensible words in a strange language.

"Huh? What a coincidence?" Vincent crossed his arms over his chest and exclaimed in an odd tone.

"You really believe in the saying: If you want to take a nap, someone will hand you a pillow? Our captain has been struggling with that Weather Mimicry System that won't shut down or dismantle. And now you appear out of the blue, claiming you can fix it?"

"Coincidence has nothing to do with it," Onyx explained with a righteous tone.

"T014 was due for its annual inspection. Headquarters sent us on a business trip, and we arrived in Flower City just in time for a heavy rainstorm. I suspected T014 was malfunctioning, but the city was swarming with zombies. I accidentally got separated from my colleagues and couldn't contact anyone else, which caused the delay."

Separated? Didn't you eliminate all your colleagues one by one?

Cora inwardly mocked, recalling vividly how he had dispatched them with ease.

Jeremy's sharp gaze studied Onyx. From the man's expression, he couldn't discern whether he was lying.

The work ID had been verified as genuine, and the photo indeed matched the person before him.

Onyx probably didn't know that if he dared to lie about this matter. He would be exposed in no time.

Jeremy's primary concern was, "Can you fix it on your own?"

"Yes."

"Good. I'll give you the time you need to restore T014 to its original state."

"Hold on a moment, Captain," Onyx smirked faintly.

"Under what capacity are you currently commanding me?"

Jeremy's head snapped up abruptly.

Wearing the NPA's regular combat attire, he exuded a solemn and eerie vibe.

His voice was low and commanding.

"I am Captain Jeremy Wolfgang of the New Pacific Alliance's specialized armed force, Azure Force, 11th Squad. I am currently carrying out a crucial military mission. I ask for your cooperation to restore the normal functionality of T014's weather mimicry system."

Over a decade ago, NPA Azure Force and Arashi Research shared intelligence and collaborated closely for a time.

Requesting the cooperation of an Arashi researcher under his military identity didn't sound entirely unreasonable.

However, unfortunately, that was over ten years ago.

Their relationship now... Onyx sneered inwardly.

Of course, outwardly, he remained courteous.

"Oh, it's the Azures' people. I'll definitely cooperate then, Captain Wolfgang. Could you kindly take us to the control center of T014? Oh, the central hub should still be at Arashi's nearest branch. The exact location..."

"No need," Jeremy interjected.

"Huh?" Onyx blinked.

"The central hub has already been brought here."

Jeremy raised his wrist and tapped, bringing up the projection interface of a communication device.

The surrounding air distorted for an instant, and in the next second, the real-time feed of Azures' logistics team appeared, showing a giant terminal being escorted by four or five people as it moved slowly forward.

Cora's head drooped drowsily, barely keeping up with their conversation. Once she relaxed, exhaustion swept over her like a tide. She was on the verge of falling asleep, but upon seeing this novel contraption, her eyes instantly widened.

What was this? It looked so impressive!

Onyx gazed at the giant terminal in the projection, and his previously impeccable expression finally showed a crack.

So, this was what he meant by "brought here." Were all the Azures personnel this way now? Since they couldn't establish a connection to the back-end terminal, they just forcefully dismantled the central hub of T014?

These brute soldiers...

The fact that the torrential rain in Flower City had lessened but not stopped completely was expected.

Onyx took a deep breath, struggling to swallow the mockery that was about to burst forth. "If I can't connect to the internal system, I'll need to troubleshoot the issues one by one. It might take a few days."

"That's fine. We'll stay here for a few days," Jeremy nodded, then gestured to Cora with a finger, "However, until you've fixed T014, she needs to stay with you."

The Azures captain maintained caution and hadn't completely abandoned his suspicion of Cora. Leaving her behind was a way of monitoring her in another form.

And so, Cora and Onyx followed Jeremy's group to Azure's temporary camp.

Although it was called a camp, it was quite rudimentary, even set up hastily by clearing an area using Anopower.

It was a single-row residential building.

It would take some time for the logistics team to bring the central hub over. Cora found an empty room and, under Onyx's "strong" insistence and disdainful looks, cleaned herself up, washing away the goo from her battle with the cockroach swarm.

After tidying up, Cora collapsed onto the bed like a boneless cat, limbs splayed out, finally able to rest. Then she rolled over and stared at Onyx, unmoving.

"About that T, T014. Are you really going to fix it?" Cora expressed strong doubt. What if Onyx was just bluffing? What if he couldn't actually fix it? Grandpa always said that some guys loved to brag.

Onyx grinned. "You really don't trust me?"

"You also said you're a medic, a pharmaceutical researcher," Cora countered logically.

"Well." Onyx remained composed.

"That's true. I am a pharmaceutical researcher, but it's a part-time gig."

"Hmph." Cora remained unconvinced.

"Actually, being a senior maintenance technician is also part-time."

Onyx chuckled and then dropped a bombshell.

"You guessed right. I don't know how to fix a Weather Mimicry System."

Cora became frozen.

Seeing her stunned expression, Onyx continued to fan the flames.

"So, I was just lying to them."

Cora kept frozen.

Discreetly, she moved her hand towards the bag strap near the bed, ready to escape quickly.

Onyx noticed her slight movement and laughed, his eyes sparkling like sunlight.

"Don't worry. T014 doesn't need fixing. Just shut it down."

"However, I might need to put in some effort to bypass the firewall. After all, it's not my area of expertise."

He winked mysteriously.

"This time, I'm telling the truth."

The Synoptic Mimetic System (SMS) was a revolutionary technology developed by Arashi Research. In the year 20 of the New Era, along with starships, it was unveiled as a major success of the "Glorious Thirty Years."

The main purpose was to observe and enhance the weather.

In case extreme weather values neared or exceeded human tolerance, the AI would calculate and adjust them to uphold climatic equilibrium.

For example, with extreme heat, SMS could release rainfall and cooling measures to change local weather and maintain climatic equilibrium.

Currently, over a hundred weather mimicry systems had been deployed by the NPA, scattered between B and D-grade cities, covering nearly 90% of the regions.

They numbered the one near Flower City as T014.

T014's loss of control handled the torrential rain in Flower City.

Onyx's explanation triggered a sudden memory of Cora of the Starship crash on the day of the rainstorm.

Could the two events be connected?

She quickly shared her speculation with Onyx.

"You think the crash of Starship caused T014 to go haywire? Mmm... That's a possibility," Onyx replied after a moment of contemplation, offering a vague response.

Cora still had one more question.

"Why did those people want to fix it?"

"If the out-of-control T014 continued to run indefinitely, it would lead to flooding not just in Flower City but in all the areas it covers. By then, sacrificing only Flower City wouldn't be enough to solve the problem."

"So complicated..." Cora scratched her head, feeling a bit lost in all the information.

Onyx mischievously reminded her, "You haven't used up all your questions for today. Do you have more?"

She had more, but...

Cora rubbed her wrist through the air, hesitated for a moment, and then couldn't hold back, "That, that thing you pointed at earlier that created a screen when you tapped it. What is it?"

Her little legs kicked rapidly, and she excitedly opened her hands wide while miming.

"Girl," Onyx chuckled. Only kids would be interested in new toys. "That's a communication terminal used in the B District."

"Oh." Cora's enthusiasm deflated as soon as she realized it was something from the B District.

B District... The CDEF districts separated it so far away. Grandpa wouldn't let her go there.

"Do you want it?"

Cora blinked, neither confirming nor rejecting it. Onyx's right hand moved, producing a small, feminine communication terminal from somewhere, as if teasing a little cat. "Here, take it to play."

It was a silver-white miniature terminal.

Despite the forced disabling of communication and tracking, other functions remained usable.

Cora fiddled with the built-in camera, trying to project it onto the floor, thoroughly enjoying herself.

"Is it fun?" Onyx asked from the side.

"Mmm."

"Do you know whose it is?"

Onyx added lightly.

"Whose, whose?"

"Yara's."

"Oh, right, you also know her."

"Remember her now?"

Cora nodded.

It seemed, maybe... perhaps... she had a vague impression?

Cora's memory rapidly retreated to the day she first met Onyx. He had taken advantage of the chaos and looted something from the bodies of two people. She vaguely remembered expressing strong disdain for such behavior.

It's coming back to her.

Cora wasn't feeling too good about this.

CHAPTER 26

Little Diamond

While Cora was running after Onyx, a faint noise emanated from the doorway.

A young boy secretly observed them as he peeked in through the gap in the mostly broken door.

Upon locking eyes with them, the boy's shoulders trembled, and he quickly fled out of fear.

Embarrassed, Cora put down the half-table she was holding.

Did she scare him away?

After about half an hour, the boy timidly approached again, still staying outside the door and not daring to come in.

His curious, beady eyes lingered on Onyx's right leg and wheelchair for two seconds before quickly moving away and turning to Cora. He looking at her with curiosity.

Cora felt stiff under his gaze and refrained from making any sudden movements. Dealing with soft-spoken human kids wasn't her strong suit, except for Little Travers, Ben Travers's son.

However, that little troublemaker always threw stones at her, leaving Cora with a poor impression of him. Whenever she saw him, she just wanted to kick his butt.

This boy differed from Little Travers—he seemed even more timid.

Cora awkwardly sat down on a chair and unexpectedly made eye contact with him.

The boy had soft brown hair, with curly ends brushing against his ears. His fair face was clean, and he wore finely textured long-sleeved pants, looking like a model from a magazine.

Cora glanced at him, then did a double-take. Wait, she remembered now. Wasn't this Victor Blackwood's son? His name was... Damian?

The day Cora left Zone F199 at Fool's Dock, Damian had been frightened along with Mrs. Travers and Little Travers when Anopower went haywire. He was taken away by Jeremy's group. Cora hadn't expected to meet him here again.

It seemed they were a sort of fellow townspeople!

Rubbing her clothes nervously, Cora spent a considerable amount of time psyching herself up. Finally gathering her courage, she wanted to greet Damian. But as soon as she raised her head, he ran away.

Words failed Cora.

The next day, and the day after, and the day after that...

For the next week, Damian would come to Cora's door, pacing around to check if she was there. Sometimes he'd catch Cora experimenting with new Ethereal Artifacts, and he'd stand by the door for a while, his eyes sparkling as he smiled at Cora with innocence. Yet, he never dared to enter.

During this time, Onyx often wasn't in the room. They successfully transported the central control of T014 to the base, and he would escort it while Maeda glared at him, to "investigate and fix issues."

Of course, according to Onyx, he was actually "breaking through the firewall."

Cora thought he was simply being lazy, spending just a few minutes typing on the screen each day and then confidently passing off the rest with, "The terminal can run automatically."

Maeda and the others were skeptical, but their technological challenges limited their ability to take action.

If they hadn't done a thorough check on Onyx's work badge, they would likely have given up on him a while back.

As for Jeremy, he led his team to clear out zombies, remove

obstacles, and rotate shifts for rest. They were constantly busy.

The towering figures of Azures weren't easy to get along with.

If you were looking for someone reasonable, Vincent was the closest.

After observing them for a few days and with the occasional prompting from Onyx, Cora gradually learned about the specifics of this Anopower squad, Azures.

Just like the legends foretold, Azures was an army composed entirely of Aberrants.

Jeremy led a team of eleven.

But in reality, it comprised a whopping forty people.

The highest-ranked Anopower in Azures was Captain Jeremy, an A-class speed-based Aberrant.

Vincent claimed that the teleportation Cora saw was just a small part of what he could really do.

Jeremy's true strength was beyond comprehension.

Vincent was a B-class lightning-based Anopower. His primary focus was on dealing with large-scale crowd damage, and he took the lead in clearing out the bug swarms.

Cora once secretly climbed up to the roof to observe.

When Vincent unleashed his Anopower, the area within a two-kilometer radius darkened as if it were night, occasionally illuminated by lightning and rainbows.

Thunder roared, and the pure purple light almost seemed to cut through the sky.

There was no denying the astonishing level of power.

If B-class Aberrants were this powerful, how much stronger were A-class ones? Cora's fighting spirit was eager for a challenge, and she really wanted to spar with Jeremy, to test herself.

Of course, for now, that desire was only at the "thinking" stage.

Cora had confidence in herself, but what if she got into a fight with Jeremy and lost? He might get angry and arrest her. Cora sighed, feeling it might be troublesome. Oh well, she thought, let's just forget it.

Apart from Jeremy and Vincent, the other team members were C and D-class Aberrants, like Payne with his C-class earth-based Anopower, Maeda with his C-class defense barrier, and William

Strong with his D-class wind-based Anopower, and so on.

Besides the official members, there were temporary members assigned to logistics in the base, like Damian.

They were originally civilians from different regions.

Jeremy had a device that could detect newly awakened Anopowers, and after the apocalypse, when these people had nowhere else to go, he temporarily recruited them.

They handled transportation and cleaning tasks.

Removing the logistics personnel, Cora counted.

The actual number of Azure members was now only twelve.

When Onyx revealed his identity to Jeremy, he had mentioned they were on an important mission.

However, for the details of the mission, everyone kept their lips sealed, demonstrating a strong sense of secrecy.

From Vincent, Cora learned another piece of not-so-good news: the central refuge of the defensive formation couldn't be opened from the outside.

The defensive formation was Flower City's most robust defense mechanism.

When it detected severe natural disasters outside, it would cut off all connections with the surrounding facilities, hiding the central refuge several kilometers underground.

Authorities ensured that the refuge had enough supplies to sustain around thirty thousand people for about five years.

However, since it was the last resort, once activated, people could only reopen the refuge from an internal control console, isolating it from the outside world.

Jeremy had attempted to access the refuge's communication channel, but with little success.

This frequency required specialized access.

The hasty activation of the refuge left doubts about the survival of any management personnel inside.

In short, the chances of seeing those people from the school again were extremely slim. Cora could only hope that Ray and Flame were doing well inside.

The days passed uneventfully for a week until things finally took a turn—Damian walked in.

Cora looked up at the knocking sound and saw him, a minor figure holding a big bag of supplies, only revealing his furry head. Struggling with the weight, Damian wobbled his way in, giving a shy smile.

After observing each other from across the hallway for a few days, he had gained a bit more courage.

"Mr. Anderson and the others asked me to bring some stuff."

"Thank you," Cora said as she accepted the supplies with one hand.

Both of them were not great at social interactions.

After Damian put down the supplies, Cora awkwardly said, "Sit."

Then, they soon fell into silence.

Cora looked helplessly at Onyx, the only eloquent one in the room. However, he elegantly smiled and said, "I'll go check on T014."

He just left like that? It was like he was an indifferent parent who'd rather not play with kids and had found any excuse to escape. Watching his casual departure, Cora's fingers played with her tassel dart, and they danced in the air with a hint of sharpening and throwing intent.

Damian's short legs dangled off the stool as he watched her play with the dart for a while. He clapped enthusiastically, "You're amazing!" Cora paused for a moment, and her dart play became even more erratic.

"I've seen you," Damian crashed the quiet atmosphere.

"Mr. Anderson said you and my dad were in the same pod."

He looked at Cora with his big watery eyes, a pleading look in his eyes.

"Sis, can I ask you something?" Cora couldn't possibly refuse, "Sure, go ahead."

"Do you know where my dad is?" "What?"

"My dad, his name is Victor Blackwood, contact number 80243..." Kids' memories were pretty good, and he immediately recited his parent's information.

Cora thought for a moment.

That civilian starship had last landed in a food factory in the northeast suburbs of Flower City.

If Mr. Blackwood had encountered none unforeseen events, he should still be there. But that was assuming nothing unexpected happened during the apocalypse...

No one could say for sure what happened during those apocalyptic times.

Seeing that she hadn't responded for a long time, Damian's eyes filled with tears, and he sobbed like a pearl dropping.

"Sis, I want to find my dad. Dad..."

Don't, don't be like this. How did he cry while speaking?

Onyx hadn't been resting well during this time.

During the day, he had to deal with Maeda's gloominess and also focus on breaking through the firewall of T014.

Onyx hadn't lied about this; he'd once studied topics like "how to bypass the AI surveillance of the Star Network," although he wasn't an expert in that field.

Each step had to be taken carefully, and he had to make Maeda think he was "repairing and troubleshooting."

It wasn't easy at all.

At night, when he stayed in the same room as Cora, the girl simply went to sleep without a care.

But Onyx was different. He had been extremely cautious from a young age. When he was resting, he wouldn't allow anyone nearby, or he wouldn't be able to sleep no matter how hard he tried.

If he told Cora this, she'd probably look at him with wide eyes and mumble, "So... troublesome."

Onyx wearily pinched his brow bone and tilted the back of the wheelchair 45 degrees, turning it into a reclining chair mode. He relaxed into it, placing his hands gently on his abdomen and allowing his psychic energy to envelop him. Then he closed his eyes.

Outside, raindrops pitter-pattered.

Amidst the monotonous white noise, his breathing gradually calmed down.

A clear and crisp child's voice suddenly echoed, "Mr. Anderson, can I continue to monitor those two tomorrow?"

"Little Diamond, so enthusiastic?"

"Yeah, I'll help you with more work, so the uncles can rest more!"

"Very good."

Vincent patted Damian's head.

"Mr. Anderson, when are we leaving here?"

"You'll have to ask the captain."

"Sob, the captain's so stern. I'm scared."

"Mr. Anderson, are you hungry? I have cookies here. Want some?"

"Mr. Anderson..."

Onyx's eyes opened as he extended his psychic energy, swiftly locating the origin of the noise.

The place where the two were talking was far from Onyx.

Damian followed behind Vincent, hopping around like a little bird.

The sunlight was bright, his words sweet, every other word being "Mr. Anderson."

It made Vincent smile, a stark contrast to the timid appearance he'd shown in front of Onyx and Cora for the past few days.

Tapping his fingers on the wheelchair, Onyx gradually squinted his eyes.

Well, it seemed like there was a little elf here.

CHAPTER 27

The Bad Boy

"Damian wants you to go with him to find someone?"

"Yeah."

"You agreed?"

Cora nodded. She had no resistance against the soft and innocent human cub. When Damian cried, she surrendered without hesitation.

"With so many people in Azures, Damian didn't ask them for help but came to you?"

"I, I don't know," Cora thought for a moment. "Maybe he's timid?"

Thinking about Jeremy's stern face, it was indeed quite intimidating.

Onyx let out a soft hum from his nose, as if Cora was a foolish person hypnotized by a magician.

"Timid? Didn't you say his father was a smuggler? A slick and cunning merchant can raise an innocent and naïve son? Have you heard an old saying from the old civilization? 'Like father, like son.'"

"What?"

"Don't understand?"

"You don't even understand this, yet you dare to trust strangers so easily?"

Cora looked at him with innocent eyes and muttered softly, "I also trust you."

When we first met, weren't we strangers too? You even lied to me. You were a pharmaceutical researcher!

Onyx paused for a moment, clearly finding this example quite unsuccessful.

"Aren't you afraid of him deceiving you? That kid is an ice-type Aberrant with an unknown level."

"Not afraid."

What was there to deceive her about?

She had no money and didn't know everything, like Onyx did.

Apart from being good at fighting, oh no, superb at fighting, anyone who wanted to deceive her should think twice.

Cora spun her lance in her hand, forming elegant lance patterns. "Anyone who tries to deceive me, I'll, I'll beat them!"

Such a straightforward... way of thinking. Onyx choked.

"Suit yourself."

Cora zipped up her backpack and turned to him.

"Are you coming?"

Onyx was reading the old fluorescent screen she had. He coldly refused without looking up.

"Not going."

Cora stared at his profile for a few seconds. She felt he didn't seem too happy, and he wasn't like that time in the safe zone when he insisted on walking her to the door, saying cheesy things. Cora felt melancholic. But then she realized, wait a minute, she had done nothing wrong.

Why should she feel guilty? Speaking of which, it's all Onyx's fault!

After days of effort from Jeremy and the others, the roads around Flower City had been cleared, and even the number of zombies had slashed.

Cora had ventured out twice in the past few days. Disappearing for half a day wouldn't raise too much attention. If she hurried, she could make it back before dark.

Within the ruins of steel and concrete, Cora moved swiftly. She occasionally stopped and asked, "Are you tired?"

Damian was chasing after her, his small face turning red, panting heavily, but he didn't fall behind. "Sis, I'm not tired."

Almost forgot, he was also an Aberrant, an ice-type with strong offensive capabilities.

Cora always treated him like a harmless child, but in fact, Damian's physical fitness had already surpassed that of an average adult man.

The outskirts of Flower City, a food factory.

The guard post two kilometers away had collapsed and been abandoned. The warehouse, covering an area of 500 square meters, stood silent.

Cora had a bad feeling about this.

She whispered to Damian, "Wait here. I'll go in and look."

Damian clenched the straps of his backpack, obediently nodding.

Cora moved agilely along the wall, lightly stepping a few times, and smoothly climbed onto the roof. Peering through a skylight, she saw the interior of the warehouse resembled a garbage disposal site, with rotting food covering the floor. When she scanned the area, she saw a sea of people, and shockingly, they were all zombies!

Despite her efforts to spot Mr. Blackwood's figure, Cora found it difficult to discern anything amidst the tightly packed zombies.

A faint noise came from behind her. Cora turned her head and saw Damian had climbed up as well.

She signaled him to be quiet by placing a finger to her lips, and Damian immediately understood. He covered his mouth with his little hand, and then his gaze wandered around. As he saw the massive number of zombies inside, his eyes widened in shock.

Luckily, Damian was only frightened, and he didn't shout out. He wiped the condensation off the skylight glass with his sleeve. Together with Cora, they leaned down to search for Mr. Blackwood. After a while, Damian pointed to a distant figure and excitedly cried out in a low voice, "Dad!"

"It's dad! That's my dad!"

Cora followed his direction and saw a man with a shiny gold belt around his waist. No wonder Damian could recognize him at a glance. But the man's figure had swollen several times, making him look abnormal.

Sure enough, after Mr. Blackwood turned around, his pupils were grayish-white, his face twisted, evincing the features of a zombie.

Damian's "Dad—" stopped abruptly in his throat. Perhaps he was shocked beyond words. He sobbed nervously, struggling to hold back hiccups.

The surrounding temperature seemed to drop. Cora touched her head and realized that raindrops had turned into snowflakes, falling gently. It reminded her of the tragic scene on the dock that day. No, Damian, please don't use Anopower again.

"I'm sorry, sis. I, I can't control it."

Damian also realized that his Anopower was leaking out. He was so nervous that he stumbled over his words. But the more he tried to suppress it, the less it listened to him. The sky filled with snow and ice; the temperature dropping rapidly. Cora shivered.

"Hey, you..." She was about to remind Damian to control himself a bit and not attract the zombies.

It was too late.

The sudden drop in temperature caused the fragile skylight to crack, and with a snap, a piece of glass fell down, making a crisp sound. All the zombies in the warehouse lifted their heads to look at the ceiling, their thousands of white eyes fixated on it. The feeling was incredibly eerie.

Cora sighed inwardly.

"Hide here, protect yourself," she reminded Damian.

With a loud bang, Cora jumped into the warehouse through the skylight. She landed with one hand supporting the ground and the other gripping her lance.

A clean and handsome posture.

She slowly looked up. Although it was troublesome for her, dealing with these zombies was only a matter of time.

The enemy was the target of the chilling tip of her lance, and the zombies rushed at her wildly. The situation was about to explode suddenly!

Countless ice shards descended from the sky, like a storm sweeping away leaves, wildly swirling around, with no order, stabbing any zombie they met.

This large-scale Anopower attack, coupled with the closed small space, left the zombies with no escape. The zombies became completely trapped, and within a short while, ice shards filled them and caused their complete demise, leaving only a few wandering around aimlessly.

Cora maintained her lance stance, her eyes wide in disbelief.

Unable to explain, she turned around and saw Damian near the skylight, crying heavily, his breath ragged.

"I'm sorry! I don't know what's happening either!"

Cora. "..."

On the way back, Damian's mood was unusually downcast.

In the end, Mr. Blackwood stayed behind at the food factory. After Cora dealt with the other zombies, she asked Damian what to do. His eyes were red and teary.

"Sis, could you not kill my dad, please? Just let him stay here."

Keep him?

But Mr. Blackwood had already turned into a zombie. He couldn't revert to being human.

Damian seemed very upset.

But Cora, who was an orphan, was always emotionally dull. She couldn't understand his feelings.

Hmm, maybe if Onyx was here, he could explain it to her.

In the end, she agreed with Damian's request and locked up the food factory with an iron chain. The two hurried back to the camp ahead of Jeremy and the others.

After wiping away his tears, Damian thanked Cora, "Sis, thank you for taking me to find my dad. I'm sorry, I know I'm useless..."

"It's okay," Cora asked him, "Is your Anopower okay?"

Damian lowered his head gloomily.

"Whenever my emotions get too intense, I can't control my Anopower. Mr. Anderson said my focus is too scattered, but I'll definitely improve! I won't cause trouble for you guys!"

Cora replied somewhat awkwardly, "Alright, alright then."

Damian's tendency to use his abilities without considering the situation was troublesome from a certain perspective.

For example, because of her shock just now, she accidentally ended up squatting down, and her tailbone was still aching.

As soon as Damian stepped out of the room, he stopped crying. He put his hands in the pockets of his hoodie and hopped around the corner.

A silver-white wheelchair was positioned at the hallway's end. Leaning against it at a slant was a tall man.

He had a languid posture, and his handsome profile looked pleasing in the misty drizzle.

Damian gave a wry smile and a shy, awkward expression.

"Sr. de Montclair."

Onyx turned around. "Oh, it's you."

"Sr. de Montclair. What are you doing here?"

"Waiting for you."

"Waiting for me? Do you have something to tell me?" Damian's head tilted slightly, looking cute.

Adjusting his wheelchair, Onyx faced Damian.

The child still appeared curious, with a hint of innocence on his face, but the corners of his eyes darted around, obviously not fully focused on this.

"Kid, you knew all along, right?"

"Knew what?"

"Your dad is dead."

Onyx's statement, although it may have come across as an insult, was delivered calmly and factually.

"You didn't hear me? Let me say it again. Your dad is dead."

Damian froze, his entire little face crumpling, and his red-rimmed eyes fixed intently on Onyx.

Onyx chuckled softly, "The Flower City uprising, Jeremy couldn't possibly be unaware. He probably sent people to the food factory a long time ago to check, and he must have told you that there's no need to go find your dad again, right?"

"What's wrong? Can't let it go? Insist on dragging a sucker along to confirm?"

Damian's hands emerged from his pockets and hung at his sides.

He muttered softly, as if grumbling like a sulking child, "Sr. de Montclair, you really love meddling in other people's business."

A sharp ice shard targeted onyx's right leg, piercing through the gap in the wheelchair with bone-chilling coldness.

Onyx sneered.

Young people, they just can't hold back their temper.

A second before the ice shard hit Onyx, an invisible force lifted Damian!

Caught on the ceiling beam, his hood caused him to plummet, with his head getting trapped in his hoodie's collar. With wings held tightly, he appeared as a young chick struggling to stay afloat.

"Let go of me! Put me down! You villain!"

Damian finally started panicking, flailing his limbs wildly, baring his teeth and claws like an angry little lion. The innocence and simplicity on his face were gone, replaced by a gnashing anger.

This person, this person, he's clearly disabled to the point of needing a wheelchair, yet he's an Aberrant!

Damn it! Damn it!! So infuriating!!!

Onyx enjoyed his predicament and earnestly advised, "Kid, you need to learn to stand on your own. Don't always rely on others."

"Especially, don't rely on others' support."

CHAPTER 28

A New Start

The day after, Onyx successfully bypassed T014's final security measures and reached the control port.

It took him a full fourteen days, but he finally shut down the out-of-control weather simulation system.

Witnessed by everyone, the mist that had shrouded Flower City gradually thinned and disappeared. Brilliant sunlight burst through the darkness, instantly dispelling the gloomy days.

The taller members of the group looked at Onyx with noticeably different expressions.

"You've got some skills, kid! Did you really fix it?"

"We finally get to see the sun. It's been zombies or stink bugs every day. I'm getting all emo!"

"Hey Payne, wanna go sunbathe together?"

Amidst the cheerful atmosphere, a team member rushed in with a hurried look and leaned close to Jeremy and Maeda to whisper, "Witness... District 83... can't confirm... suspected key appeared."

Jeremy's expression tightened, and he immediately gave orders, "Everyone! Speed up the process. By tomorrow at the latest, clear the road out of the city."

The team members who were just talking about sunbathing

immediately snapped to attention, responding in unison, "Yes, Captain!"

Cora supported herself in Onyx's wheelchair, clutching a small, slender pear, asserting she was overseeing his coding (despite not comprehending a word). She caught on to his decreased typing speed and glanced down at him.

Onyx's eyes were locked onto the conversing individuals, wearing an inexplicable look.

"What's... wrong?" Cora took a bite of the pear. It was so sour!

Onyx withdrew his gaze and pointed at the massive terminal in front of him. "What's this?"

"T... T014."

"No, this isn't T014. The real T014 is still above us. This is its control center."

"Huh?" Was there a difference?

"This control center has been stored near Flower City at the Arashi Research facility."

"Oh, right."

Wasn't this something everyone already knew?

"But you mentioned earlier that Jeremy and the others came from District F199."

Arashi Research and District F199 were located at the endpoints of a line segment, with Flower City roughly in the middle.

"Jeremy left Flower City before the heavy rain. It's clear that T014 was just something he brought along."

"In that case, it's interesting. You said the Azures people took such a big detour to go to Arashi Research. What could they want there?"

"Or rather, what reason could they have that's so compelling?" Cora was baffled.

How would she know?

Onyx was speaking in terms she couldn't understand again.

Seeing her puzzled expression, Onyx patted her head with a meaningful look.

"Keep eating your pear."

That evening, Jeremy officially announced that once the road was clear the next morning, they would leave Flower City.

Because of their upcoming mission, it would be inconvenient for logistical personnel to be involved. Therefore, once they reached the next destination, the twelve Azures members would part ways with them.

Dinner was like a farewell meal. They created temporary stoves in the courtyard and cooked their own meal.

Vincent held an unlit cigarette, brushing sauce onto a steak as he asked Cora, "Little sister, now that T014 is fixed, what are your plans?"

Cora stared unblinkingly at the sizzling steaks, absentmindedly shaking her head. She didn't have any place to go. She would just ask Onyx later.

She caught sight of a familiar figure—Damian in a pale yellow sweater, tilting his soft face to listen to Payne. He looked cute and obedient. Cora waved at him, wanting to invite him over to eat.

However, when the little guy saw her, he first seemed pleased, but then his expression turned as if he had seen a ghost, and he scampered away.

Confusion filled Cora's mind.

A familiar and relaxed voice came from behind.

"Hey, everyone's here?"

Cora turned around to see two figures gradually approaching—Onyx and Jeremy.

After spending this time together, Jeremy hadn't completely let his guard down around Cora.

However, given that she had been "keeping to herself" and acting like a "law-abiding citizen" these days caused no trouble, Jeremy's attitude wasn't as hostile.

He also wasn't as quick to detain her for no reason.

"Captain Wolf, do you have any sensible suggestions for our next move?" Onyx deliberately ignored someone who had bolted away, smiling as he asked.

Jeremy glanced at Cora, his tone icy as he replied.

"The NPA has regulations governing Aberrants. Since you've awakened, register as soon as possible. Only registered Aberrants can gain official recognition from the NPA. Otherwise, you'll forever be an unidentified person."

Cora, with her eighteen years of being unidentified, felt like a knife was being stabbed into her back.

However, if registering as an Aberrant could grant her official status...

Cora's interest was piqued.

"Where can... can I register?"

"Any C District will do. The C Districts had Aberrant bases before. They just weren't publicized," Vincent flipped the steak over with a casual air, continuing, "But given the current situation, starship's halted, and roads aren't easy to travel. Hey, by the way, we're heading to District C83. You could ask the Captain to give you a ride."

"C83 District? Felalakas, the City of music and art?" Onyx suddenly spoke up.

"Yeah, you know about it?" Vincent was surprised.

This guy either had excellent memory or was well-versed in NPA's regional information, enabling him to remember the city's name just from the number.

Alternatively, he had been there or heard about it before, making it familiar.

"I haven't been there, but I've heard of it," Onyx replied modestly.

In the New Era Year, the NPA officially divided the entire territory into over 200 regions, rated from A to F based on comprehensive development levels.

E District was developed into various functional areas to use its unique ecological environment.

F District only had numbers and no place names because of its extreme backwardness.

All the ABCD Districts had a pyramid distribution, except for the elusive and mysterious A District.

The B District is affluent and bustling, while the D District is numerous yet unremarkable, leaving the technologically advanced and well-managed C District as the desired "ideal country."

C District had 50 cities, each with its own irreplaceable uniqueness. For example, C83 District—Felalakas.

Felalakas not only had nearly a thousand grand and small vintage opera houses, but had also achieved a pinnacle in holographic projection technology.

In this land filled with floating and leaping notes, brimming with creative ideas, singers, poets, painters, playwrights, from all around the world gathered together, hoping to step onto the brilliant stage and achieve their lifelong goals someday.

Felalakas also had the NPA's most "liberal" governor.

"Do you want to go to Felalakas?" Onyx asked Cora.

Cora nodded. Registering as an official Aberrant, getting an official identity, the allure was too strong. She wouldn't have to hide for the rest of her life and could proudly show others her "proof of identity."

Onyx easily understood Cora's thoughts and smiled, turning to Jeremy. "I don't mind. It depends on whether Captain Wolf agrees."

Though Jeremy had a stern demeanor, as a soldier from the lower ranks, he possessed a sense of compassion for people. Otherwise, during their time in District F199, he wouldn't have allocated half of the Starship to civilians.

"Fine," Jeremy nodded coldly, "but I'll only take you to District C83." Meaning, once they reached District C83, they would have to find their own way, just like the logistical team members.

Onyx fully understood this and expressed his gratitude, "Of course, thank you, Captain Wolf."

"Little sister, are you willing to join us this time? Come, eat!" Vincent's grilled steak was finally ready. After being declined by both Jeremy and Onyx, Cora took a skewer.

She stared at the bright red surface for a while before taking a bite. Ugh! So spicy!

The departure day arrived quickly.

When the first light of day broke, a faint rustling awakened Cora —footsteps! Although these footsteps were varied, they were not chaotic, well-trained, with barely any sound upon landing. If she weren't so perceptive, they could have easily gone unnoticed.

She rubbed her eyes, tossing off her sleepiness as she got out of bed. But the next moment, she realized the single bed across from her was empty —Onyx was nowhere to be seen. On her second glance, she found him sitting by the window, lifting the curtains to look outside.

Cora was slightly surprised. Onyx surprised her by being more alert and waking up earlier than she did.

"Who is it?"

"Members of Azures."

Cora suddenly became nervous.

"Are they trying to sneak away?"

Her unexpected thought process left onyx speechless.

"No," he said with a serious expression, "come see for yourself, the Central Shelter has opened."

Cora jumped up and hurried to the window.

Flower City's familiar aerial structure reappeared in the dim morning light.

However, the former prosperity was gone.

The once grand building was now dilapidated, leaning against the ground near a crater.

A significant number of people were drawn to it as dark shadows loomed.

Cora put on her coat. "Let's go look."

The two arrived at a nearby hill and looked down from above. As expected, people were coming out of the various entrances.

In contrast to the frantic escape during the day the Central Shelter contracted, these individuals emerging now appeared despondent and unusually quiet. Some had blank expressions, others looked desolate and miserable, while some had bloodshot eyes, lost and dazed. Their houses vanished, their city demolished, and even the final sanctuary was lost. From today onwards, they had truly become rootless drifters.

Besides people, many zombies were also running out, even some in the process of mutating into half-human, half-zombie beings. Cora didn't know exactly what had happened inside, but this scene was disturbing. She had a feeling that from now on, this city would probably coexist with zombies.

They were in a noticeable position. After a short while, a low, hoarse voice called out behind Cora, "Cora."

The night wind made her oversized coat flutter as she turned around.

Ray was staring at her, feeling as if time had passed like a river. It had been less than half a month, but seeing Cora again made it seem like a lifetime had gone by.

She was still alive, which was great.

But him? Given his condition now, could he even be alive?

These experiences were like the cruelest purgatory, shattering

Ray's innocence completely.

If Ray could have foreseen how things would turn out, he would have never chosen to enter the Central Shelter.

The collapse of Flower City's defense formation was engulfed in absurd chaos from beginning to end.

DAY 1

This landmark mall at the center of Flower City had eleven floors, with an atrium in the middle and rows of shops and restaurants on either side. The crucial control center was on the bottom floor, separated from the primary structure. As one ascended, the space increased.

When the gangway entrance closed, all survivors were scrambling for territory, resorting to physical confrontations. Ray and his group secured a small shop, largely thanks to his intimidating Anopower. Without Ray, they might not have even kept this tiny space.

"I'm so stupid. How could I be this dumb?"

Siegfried's death had hit Angela hard.

She had lost her usual vivacity and spent her days in tears.

"Ray, whether you believe it, three years ago, it wasn't me who started the bullying against Cora." Angela's eyes were red as she revealed the truth behind that brawl.

"It was Irene who kept telling me that Cora was a slut, intentionally flirting with you. I lost my senses because of her, but I just wanted to give her a piece of my mind—throwing dead mice into her bag, discarding her uniform, pouring soup on her... these were Irene's ideas."

"Those intimate photos of you two? She sent those to me. I thought she was my friend..."

Angela was full of regret, covering her face and crying.

Though she was overbearing and indulgent, she had never intended to harm her classmates like this. She never could have imagined that Irene would be so heartless.

"She told you to do something, and you just did it? You're quite a useful tool, targeting wherever she pointed at you."

Others who were still alive couldn't stand it, and mocked her coldly.

"Who do you regret showing this to now? Who knows if you're just faking it," even Flame, who was usually easygoing, couldn't help but stand up for Cora, "You! You're just trying to shift the blame!"

Irene's betrayal had made them hate her to the bone. The mere mention of her name made them wish they could tear her apart.

"What bullying? Wasn't it just a minor conflict..." Ray suddenly stopped, remembering that "minor conflict" was a term Irene had used.

So that was it. He had been kept in the dark all along. He realized that, just like Angela, he was a complete fool.

When he got injured in the past, he had actually resented Cora a bit for not knowing her limits and not showing remorse for her mistakes. So when the school wanted to hold him accountable for the fight, although he had his family help smooth things over, he soon learned from Irene that Cora had dropped out. From then on, he felt disillusioned and never sought the truth, refusing to contact her out of spite.

Because of one comment from Cora, he had held a grudge for a long time. In your eyes, am I the same as everyone else? So you can ruthlessly lay your hands on me, too.

Ray closed his eyes, silently chuckling with a bitter smile. He thought of Cora, who had stayed outside to save them, and realized it was all too late now.

DAY 3

The conflicts continued to escalate.

In just half a day, there were several disputes on the third, seventh, and ninth floors. Friction arose wherever there were people. In this confined and stifling space, even the smallest things could explode like dynamite.

Survivors pushed and shoved, verbal disagreements quickly escalated into physical conflicts.

The piercing screams reached Ray and the others on the eighth floor, and they learned some bad news—someone had mutated into a zombie.

DAY 4

Chaos, chaos, chaos.

No one knew why zombies had infiltrated. All they knew was that their impending doom was inevitable. The number of mutated individuals kept increasing, the situation worsening. Holden and the others locked their shop's door, guarding it to prevent anyone from breaking in.

DAY 5

Worse, news arrived: the personnel responsible for distributing supplies were dead.

They had been murdered, and the stored supplies had been looted. The items that were hard to preserve and carry had been trampled and shattered. The once-safe shelter had become an absurd hell of slaughter.

DAY 7

The number of zombies kept growing.

Flame unexpectedly spotted Mr. Sheridan, or rather, "The zombie Mr. Sheridan."

He had already told Ray and the others about Mr. Sheridan's actions. Irene's betrayal had left them numb. Yet, when they discovered that the teacher they respected was actually a heartless monster, Holden and the others punched the wall.

"Zombie Mr. Sheridan" blended in with a group of zombies. Its head twitched neurotically, slowly passing by the shop. When it turned around, Flame noticed a festering, pus-filled wound on its shoulder, a clear bite mark.

Flame thought of those classmates he had pushed out to their deaths. He thought of Jacky, his best friend.

He silently shed tears while muttering, "Serves them right! Well bitten!"

DAY 8

Ray and the others finally reached the first floor, following the route Jacky had given them to find the "hidden door." However, things didn't go smoothly.

In addition to a password, biometric recognition was also necessary to open the secret door.

But with most of the shelter's personnel dead or injured, the remaining were nowhere to be found.

DAY 10

No one expected they would encounter Irene again.

Eventually, those who abandon their companions will be left abandoned themselves.

Irene wasn't doing well inside. Her tricks were useless in the face of madness. When Ray and the others found her, her hair was messy, her clothes were torn, and several repulsive men pinned her down. When she saw them, her eyes lit up, and she struggled to break free, crawling over with difficulty.

"Ray, Angie, save me! Save me!" The group stopped in their tracks, gazing at her with indifference.

Four or five men stared at them with apprehension, especially at Ray's whip. They didn't dare make a move.

Irene didn't get the rescue she hoped for.

The light in her eyes gradually extinguished, and she hysterically yelled, "We're companions! How can you do this? How can you watch someone die without helping?"

Then she was dragged back.

"You'll pay for this!"

"I won't let you off the hook! Ray, Angela, all of you should die!"

Irene's curses from behind were relentless, growing more venomous.

"What... will happen to her?" Charlotte turned away, gripping Angela's hand.

If she didn't restrain Angela, she might have lunged forward to tear Irene apart.

"The person dragging her had bite marks from zombies on his leg," Holden said.

The group fell into silence.

DAY 13

Ray tried to break through the secret door again, with no success.

On their way back to the eighth floor, they unexpectedly saved a clerk from Flower City's city hall who was surrounded by zombies.

He was emaciated and barely clinging to life. Flame gave him water and food, barely keeping him conscious.

In the evening, the man finally woke up. They learned from him he had been the designer of the defense formation project, responsible for the structural design of the entire central shelter.

"The defense formation is Flower City's best shelter, the best!"

"Why? Why can it withstand natural disasters but not human nature?"

"I don't want to die here."

"This place is already hell."

The clerk, Tom Lee, had empty eyes and murmured to himself while staring blankly.

DAY 14

Tom, who had regained consciousness, led them to the control room.

Even though they all knew that opening the central shelter might lead to an endless tide of zombies and insects, Tom firmly pressed the button.

Cora and Onyx listened quietly to the students' account.

Even within the central shelter, they were caught off guard by an unexpected tragedy.

Angela gathered her courage and walked up to Cora. The once proud princess had learned to lower her head after her experiences.

She finally said, "Although I still dislike you, I'm sorry, I'm sorry... I'm, I'm sorry..."

She apologized to Cora, repeating "I'm sorry" over and over, trembling and choked with tears.

In the end, she wiped away her tears and stubbornly said, "I didn't force you, and you don't have to forgive me."

Cora sighed deeply in her heart and responded, "Okay."

Onyx asked, "What are your plans now?"

Ray replied, "We're planning to go north with Mr. Lee."

Tom had insider knowledge of the locations of various NPA shelters. Ray felt responsible for guiding Holden, Charlotte, Flame, and the others to survive.

They could either find a shelter to settle down in or keep searching until they found a welcoming place.

"What about you?" Ray looked at Cora.

"We..." Cora lowered her head, and Onyx was looking at her.

"We... are going to C83 district."

From further up the slope, Vincent's loud voice could be heard, "Girl, get ready to leave!"

His voice startled the nearby zombies, making them converge on him like a compass pointing north.

Vincent, using profanity and a purple light, fought off his attackers.

The time to part had come.

Flame and Charlotte looked at her with teary eyes.

Cora nodded at them, saying, "Goodbye. I hope to... see you again."

Then she turned to Ray, "Goodbye."

"Goodbye, Cora," Ray's voice was hoarse, but there was a certain resolute core in his gaze. "Take care."

Cora turned away and left.

Onyx, not knowing what to say, earned a kick from her that made him jump, chasing after her wheelchair.

Their figures merged with another group of tall individuals, quickly disappearing into the darkness.

Cora possessed the qualities of grace, carefree spirit, and adaptability, much like an untamable wind.

And Ray, once naïve, arrogant, ignorant.

At this moment, he finally understood.

They were never meant to be on the same path, like Changming's lighthouse and drifting ships. Even in a temporary meeting, they would say goodbye for eternity.

So it was better to say a proper farewell.

To Be Continued...

About Me

This is Jennifer. I have a deep passion for young adult romance and science fiction, with a penchant for weaving in the extraordinary, like zombies, into the ordinary.

About the Series

"Ethereal Artifacts" was originally serialized via a web novel platform. It's my first long series with all elements I like in my life: post-apocalypse, zombies, dystopian, cyberpunk, and of course, strong female leads.

Please Review

Your opinions matters! It is important for authors to improve themselves.